The Sex Bucket List

by
PRESCOTT LANE

*Kristine,
Live, Laugh, Love!
Prescott Lane*

Copyright © 2017 Prescott Lane
Print Edition

Cover design © Perfect Pear Creative Covers
Cover image by Alina Cardiae Photography / Shutterstock.com
Editing by Nikki Rushbrook

This is a work of fiction. All characters, organizations, and events portrayed in this novel are either products of the author's imagination or used fictitiously. All rights reserved. This book or any portion thereof may not be reproduced or used in any manner whatsoever without the express written permission of the author, except for the use of brief quotations in a book review.

TABLE OF CONTENTS

Chapter One: The List Emerges — 1
Chapter Two: Ask a Man Out — 14
Chapter Three: Multiples — 22
Chapter Four: Sex with an Ex — 30
Chapter Five: Pole Dancing 101 — 35
Chapter Six: Orgasm Meditation — 44
Chapter Seven: Public Display — 52
Chapter Eight: Naughty Pics — 60
Chapter Nine: Selfish Sex — 68
Chapter Ten: Cougar Denied — 72
Chapter Eleven: Panties to a Stranger — 78
Chapter Twelve: Porn and Beer — 87
Chapter Thirteen: List Emergency — 94
Chapter Fourteen: Unselfish Sex — 107
Chapter Fifteen: Reverse Cowgirl — 114
Chapter Sixteen: Why Me? — 126
Chapter Seventeen: The Talk — 140
Chapter Eighteen: No Threesomes — 145
Chapter Nineteen: Spanking — 159
Chapter Twenty: Sex Tape — 166
Chapter Twenty-One: Sex, Interrupted — 172
Chapter Twenty-Two: Quickie Queen — 181
Chapter Twenty-Three: Complications — 193

Chapter Twenty-Four: Man Sandwich	200
Chapter Twenty-Five: The List Returns	211
Epilogue	215
Also by Prescott Lane	224
Acknowledgements	225
About the Author	227

CHAPTER ONE
THE LIST EMERGES

EMERSON

I DON'T CARE what they say, forty is *not* the new twenty. You can name a cocktail that, or have a social media page with the title, but that doesn't make it true. When my kids were little, we used to say *fat* was the "F" word. Then my boys thought the "F" word was *fart*. But maybe we were all wrong. Maybe it's not a word at all, but a number—the big four-zero.

And I'm in my early forties, so I'm super screwed. Who even thought of that lying phrase? *Forty is the new twenty*? I don't know a single twenty-year-old who gets sleep wrinkles. Come on, you know what I'm talking about. The little lines left on your face in the morning from your sheet or pillowcase. In your twenties, they bounce back by the time your feet hit the floor. At forty, you're hoping they disappear by the time you walk in the office.

And what twenty-year-old gets gray hair? And I'm not talking about on your head. Everyone remembers that *Sex in the City* episode when Samantha found her first gray pubic hair. At the time, I thought that was just good television. Unfortunately, now I know it actually happens.

Aside from getting older, the three reasons for my wrinkles and gray hair are upstairs getting ready for their week with their father, my ex-husband. That's the worst part about divorce, splitting time, missing out on whole weeks of their lives. Sure, we call and text, and I go to their activities, but it's not the same as kissing them goodnight. But that's divorce these days.

I tend to keep myself busy while they're gone, working more, exercising, spending time with friends and family. I even clean to avoid feeling the loss. That's how bad it's been the past year and a half or so.

On today's agenda, clean out my wallet. I did the purse two weeks ago when they were gone. And if your wallet is anything like mine, you've got some kind of discount card for every store within a twenty-mile radius.

I begin sorting through them. A pet store? We don't have pets. Why do I have that? A punch card for a packaging store from two years ago? Toss. An expired coupon for a car detailing? The list is endless. Between my Victoria's Secret credit card that I never use, and the yogurt frequent buyer card that I use too much, I find a folded-up, tattered piece of paper.

Emerson's Sex Bucket List.

I have a vague memory of writing this with my friend, Poppy, and sister-in-law, Layla. It was at Layla's bachelorette party a couple years ago shortly after Ryan and I separated. She and my baby brother, Gage, were getting married then. They just recently had their first baby.

At that party, the three of us were well into our third bottle of wine, when Poppy suggested I had a case of mono-penis, as she called it, and needed to get back out on the market. But dating wasn't on my radar. I didn't even know what Tinder or Plenty of Fish were. And I didn't think ChristianMingle would take me.

Poppy suggested I make a sex bucket list. At first I thought she was joking, but she was dead serious. Layla provided the pen and paper, and Poppy started firing ideas at me. Layla chimed in here and there. We must've really been loaded when we came up with some of these. There are over twenty ideas on the list, and I vaguely remember it being hard to come up with them. I was with Ryan for over twenty years, so I'd accomplished a lot already. I'm no Poppy, but not half bad. The longer the list got, the more we laughed.

I'm not sure if it's because it's been a couple years or because of the amount I drank, but I can't remember much else from that party.

I see twerking is scratched off, so I must have done that when we went dancing later that night. I know I haven't done it since. Sadly, that's the only thing scratched off the list. It's the only action—if you can even call it that—I've seen in a long time.

It makes sense I'd have a sex list, though. I mean, why not? I've got grocery lists, Christmas lists, to-do lists, even honey-do lists—minus the honey. I'm the queen of list making. It helps me keep some semblance of order in my life. Those of you with kids and a job and countless after-school activities know what I'm talking about.

So why not a sex bucket list? The doorbell rings, and I quickly fold it up.

I'm not sure if it's just my kids, but they never answer the door. Maybe I enforced that too much when they were little. *Don't open the door to strangers.* Hell, I still tell them that. But I've created monsters, because they don't ever answer the home phone, either. They think if it's important, their cell phones will ring.

Still, it's weird my ex-husband rings the bell. I've always told him he can just knock and come in, but he doesn't. We shared this house for close to twenty years. When we bought it, it was a complete disaster, but Ryan carefully brought it back to life. It's beautiful: two stories, painted a cheery yellow color with a white wrap-around porch and red door. Ryan thought I was crazy when I suggested red; he teased me mercilessly that it would look like scrambled eggs with ketchup.

Opening the door, I lift my glasses to my head, completing my messy bun look. It goes with my oversized shirt and yoga pants—the mom uniform for the twenty-first century. And the glasses are a necessary evil of being forty-something. I shouldn't complain, I really only need them for reading and when my eyes are tired.

Ryan smiles at me, and it still hurts. But I'm glad we've gotten to this place—the friend zone. "Morning," he says. "They almost ready?"

I motion for him to come in, yelling up the stairs for the kids. All their bedrooms are upstairs, and the master bedroom is down. That was perfect when I was married, for privacy. But now when the kids are gone, I barely even go upstairs. "I'm sure the boys are," I say. "But you know Ava. She's trying to match her nail polish to her clothes."

He chuckles, sticking his hands in his pockets, and takes a few steps inside but stopping at the edge of the foyer. He never comes in any further than that. It's like there's lava past that point. "How's the baby?" he asks. "Ava texted me a picture of Gage and her."

"Greer," I say. "That's her name."

"Pretty. It's different."

I nod, hating how we just make stupid, polite, awkward conversation now. The man has fucked me every which way, and even had his finger up my ass. Now we just discuss the weather.

One of the most difficult things to get used to when Ryan moved out was that I didn't have anybody to share things with. I'd see some silly news story or hear some gossip about a friend, and I'd want to tell him—but I couldn't. He was gone. It's the strangest feeling to go from sharing everything with someone to sharing nothing.

"She's adorable," I say. "I'm going over to see Layla and Gage later. They plan on spending most of the summer in Savannah, so they'll be close to family while the baby's so little."

"Gage told me. I called to say congrats," Ryan says, and that doesn't surprise me. Gage and Ryan always got along. It's not like they hang out anymore, but there's no hard feelings between them. Still, Gage is my brother, and he stood by me through the divorce.

"He's so happy," I say.

"Remember when we brought Ava home," he says, looking away for a second, smiling. "God, that was over sixteen years ago."

"We had no idea what we were doing."

"We've got three great kids."

"They are," I say, "even though I did a lot of things wrong."

"*We* did a lot of things wrong," he says.

I almost fall over in shock. It's the first time I've ever heard him take any blame for the destruction of our marriage. Why would he say this now? My mouth is open, and I'm trying to think of something to say, but before anything comes out, our seven-year-old comes flying down the stairs.

"Daddy! Daddy!" Connor says, giving him a high-five, followed by some odd handshake and ending with fist bumps. "Did you get the new video game? The one with the zombies?"

"Shh!" Ryan says. "Your mom's not supposed to know about that."

In truth, Ryan cleared it with me. We are the two most responsible and considerate divorced people in the history of the universe.

Connor flashes me a big toothless grin. "Jacob, Dad got the game," Connor says as his older brother approaches.

"Cool."

Jacob's fourteen, so he only provides one-word answers, and that's on a good day. Sometimes he just gives a shrug or an eye roll or a grunt, and not just to me and his siblings. He does the same to Ryan. "Where's your sister?" I ask Jacob, sneaking a kiss on the side of his head.

"If you'd get me a car, then I could just drive myself over," Ava says, coming down the stairs.

Ryan holds out his keys. "You can drive mine."

Ava ignores him, stopping in front of me. He gets the brunt of her attitude. "Could I spend a night here with just you?"

Glancing over at Ryan, I say, "Your dad misses you, honey."

"Doubt that," she mumbles.

"Jacob, take your brother to the car," Ryan says and hands Jacob the keys. "Don't drive off." Both boys laugh and bolt outside.

"Ava, honey," I say and comb my fingers through her long hair, "what's going on? I know this isn't about a car. You've never been spoiled."

"I just want to stay with you. I worry about you here alone," Ava says, leaning her head on my shoulder.

I wrap her in a hug and can see Ryan is agitated. He values his time with the kids and doesn't want to hear all this. I get it, and I'm surprised by Ava. We all went through some growing pains when Ryan and I first separated, but I thought we were past much of it.

Maybe she's having trouble with her own boyfriend, Justin. Maybe that's where this attitude is coming from. I try to reassure her. "I've got an alarm and a good book, and I'm going over to see your new cousin. I'll be fine."

"Please," she begs.

"Let's go, Ava," Ryan says. "We aren't going to cater to this behavior."

He stops when Ava stares daggers at him, like only a sixteen-year-old girl can. "You might have the boys fooled," she barks, "but I see right through you."

"Ava!" I scold. No matter what, Ryan is her father, and he deserves respect. He'd demand the same for me.

"He's dating!" she blurts out. "Some *blonde* woman!"

She says the word *blonde* like it's a cuss word. And maybe she has a point. Gray hair doesn't show as easily in blondes, and supposedly they have more fun. I'm sure they're better at twerking, too. Sighing, I mess with my brown hair, pulling on my messy bun. The only word I can manage is, "Oh."

"Ava, we can talk about this later," Ryan says, his eyes flashing to me.

"Mom doesn't date," she says. "She's always home. Alone!"

Somewhere deep inside, I appreciate her concern for me, but not to the point that Ryan hears I'm some kind of hermit, that I have zero social life.

"Mom, she drives a *hybrid Mercedes* and wears *stilettos* and carries a *Prada* bag. And I *hate* her."

Apparently, Ava now hates hybrids, Mercedes, Prada, and stilettos. I look over at Ryan, not knowing what to say. "Ryan, I thought we said we'd talk before bringing someone new into the kids' lives." Mentally, I pat myself on the back for sounding so mature though I'm feeling like I could be sick.

"She's practically my age," Ava piles on.

I wish Ava would stop talking and leave. Now I feel like I could throw up.

"Emerson, I didn't bring her around the kids. We were out at the movies, and Ava saw us." Ryan turns to Ava and asks, "How'd you know what she drives?"

We both look at Ava, who's looking at her feet. "I might have had Justin drive by your house."

"Ava," he yells, and she dissolves into tears.

I pull her into my arms and let her cry. I may need to suppress my emotions about this, but I won't make her.

Ryan steps towards us, rubbing our daughter's back. "I'm sorry, baby girl. I shouldn't have snapped like that."

"But you can't stalk your father," I tell Ava, feeling her smile a little.

"For the record, her name is Christine," Ryan says gently. "And she's thirty-five, not sixteen."

That's still almost ten years younger than me. Wonder when her birthday is? Maybe she's almost thirty-six.

"Are you going to marry her?" Ava cries.

"Honey," he says, rubbing her back some more, "we've only been out a few times."

Ava turns around. "But you like her?"

"So far," he says.

She looks up at me, and I give her a smile, reassuring her that I'm fine. "I just always hoped you and Mom would get back together."

I guess I always hoped that, too. Ryan is the only man I've ever loved. I don't think it's possible for me to love anyone else. I never wanted this—a broken family. I know my kids wish we'd get back together, and it hurts my heart that I can't give them what they really want.

Ryan looks at me with his *help me* eyes. "Sweetie," I say, "I want your dad to be happy, and he wants the same thing for me."

Ava nods a little, drying her face with her hands, and Ryan gives her shoulder a little rub. "Can you go make sure your brothers aren't drag racing down the street? Give me and your mom a minute." Ava gives me another big hug then disappears outside.

"Maybe you should let her stay with me," I say. "She might need me right now."

He shakes his head. "I think she needs to see that this doesn't change anything between me and her."

"You're probably right," I say. He sits down on the stairs, his head in his hands, then looks up at me, his blue eyes piercing. "Sorry about that. You okay?"

It's sweet he even bothered to ask—and his dimples popped out when he did. I've always had a thing for dimples. It's a genetic thing. My brother Gage loves Layla's dimples, and I've always liked Ryan's dimples. It's part of what made me fall for him.

There's actually not much about him that a woman wouldn't fall for. Even in his forties, he's maintained his lean, muscular build. And even with a few gray strands in his brown hair, and a few lines around his eyes when he smiles, he still makes my heart speed up. I guess that shouldn't happen anymore, but it does.

"Why do I feel like I just got caught cheating?" he asks.

What's gotten into him? I'm not quite sure how to answer, or if he's even looking for an answer. I suspect he's fucking this Christine woman; maybe that's why it feels different for him. But I'm not going to offer that opinion out loud, and it's probably wrong anyway. I'm sure he's had sex since the divorce. Well, I can't be sure, but it's more than likely. I could carbon date my vagina, it hasn't been used in so long.

He adds, "It's not like I haven't been on a date since we split up."

I figured as much, but didn't need to hear that bit of information. "I might not be the best person to discuss this with."

He shakes his head, getting to his feet. "It's just easy to fall back into that place."

"Same here," I admit.

He starts for the door then turns back. "You're a hard woman to get over, you know that?"

But before I can answer, he's gone.

I REMEMBER THE day my marriage fell apart. It was October 22, a year before either of us said the forbidden d-word. But it was the day

I knew we were in big trouble. We'd had another fight the night before, which extended into the morning and past lunch the next day. I called Ryan at work, trying to make peace, begging him to go to counseling, for us to get some help. He refused.

Heart mangled.

That's when I knew. He didn't seem to care. He wouldn't fight for me. Every woman needs to know her man will fight for her, protect her, go to battle to keep her, but I knew in that moment Ryan would just let me go.

Through my tears, I told him to remember this day—the day he broke us.

Discovering your husband doesn't care enough about your marriage to fight for it is a tough pill to swallow. You want to pack your bags, ask for a separation. And if it were just about you, you would.

But you've got three kids sleeping upstairs, and you've devoted your entire life to raising them. So it's not so easy. You don't want to split time with them; you want to tuck them in every night. Plus, you have no idea what divorce looks like.

So you tell yourself it's not worth it. You swallow your pride and say you're sorry, but you aren't sure for what exactly. And you know you'll have the same fight again in a week.

Every time your phone dings with a text or email, your heart jumps, hoping it's him, hoping he's reaching out, hoping he's changed his mind, hoping he still loves you enough, hoping he wants to fight for you. But it's never him.

And you feel stupid for even hoping. You know better.

So you decide to suck it up and stay, putting on the fake smile, tying your hair in a messy bun, putting on your yoga pants, facing mommy duties, doing everything alone, even though you and he are still living under the same roof.

Then it happens one day: a nice-looking guy in your boot camp class smiles at you.

Really fucking smiles.

Your husband never smiles at you like that anymore.

And with that smile, and in that moment, something inside you clicks.

I *am* worth fighting for. There just might be someone who thinks I'm good enough the way I am, who doesn't say I'm selfish, dramatic, overly sensitive, nagging, bitchy, or crazy.

Your day's made by a total stranger. If only your husband ever looked at you like that, the way he used to look at you.

What you wouldn't give for one glance full of love.

I KNEW AS soon as I dialed and heard his voice that he was still pissed off from the night before. Clearly, I'd fucked up again. This time he didn't like the way I exhaled. Apparently, breathing was another thing I wasn't getting right.

It was a Sunday, and his car wouldn't start. He was storming around, aggravated because we had so much to do. Our son needed a haircut, and to be dropped off at a friend's house, and we needed to get to Mass, and it seemed we were going to miss now. It was the third time the car had given him trouble in two months. It was understandably frustrating, and I wanted to help. I grabbed my phone to try to figure out where we could have it towed, and in doing so, I let out a deep breath. That's when the shit hit the fan.

"What's that for?" he barked.

I wasn't sure what to say. I just needed a deep, cleansing breath. That's what every self-help book in the world says to do to relieve stress. But I knew more stress was coming now. My chest got tight, and I braced myself.

He started ranting. All I could think was that I really felt like I was trying, and yet once again, I was falling short. Maybe because I was trying for two people.

We hadn't been getting along for a while, and I felt I was the only one trying to make things work. So I did what I had been doing, what seemed necessary: I apologized again.

It made me cry to say it, made me feel small and stupid because he was the one who was cursing, waking up our daughter, going on and on about my breathing and the stupid car.

But I did it anyway. And I hated myself for it.

"I'm canceling our trip to New York," I said.

"That's my birthday trip," he said. "I swear, you are so selfish."

"I don't want to go and fight the whole time."

"We won't."

"I don't want to go and pretend we are alright. We are in trouble. Our marriage is in trouble."

"You are always so dramatic, Jesus Christ."

Maybe it was the wrong thing to do, but because I'm not a quitter, we actually went to New York a few weeks later. And as expected, everything was fine for the three whole days we were gone—good hotel, good conversation, good food. But when it was time to come home, time to come back to reality, and there was a little chaos at the airport—typical, stupid travel stuff—he got frustrated and snapped at me at the ticket counter.

Right before I hung my head, I caught the eyes of the woman agent behind the counter. I'll never forget that look of pity. I felt so small, ashamed. As we were going through security a few minutes later, Ryan gave me a halfway apology, which I just smiled at in return. I was so sad we couldn't hold on to those three days. But I never expected we could.

I closed my eyes on the plane and tears rolled down my cheeks. I don't think he even noticed. Up in the clouds, I whispered, hoping God could hear me because we were so close, "Please help me."

I was tired of feeling so bad, when I was the only one trying. I didn't want to be sad or hate myself anymore. I deserved better than that. I didn't want to pretend for one second longer. I wasn't going to try to be perfect anymore.

THESE ARE JUST a few examples of the kind of bullshit that infected our marriage. There were so many little things like this, stupid things, really. I can't say there was a big, life-altering thing that destroyed us; I mean, there was no asteroid that crashed into us.

No, our marriage died a slow death by bullshit, bit by bit. And there came a point—I can't remember exactly when because it was a gradual thing—that I decided I wasn't going to give Ryan any more bits of me. When we got married, I made sure to scratch out the *obey* part in the standard vows, and I know there wasn't a part about promising to kill my soul, either.

A few weeks after New York, I made the biggest mistake of my life. I started flirting with the hot guy from boot camp class. I told myself it was innocent—a smile, nothing more. And for those few minutes each day, I felt special, wanted, desired. It was addictive.

I let it go too far.

One really good, passionate kiss after class—that was it.

But that was too far.

Afterwards, I sobbed in my car the whole drive home. I sobbed because of what I'd done, but also because I wished I could've had the kiss with my husband, not another man. My marriage had become more like a business arrangement than a marriage, and I wanted more.

I pulled into the driveway, walked into our home and told Ryan what I'd just done. Of course, I apologized over and over again, the most sincere apologies of my life. It was the right thing to do—but since we're divorced, you can imagine my words didn't fix things.

"I was happy," he said. "I thought you were, too."

I really didn't know how that was possible—maybe Ryan had a lower threshold for happiness than I did, or maybe he, like many other men, was just clueless. "I'm *not* happy," I said.

"Why aren't you happy?" he snapped. "Tell me, what's so bad about our life that you're not happy?"

"We're fighting every week. It actually seems like every day."

"And that's my fault, right?"

"I didn't say that."

"Nothing I do is good enough for you," he said, throwing up his hands.

"That's not true."

"You have no idea how good you have it. So many guys are jerks—staying out all hours of the night getting drunk, cheating. All I do is go to work, come home, take care of you and the kids."

"I appreciate that."

"Doesn't seem like it."

"Look, something's wrong with us."

"What's wrong is that you want for nothing, you give me no credit, and then you go kiss some other guy! You are so selfish."

"I know," I said. "You've told me enough."

"What?" he cried. "After what you've done, now you're going to play the victim card?"

We went round and round in circles for a while, the fight taking a variety of twists and turns, all of them ugly. It was like a bad road trip, constantly getting lost, with speed bumps and warning signs all over the place, and never reaching the destination.

We hung on for a little while for the kids, but Ryan never could forgive me. Eventually, he moved out and asked for a divorce. And through it all, I loved him.

CHAPTER TWO
ASK A MAN OUT

GAGE AND LAYLA have a place in Atlanta, but they visit Savannah enough that they kept Layla's cottage here to use when they're in town. I step up to the front porch and find Gage sound asleep on the swing. Layla must see me coming and opens the front door. She has her finger over her mouth. "Shh!" she says. "He went out to check the mail an hour ago."

I walk inside and give Layla a hug. My brother did well marrying her. She's one of my best friends, and a beautiful woman inside and out. "You look . . ." I stop because I can barely breathe. My nose wrinkles up. I can't help it. I know it's the rudest thing ever, but something smells terrible.

"It's the cabbage," Poppy calls out from the kitchen. "Smells like piss."

"Hush!" Layla says, peeking over at little Greer asleep in her white and pink bassinet. "Let's talk in the kitchen."

I give the baby a quick glance. She's got Layla's dark hair and dimples. Layla insists she has my brother's blue eyes.

"Why do you smell like cabbage?" I ask Layla as she leads me to the kitchen.

"She's got cabbage in her bra. Can you believe that shit?" Poppy says. "No wonder Gage is outside. The smell probably killed him. Poor man will never want to suck those tits again."

I politely remind Poppy she's talking about my baby brother, and I have zero desire to think about him sucking my friend's tits. But

Poppy has no limits, no filter, no shame. She doesn't care what I think, and I absolutely love that about her.

"The lactation nurse recommended the cabbage," Layla says. "You guys know I don't have big breasts usually. I broke my D-cup nursing bra today. I literally busted the thing wide open I'm so huge. At this point, I'll try anything to calm them down."

"I know it's tough," I say. "I nursed all three of mine."

"I'm afraid I'm poisoning her," Layla says. "My nipples are cracked and bleeding."

"It'll get easier," I say. "How's Gage been?"

"He's so great," Layla says. "He's so happy to be a father. It's tiring, of course—you saw him outside—but he's thrilled." Layla just beams talking about Gage, and he always does the same when talking about her. I wonder if I'll ever have that again.

"Does he like the taste of breast milk?" Poppy asks.

"It's actually not so bad," Layla says.

"You tasted it?" Poppy asks.

"I want to know what my baby is tasting," Layla says.

"I always knew you were kinky," Poppy says.

We bust out laughing. There's something about hanging out with girlfriends. No matter what's going on, you can be yourself, and they love and get you. It's the best feeling in the world. It makes me feel safe, happy—rare things these days.

"Gage is counting the days until my six-week appointment," Layla says.

"Why?" Poppy asks.

"You aren't supposed to have sex for six weeks after having a baby."

"No shit?" Poppy cries.

"Yep, I actually think Gage is getting sick of blowjobs."

I close my eyes and stick my fingers in my ears before quickly changing the subject to something about work. Poppy and I work in Atlanta at my family's airline, Southern Wings. I'm the head of PR and marketing. Poppy is my right hand. She lives in Atlanta, and I commute back and forth a few times a week and work from home in

Savannah the rest of the time. Gage is the CEO of Southern Wings, and he and Layla split their time between the two cities. Between our work commitments and commutes, Layla being a married mom to a newborn, Poppy doing whatever she does with her boyfriend, and my three kids, it's hard for the three of us to get together. But we make time as much as possible.

"How is it living with Dash?" Layla asks Poppy.

Poppy and Dash have been together about two years. Poppy's got no desire to get married or have kids. Dash is a pilot at the airline, a longtime friend of Gage, and a former player with the ladies—but he met his match with Poppy. Normally, I'd tell a woman you can't turn a bad boy into a good guy. That's something that only happens in romance novels—when the fierce woman captures the heart of the lifetime bachelor, they get married and live happily-ever-after. Come to think of it, it also happened with George Clooney and his wife. But that's it. Except for Poppy, too. She successfully captured that unicorn.

And Dash is a great guy. At this point, he'd like to do the traditional thing—marriage and kids—but Poppy's having none of it. So things between them haven't exactly been smooth lately, but her hair is still holding up. She's got this weird thing where she abuses her hair with different colors, cuts, and extensions depending on her mood. It's been its natural dirty blonde color in a cute pixie cut for a good while, but I'm sensing she may soon be hitting up the hair dye aisle and taking a meat cleaver to it. Still, they've had their share of nonsense to deal with, the most ridiculous of which is the crap they take for being an interracial couple. It turns my stomach the stuff they've had said to them. Dash usually handles it better than Poppy, probably because he's dealt with it his whole life.

"We only had sex three times this week," Poppy says. "I think something's really wrong."

"Three times, huh?" Layla says. "That's like twelve hours in Poppy and Dash world."

"It would've been four," Poppy says, "but he slipped himself inside me without a condom. I reminded him because you know guys, they forget. Only he didn't forget. He wants to get me pregnant."

"But you aren't married," I say, sounding like the old fogey I am. "I just meant, I thought he wanted to get married."

"I think he thinks if he knocks me up, I'll marry him."

"Why won't you?" I ask. "He adores you."

"He wants kids, and I don't," Poppy says. "He's so happy Gage and Layla had a baby. He thinks that will make me want one. Like having babies is contagious."

"What's contagious?" Gage says, stumbling in the kitchen and giving me a kiss on the cheek. "If someone is sick, I don't want them around Greer. Did you wash your hands?"

Layla pats his hand. "No one's contagious."

The baby starts crying. "I'll get her," Gage says. "You keep doing whatever you're doing. I'll take her in the yard. She likes that. I'll bring her to you in a little bit to eat."

I always knew my baby brother would be a great dad. We had a great father ourselves. "So what are you going to do about Dash and babies?" Layla asks Poppy.

"I keep telling him that squeezing a watermelon out of my vagina will ruin our sex life. I'll never be tight again. So instead of sending him sexy pics, I'm sending him episiotomy photos."

"You are not!" I cry.

Poppy nods, pulling out her phone to show us, but we cower away in horror. Thankfully, Layla quickly changes the subject. "Ryan got the kids this week?"

Nodding, I say, "He's dating someone—some stylish younger blonde who's environmentally conscious to boot." Poppy and Layla exchange a glance. We don't discuss it, but they both know I'm not over the loss of my marriage.

"Why aren't you dating?" Poppy asks.

"Because I'm a working mom raising three kids."

"What a load of shit," Poppy says. "The kids are gone every other week. Heck, they're gone now. You should be running through some dick."

Layla gently touches my hand. "Poppy's choice of words leaves something to be desired, but she's right. You should get back out there. You've got a lot to offer someone."

"Like three kids, stretch marks, cellulite, and wrinkles?"

"Stop it," Layla says.

"It's true," I say.

"Not true," Layla says. "You're just punishing yourself for what happened with Ryan. You paid for it ten-fold already. That's enough."

"Is it?" I wonder aloud. "I'm a cheater. How am I supposed to date? The next guy is going to ask me what happened to my marriage, and I'm going to have to say I cheated."

Layla and Poppy look at me with a strange sadness. I'm not sure if it's saying what I did, or seeing their faces, or knowing Ryan has moved on, but I start to tear up. I'm usually not a big crier. Perhaps it's the lingering cabbage stench. Yeah, I'll blame it on that.

"Maybe you're a closet masochist," Poppy says. "Beating yourself up over this. It was one kiss."

Layla reaches for my hand. "You've been through enough pain. Let it go."

"Just go out and have some fun. Nothing serious. No explanations. Just get your feet wet—and your pussy, too," Poppy adds.

And just like that, I crack up, and the mood is light and fun again. Thank God for Poppy. "That reminds me. Look what I found when I was cleaning out my wallet this morning." I reach inside, pulling out my sex bucket list. Poppy quickly takes it from me, and she and Layla begin to peruse it.

"This is great," Poppy says. "It's like some sort of sign from God."

"A threesome is hardly a divine sign," I say.

"You've got to work your way up to a threesome. You can't just start there," Poppy says.

"Wait, you think I should do all this?" I wonder.

"Of course," Poppy says.

"Definitely," Layla says.

"You guys are crazy," I say. "I've got kids."

"Start with this one," Layla says and points to the list. "Number 12—Ask a man out."

"I don't even know who I could ask."

Poppy waves me off. "A guy at the grocery store, on a plane, at the coffee shop, on the side of the road! Who cares? You've got to start somewhere. And if he's more than ten years younger than you, that takes care of number 20, too." Poppy reaches in her purse. "This should help get you started."

She pulls out a handful of condoms—like six or so—and hands them to me. Yes, Poppy is *that* friend, the one who doesn't think twice about providing contraception no matter the time, day, or place. "Um, thanks," I mutter, wondering how many condoms she actually has in her purse, whether she gave me her whole stash, and why she carries so many at one time.

"Those aren't just any condoms," Poppy says. "I'll have you know they are super innovative ones. They sell for like fifty bucks for a few dozen. That rubber is special. They're extra large, too."

"I'm touched," I say. "I'll pay you back."

"No, it's my treat," Poppy says. "I just expect details. With Dash being a little pissy of late and Layla's pussy still on the mend, I'm counting on you."

POPPY LEFT HOURS ago, but I'm still hanging around Layla's place, way longer than I should. I usually don't mind going home to my empty house. I've gotten used to being alone. Actually, it wasn't that hard. I was alone in my marriage for a long time, so it wasn't a huge adjustment. Being alone doesn't have to equal loneliness. I've never been more lonely than I was the last few years of my marriage. Something just feels different tonight, so I volunteer to do some laundry and other chores to help out the new parents.

Last chore for the night is to give their dog, Pippa, a quick walk around the block. Poop bags in hand, I make my way down the Savannah streets. It's not quite summer yet, but it's still warm outside, so it seems the whole city is out biking, walking, or sitting on their porches, enjoying the weather before the oppressive Georgia heat barrels through.

I come upon one of the square parks Savannah is known for, and I find several couples strolling together. In fact, it seems like everyone is a couple. Why is that? When you're single, why does it seem like you've got a neon sign over your head?

When you're young, you can have a reckless love. It's like no one else in the world exists but you and your lover. Moms don't get that. There's always someone else to think about. Still, I've been okay alone these past few years, but I don't want to spend the rest of my life that way.

"Go potty," I tell Pippa, but she's simply darting back and forth, smelling every blade of grass she can find. I pull her leash a little closer, as a runner is fast approaching down the sidewalk. Like all dogs, she loves to bark and act like a complete fool. She darts right in front of the poor guy, almost tripping him.

"So sorry," I say, as my eyes land on a smile befitting a toothpaste commercial, which is attached to a man befitting a cologne ad.

"No trouble," he says, bending down to give Pippa a little pat.

This is a perfect sex bucket list challenge.

I flash a smile, hoping it doesn't look like a psycho grin. "Nice night," I say then cringe at my unoriginal, stupid comment. I truly suck at this.

He smiles when he stands up. "And getting better," he says. "I run every night. I don't remember seeing you before. You new to the neighborhood?"

"I'm visiting my brother," I say, turning and motioning down the street.

"Watch your dog!" he yells.

I whip my head around to find him yanking his leg away, as Pippa is squatting and pooping on his shoe. "Oh, I'm so . . ." I can't finish my apology before he's shaking his head and crossing the street to escape me and my dog with bowel-control issues.

What the hell? I try to commit to the sex bucket list, and this happens? Should I just embrace the spinster life? Mortified, I cut Pippa's walk short as punishment, take her home, then head to my own place. At least tomorrow is a workday. I'll be busy. Keeping busy helps me stay sane.

I'm commuting to work in Atlanta tomorrow, so I need to get up early. I slip under the cold covers of my bed. I still sleep on the same side as when I was married. My body won't let me take up the whole bed. I tell myself I'm just trained that way, but feel there's more to it. I even bought a new mattress and bedding, but that didn't help, either.

I say my prayers and list the things I'm thankful for. But my mind wanders to *the* list. While tonight was a complete bust, I have to do something to shake myself up. So I promise myself that sex-bucket-list Emerson will come out to play—or, at the very least, not shit on anyone else.

CHAPTER THREE
MULTIPLES

I STEP INTO the elevator of Southern Wings, and a hand flies out, blocking the closing door. I'd know that hand anywhere. He steps into the elevator with me, flashing a subtle smile. Mateo is a walking, living, breathing reason to pant. The man is God's gift to women—tan skin, dark hair and eyes, and muscles for days and days.

I hired him a few years ago to guard Layla when Gage was considering a run for public office. At the time, the media was insane, the public was in a frenzy, and it seemed all hell was breaking loose. Layla needed some protection, and I couldn't resist tormenting my baby brother by making his wife's security guy so hot he can melt any woman's panties.

Mateo was excellent in that role, having worked in the Secret Service before entering the private sector and ultimately being hired by us. But he never talks about that time in his life. Maybe he's not allowed or something. It turned out that Gage actually liked him. They have the same overprotective, macho, caveman vibe. When Gage decided not to run for office, he consulted with Mateo on security issues from time to time, so I'd see him around the office occasionally.

Gage recently made Mateo head of security for Southern Wings, so the man is a permanent fixture around here now. And let me tell you, we've had no complaints from our female employees. They make objectifying him part of their daily routine. They all lust over him, and I don't blame them. My personal lust level has gone up exponentially now that Mateo is full time. As far as I know, he's never dated any of the female employees. I haven't heard he's banged any of them, either.

We greet each other as the elevator door closes. He looks incredible, as usual. He's one of those men you can't miss. He most certainly could help me out with my sex bucket list. Maybe the elevator will break down, and we'd get stuck and make out in here all day.

A Monday morning hardly seems the time to start scratching things off my list, but if I should ask out any man, it's Mateo. Yeah, he's a good decade younger, but he's polite, employed, easy on the eyes. One problem, though, is he's an employee. Conflicted, I shuffle my feet a little. Any hesitation I have about asking him out because he's an employee is just an excuse—I don't care about that, whether we have a company policy or not. The truth is, I'm afraid I could actually fall for Mateo—the guy is the real deal.

"How are Gage and Layla?" he asks. "The baby?"

"They're great," I say, glancing at him briefly.

"I guess this is your week to be in the office?" he says, and I nod. The door opens, and he places his hand out, holding it open for me. I take a step out as he asks, "Do you ever stay over in Atlanta when you're working?"

I freeze and stare at him, deep into his brown eyes. Why does he want to know? Is he asking me over to his place? Does he want to ask me out? The elevator door closes and hits me right in the backside, forcing me into Mateo's hard chest, my breasts pressed up against him. His arms go around me, shoving the door back open.

"God, I'm so sorry," I say, fibbing and feeling safe and secure in his arms.

"Don't be," he says with a grin before releasing me.

We step out of the elevator into the prying eyes of the corporate office. Clearing my throat, and hoping my panties dry out soon, I say, "It's been a long time since I've slept over." He cocks an eyebrow at me. "I mean, in Atlanta."

Poppy approaches us. "Mateo, I need your opinion."

Oh, this should be good. Poppy would never cheat on Dash, but she loves to flirt and enjoys torturing Mateo with her borderline sexual harassment. As an executive in the company, I suppose I have an obligation to prevent it, but Mateo doesn't seem to mind. He's always a good sport about it.

"No, Poppy, I don't do bachelorette parties," he says.

"What kind of man slut are you?" she asks. Normally, I find her questions off the wall with no purpose, but this time I'm interested in the answer.

"Who called me a man slut?" he asks, frowning.

"Everyone!" Poppy laughs. "You're so alpha male and . . ."

"Does that mean I have to sleep around?"

She just shakes her head. "That's not what I wanted to know anyway. What I need to know is why men are obsessed with breeding."

"*Breeding?*" Mateo asks.

"Poppy, for goodness sake," I say.

"No, this is important," Poppy says. "Mateo is cut from the same mold as Gage and Dash. Gage couldn't wait to knock Layla up, and Dash wants to do the same to me. So what is it that makes you want to breed us like we're horses?"

Mateo ponders the question for a moment then turns his eyes from Poppy and looks directly at me, holding my eyes, and says, "I like kids, but if a woman I'm with doesn't want more kids, I'd be okay with that."

Poppy wrinkles her nose. "That doesn't really answer the question. You're no help, Mateo."

He gives me a small smile before walking off. "Did you catch that?" I ask Poppy and pull her into my office. "He said if the woman he's with already has kids. Does that mean he's interested in a woman with kids?"

Her eyes get huge. "You've got to ask him out!"

"I can't. He works for me."

"Then fire him," she says. "I need to know if he fucks as good as he looks."

✧ ✧ ✧

WELL, I DIDN'T fire Mateo today. And I didn't ask him out, either. In fact, I avoided him the rest of the day. The first day of my sex bucket list challenge is a complete failure.

The only list I've worked on today is my grocery list, making a quick stop at the store on my way home from the airport after flying in. Perhaps I'm going about this the wrong way.

There's nothing about my life that screams sex or sexy. I work. I'm a mom. That's my day. I don't even remember the last time I played with my vibrator. It's like my sex switch is stuck in the *off* position.

And it's my fault. I don't do anything to help myself feel sexy—no matching pretty bra and panties sets. I barely have time to have my roots touched up, much less go for a wax. Maybe that's a good place to start. Maybe I need to take personal stock before I can properly get on with my list.

Flipping up my laptop and putting on my glasses, I snuggle into bed and eye my flannel pajamas. Good Lord, I need a lot of help. First thing I do is surf around for new bras and panties, several hundred dollars worth. It's a lot of money for underwear, and I feel a twinge of guilt that it could be better spent on my kids, car insurance, or school uniforms. Even though my family is well off, my parents instilled in Gage and me not to spend frivolously and that nothing comes without hard work.

But I hit the purchase button anyway. I'm investing in my sexual future.

God, I sound like a financial planner. Could I be less spontaneous? I'm planning for the day I might have sex again. Even I know how sad that is.

I reach for my wine glass and start phase two of my plan—new vibrator. I'm out of the loop on the best brands and models, so I type *best vibrators for women* in the search box. Did you know everyone from Oprah to the Huffington Post has done articles on the subject? I decide to follow Oprah's recommendations, because if you can't trust her on matters of the Big O, who can you trust?

But damn, some of these things push a couple hundred bucks. And I already dropped that on underwear. They do seem high quality, though—I see one of them doubles as a necklace—so maybe that's worth it. I can just see myself in a board meeting with my baby brother, maybe talking about the latest federal regulations, and suddenly my necklace starts buzzing. That is something that would completely happen to me, and I just don't need that in my life right now. But maybe the one disguised as a lipstick?

I read some more. Did you know you can charge most vibrators with your computer? I had no idea masturbating has gotten so high tech. I keep surfing around and begin to see the same one over and over again. It's apparently the best bang for the buck, no pun intended. Clicking on it, an article pops up on the person who invented it—a woman.

For some reason, that makes total sense. Who better than a woman to invent a sex toy for women? I see that she's younger than me—the article says she's in her late twenties—but she looks completely normal, this female vibrator trailblazer. It shouldn't surprise me, but it does for some reason. I didn't expect a sex toy inventor to look normal.

The article seals the deal for me. I opt to buy this one. I mean, women should support other women. I'm doing it for the cause. I'm so intrigued by her that I click on her social media page, and even send her a friend request. I blame the alcohol for doing that. Hope she doesn't think I want to get in her pants.

Last order of business is to make a waxing appointment, and I resolve to go all the way. No cute landing strip or triangle this time. I'm going bare. Go big or go home, they say. Lucky for me, the salon and spa that does the hair on my head can also take care of my other unruly mane. I make an appointment online and see something else on their website, vaginal steaming.

Intrigued, I read the description touting it as a detox, kind of a facial for your lady parts, then do a quick Google search. Let me tell you, vaginal health is big these days. I had no idea. There's spas for everything. And there's no way I'm ready for what I'm seeing. Vaginal lifts? Lasers on my girl parts? Platelets shot into my vagina? No, thank you.

But I remain intrigued by the vaginal steaming. That seems harmless enough, and I make an appointment for that, too. After all, I'm starting fresh with my list. Shouldn't she?

A COUPLE DAYS ago, I had my wax and even splurged to buy some stuff called Tend Skin, which is supposedly used by bikini models to prevent unsightly ingrown hairs and red bumps. So I'm thinking I have the most pampered vagina in all of Savannah.

I have to say, it's pretty damn masochistic to have someone rip your pubic hair out by the root and then pay them sixty bucks. When the woman asked me if I wanted the backside done, I had no clue what she was talking about. I guess you learn something new every day. Apparently, I had hair by my ass, but not anymore—as smooth as can be. So today, I'm back for the steaming.

They say to do it a couple days after your period, but that didn't fit with my timetable. I'm on a mission here. There is a whole list of different herbs to use. How am I supposed to know if my vagina likes lemon or rosemary? I know lemon is commonly used in household cleaners, so I opt for that. It will certainly do the job.

I'm taken into this room where a little pot sits on a table. The spa technician fills it, adds my special blend of herbs, turns on some relaxing music, and dims the lights. If I remember correctly, this is how Ryan used to try to get me in the mood as well, minus the pot and herbs. Well, if I'm being honest, there was some pot and herbs of a different variety back in college.

The vaginal expert proceeds to give me some instructions on what the procedure entails, and then she advises me to just relax. Yeah, I don't really do relaxation well. My mind begins to wander. I wonder what training and certifications, if any, you need for this profession. How is the training done? Do women offer themselves as guinea pigs for the trainees? Do any guys go into this field?

I guess the expert can tell I'm not entirely comfortable because she says, "It might help if you massage your stomach or inner thighs."

She encourages me to sit down on the pot, and wraps a towel around my waist, creating a little barrier to hold the steam in before leaving the room. I'm glad she's gone. This seems like it should be private time—just me and my vagina.

My treatment is thirty minutes. A few minutes in, I don't think I'm going to make it. It feels like my vagina is being incinerated—like I'm literally burning it off. My entire body is covered in sweat. I feel like I'm being tortured.

But around the fifteen-minute mark, my body adjusts—and by that, I mean I'm horny as hell. I don't know if it's the heat or the increased blood flow down there, but I'm wide open and dripping. Though I haven't masturbated in light years, I remember what that's like, but this is coming from an entirely different place.

Taking a quick glance around, I make sure there aren't any cameras. The walls of my vagina start clenching over and over again, my muscles knowing what they want. My hands grip the side of the pot—or throne, really, which deserves every bit of my worship. I'm trembling between my legs when the technician walks back in.

"I need another minute," I pant, not wanting to come right in front of her.

"I'm sorry, but the time's over, and we have another client."

I stare daggers at her and curse under my breath, frustrated as hell. So I stand and clean up, and try to look on the bright side: the damn steaming has awakened something in me that I thought was in hibernation forever.

I quickly pay, leaving way over a twenty percent tip. The only thing I want to do is get home and get off. And when I arrive, as if heaven is smiling down on me, I find a non-descript package waiting on my front porch. I smile wide, knowing I'm about to finally knock something off my sex bucket list.

Number 7. Give yourself multiple orgasms.

So instead of the television, a book, or surfing the internet, I spend the night with my new vibrator. And for the first time in forever, I'm not worried about the kids walking in, how I look doing this, whether I'm a whore for it. I mean, if I want to be comfortable with a man again, I've got to get comfortable with myself.

So I don't turn the lights off. I don't hide under the covers. I lay completely naked in the bright lights of my bedroom and use my new toy. The best thing is, it's made for me to be on top. Perfect for a woman like me, who's trying to take back control of her sex life.

When I'm completely done, when I have nothing left, I fire up my laptop and look up sex toys that mimic oral sex. I also check out how to give yourself a vaginal steaming at home. These are whole new worlds to explore. Smiling, I drift off to sleep, planning out the next time the kids will be gone, so I can do this all over again.

CHAPTER FOUR
SEX WITH AN EX

"Mom!" I hear three different voices calling out to me. My eyes open, and I fly out of bed, looking at the clock. It's apparently noon already, and the kids are back from a week away. Stretching, I glance around to make sure all the evidence of my night of passion for one is stowed away. Then I start towards the door, met by my youngest in a huge hug.

Kissing Conner, I walk towards the foyer, passing Jacob and Ava both heading up the stairs. "Hey, hey," I say. "Haven't seen you in forever. Where's my kiss?"

Ava leans over the banister, rolling her eyes, but kisses me with a smile. Jacob just leans his head down so I can kiss him. Then they fly up to their rooms. Since we split time, there's not much exchange of stuff, except for the kids' school bags, which Ryan drops by the front door.

"Mommy, are you sick?" Connor asks. "Why were you still in bed?"

I know I blush, and I know Ryan catches it. "I'm fine, baby," I say. "I was just having a lazy morning." He gives me one more big squeeze then runs off.

But Ryan doesn't leave. Usually he doesn't linger. At most, we'll talk kids' schedules, but that's it. He's not saying anything now, though, just glaring at me. He hasn't looked at me like this since I told him about the kiss. "What?" I ask.

"Are you not alone?" he snaps.

"Huh?"

"You find out I'm seeing someone, and now you've got some guy hiding in your bedroom?"

"I do not!"

He steps a little closer and lowers his voice. "We were married close to twenty years. I know what you look like after you've come."

I put my finger on his chest. "And how do I look?"

"Like you do now." Ryan waves his hand over me. "Your shirt is on backwards. Your hair is all crazy. You're glowing."

I try not to smile, picturing my vagina glowing like your skin after a facial. "Ryan, I promise there isn't a man in my bedroom—or anywhere in the house."

"Did he go out the back when he heard the kids?"

"No!" I snap. "And what business is it of yours anyway? You have no say in who I sleep with!"

His lips crash into mine, forcing me up against the foyer wall. I'm a little in shock, but I don't resist, not one bit. My knees go weak, having forgotten how well this man can kiss. Neither one of us seems to care that the kids are home, that it's the middle of the day, or that we're divorced.

Still kissing me, he starts to move. And before I know it, we are way beyond his invisible barrier of the foyer. And his hands are way beyond the safe zones, tugging and ripping at both our clothes, until we reach my bedroom, our bedroom. He kicks the door closed, locking it, as we shed what's left of our clothes. Panting, his eyes lower to the bare flesh between my legs.

"I did it for me," I say quietly, unsure why I'm explaining myself. "Trying to make myself feel desirable again."

"Christ, Emerson," he says, taking me down to the bed.

Suddenly, I realize what's happening, and how confusing this will be for the kids if they find out, and how confusing it is for me. "Ryan, the kids are here."

"Don't make me stop," he says. "I just want to feel you trembling under me."

Maybe I should stop it, but I don't. Despite all my pleasure last night, there's nothing like the real thing. Telling myself it doesn't have to mean anything, I grind against him. We never had one last romp in the hay, never had the infamous goodbye sex. So I'm just going to enjoy this for what it is, even though sex with an ex isn't on my list.

It's torture not to be able to breathe heavy, to scream out. But something about having to maintain control makes my body even needier. And I want this to be special, memorable. I always wished I could remember the last time we had sex. If this is going to be it, I want to remember. I want to give him every last drop of me. I look down at his hard dick, rubbing up against me.

"I'm not on birth control," I say, which slows him down. "But I have a condom," I add, which makes him stop completely.

"You have condoms?"

"Poppy," I say, and it only takes that one name for him to understand. I reach towards my purse, knowing how thrilled she'll be we used hers. Ryan's eyes are glued on me as I find a condom and place it in his hand.

He seems impressed. Being prepared is sexy. My legs shaking, he buries himself deep between my thighs.

"Don't you dare hold back on me," he says. "I want all of it."

Oh God, I always did love his dick. It's the perfect length and width, and my body molds around him perfectly. He pulls my nipple between his teeth, sucking, then thrusts in and out of me, hard and quick.

I place my hands on his hips to slow him down, knowing I won't get off this way. He slips out, and yanks me to the edge of the bed. I can't help but smile, remembering when we bought our first mattress together, and his only concern was it was the right height for him to fuck me this way—nothing else mattered in the purchase. The little grin on his face tells me he remembers that day, too.

Standing, he glides himself back inside me, slowly, letting my body enjoy every inch of him, making sure I feel him. His hands caress my breasts, my stomach—all the parts I'm insecure about—but he's seen them a thousand times before. But at this point, there's only one part I want him to get to. Ladies, do we need to make a big X marks the spot? Maybe it confused the whole male species when they heard the term G-spot or the big O?

After almost twenty years of marriage, how can the man not know what I need? The waiting, the teasing is almost too much, too intense. I can tell he's getting close. To fake it or not? That is the question. I faked orgasming as much as I faked being happy the last couple years of our marriage, which was a huge mistake. Basically, I taught him to be lazy. At the time, I thought I was sparing his feelings—at the expense of my own. I won't do that anymore.

Right as I gain the courage to tell him what I need, he groans and falls down on me, burying his head in my neck, muffling the string of orgasmic curse words. To see him during the day, you'd never think he's dirty in bed. He's always so professional. He's a college professor, for goodness sake. We lay together for a minute, our bodies stuck from a thin sheet of sweat.

"I really needed that," he says, panting.

Ugh, this is the worst feeling in the world, with so many emotions and questions swirling in my body. I'm reminded of loving him. I'm reminded of him loving me. I wish I hadn't messed things up. I wish we hadn't gotten to the point where I was in a position to mess things up. And now, what are we going to say to each other? How are we going to act going forward? Is this a one-time deal? Should I ask him if the condom was as good as advertised? On top of all these issues, I'm full on sexually frustrated, completely horny and unsatisfied.

Ryan gives me one long, deep kiss before slipping out of me. Then he gets up and takes off the condom. Usually this is the part I hate about condoms—they totally mess up the mood. That brief loss of contact dampens the cuddling after.

But today I'm grateful when he disappears into the bathroom. It gives me a minute to get myself off. Lucky for me, it only takes about thirty seconds. I'm quite the expert after last night. Why can I give myself an orgasm so quickly and Ryan can't do it after twenty years of practice?

✧ ✧ ✧

I STICK MY head out of my bedroom door and see that the coast is clear. I walk Ryan to the front door when Connor pops out of the kitchen. "Dad, you're still here?"

"Um, yeah, your mom needed a little help with something in the bedroom," Ryan says.

I almost die laughing—I helped myself, thank you very much. "I'll be right back, Connor. Just let me walk your dad out."

We step out onto the front porch into the harsh light of day, of what we just did. It took us well over a year to untangle our lives, and now in a few short minutes, we just wrapped ourselves back up into each other like a tangled ball of Christmas lights.

"Emerson," he says, regret thick in his voice.

Eyes closed, I shake my head. "You don't need to say anything."

CHAPTER FIVE
POLE DANCING 101

HAVING UNSATISFYING SEX with my ex wasn't on my list of sexual adventures. And rightfully so—it was a mistake. Since then, the only communication I've had with Ryan is by text; he hasn't come inside the house at all. I know it shouldn't, but it's taken some steam out of my sex bucket list challenge. It's been two weeks, and I can't shake the funk it put me in.

Poppy doesn't seem to be feeling any better than I am. And the color of her hair proves it. When she came to work for us, Gage wrote in her contract she couldn't have "crazy" colors. She's been good about it. I'm not sure if it's the job or the fact that she's been in a stable relationship with Dash.

But all bets are off today. She walked in the office with extensions down to her butt, and I can tell she tried to hide the color. The under-hair is dyed a royal blue, so you only see it when her hair moves a certain way. I need to check on her.

Walking down the hallway to her office, I see Mateo heading towards me. His head is down, looking at some papers, giving me a second to admire the way he fills out his suit. Hell, the man fills up the entire space. He glances up, and I'm not sure who smiles first. "Good morning," I say.

In one long stride, he's in front of me. "Everything alright?" he asks.

The first words in my head are, "No, I slept with Ryan a few weeks back and am a mess for it," but the ones out of my mouth are much safer. "Of course, just going to see Poppy."

He raises his eyebrows. "I saw the hair."

"I'm on it."

The corner of his mouth turns up slightly, and his eyes brighten. "I knew you would be."

"Poppy's my friend."

His smile grows. "Yeah, but you take care of everyone all the time."

"I do not." I shut my mouth because the lies I'm about to spew would burn my tongue.

"You keep Gage's head on straight. You organize office parties for birthdays. You send flowers, gifts. You call when someone has a relative die. You bring people lunch when they are really busy. Hell, you even wash the coffee pot when you're in the kitchen. You take care of everyone."

"You notice all that?"

He inches closer, looking down at me, and my heart pumps hard. "I notice *everything* about you."

Oh my God, my heart's about to pump out of my chest. But I tell myself maybe he just means it's his job as head of security to pay attention, to be observant. But maybe not—after all, he sure is standing close to me. And he looks and smells fantastic. Powered by my list, I place a hand on my hip, and in my sassiest tone, say, "Are you wondering what it'd be like for me to take care of you?"

His head lowers to my ear, his warm breath sending shivers over my skin. "I'm wondering if you'll ever let me take care of you."

That's the sweetest thing a man's said to me in a long time.

I want to say something sexy back like, "Which parts do you have in mind?" But my brain isn't functioning. All my energy is solely focused on the pulsing between my legs. That's the only thing functioning. He pulls back slightly, locking eyes with me. The way he's looking at me, I'm certain he could take care of every inch of me.

A slamming door forces us each to take a huge step back, and we turn to see Dash storming out of Poppy's office. I wonder why he's here. It's rare for a pilot to be in the corporate office. I really hope they aren't breaking up. Dash spots Mateo and me in the hallway, but I don't think he picked up on anything, too caught up in his own drama. I flash a look to Mateo, urging him silently to talk Dash off the ledge.

I head into Poppy's office, and she starts yapping right away, talking a mile a minute. "Dash is driving me nuts," she says. "On top of lots of sex, I've given him like twenty blowjobs the past week. I've been an excellent girlfriend like that." She goes on for about ten minutes, describing the locations of the blowjobs, different techniques she's used, and so on.

I listen until she's quiet, until her battery is dead. "So what's the problem?"

"He's all pissy because I got my period now," she says.

"Never thought that would stop you guys," I say, wondering how Mateo feels about period sex. Ryan was adamantly opposed.

"It's not that," Poppy says. "I was a couple days late. Stress, I think. Dash got his hopes up."

She keeps talking, but my mind is stuck on her period being late. Poppy, Layla, and I generally run on the same cycle—freaky, but true. I know it's rude—I'm supposed to be focused on her—but I pull out my phone. I mark my calendar when my period starts every month.

Counting the days, my skin starts to sweat, my heart thumping like a freight train. "Emerson, you alright? You look like you're about to pass out."

"This is your fault!" I cry out, jumping to my feet.

"Huh? What are you talking about?"

"I had sex!"

"You did? I'm so happy! But how is that *my* fault?"

"You gave me the condoms!" I say. "One time! I did it one time with the condoms you gave me—and now I'm late."

Poppy flings open the door to her office and finds Mateo talking to Dash in the hallway. "Dash," she screams so loudly I swear the building shakes, "did you poke holes in the condoms to get me pregnant?"

Left and right, employees begin to pop out of their cubicles and offices, taking in the free show.

"Are you insane?" Dash asks. "Men don't do that shit! That's shit *women* do."

"You think I did it?" she snaps back. "You accusing me? Why would I do that? I didn't poke a hole in them!"

"What are we even talking about?" Dash asks. "Are there holes in them? Are you pregnant?"

"No!" Poppy barks. "You know I'm on my period!"

"I know! So I don't even know what we're talking about!"

"I gave some of the condoms to Emerson!"

Poppy says it so loudly I think all of Atlanta hears. Mateo seems to have a slight grin on his face, but I'm fully mortified with all the employees around, and I'd like to just crawl under a desk and die. My mind quickly wanders to things outside the office—Ryan will think I got pregnant on purpose to get him back. Holy hell, I've really got myself freaked the fuck out now, and I start to pace. Every other time I've been pregnant, it had been planned, thought out, like everything else in my life. Ryan and I had talked about it. I had cute ways of telling him. It was never a surprise, never a shock. I tell myself over and over again there's no way I could be pregnant. I'm supposed to be working on my sex bucket list, not a baby registry.

Poppy tells everyone to get back to work, and then she pulls me and Dash into her office and closes the door. She grabs my arms to calm me, and I reward her with my word vomit. "I didn't poke a hole in your condom," I pant out.

"Of course you didn't, honey," Poppy says. "And I didn't. And Dash didn't, either. So everything should be good?"

"I don't know. I'm late. I doubt Ryan will think everything's good."

"Who gives a fuck about him?" Poppy asks.

"We slept together," I say, "with your condom."

"Oh," Poppy says, and her eyes flash to Dash, her silent order to keep his mouth shut.

"I need to go," I say.

"You're shaking. You need to calm down."

"I can't be forty-something and pregnant," I cry, pulling away. "No, no, no, I can't be *unmarried* and pregnant. I mean, I preach to Ava and Jacob all day long about waiting until you're married. They will know what we did. Oh God, Connor! He thinks you can get pregnant *only* when you're married."

She grabs both my arms and motions with her head for Dash to leave. "Maybe it's early menopause."

"You did *not* just say that!" I cry out.

She laughs so hard that she actually snorts like a pig. "What's so wrong with menopause? I'm looking forward to it." She nudges me, but I don't crack a smile. I'm in no mood.

I tell her I need to be alone and walk out of her office.

IN THE MOVIES, when someone's life is upside down, they often end up at a bar. But given my potentially delicate condition, I can't really go tie one on. So instead of drowning my sorrows in a bottle of whiskey, I decide to get drunk on carbs and make a beeline for my favorite Italian restaurant. That seems a sensible thing to do right now, and I have a few hours to kill before my flight back home to Savannah.

I polish off a pile of breadsticks while I wait for my spaghetti then push the basket to the side of the table and tell the waiter, "Keep 'em coming. I don't want to see the bottom." He raises an eyebrow like I've lost my mind. "Don't judge me," I say.

He laughs, leaving a bottle of olive oil for me to dip. Good man. I know there are all kinds of diets that tout giving up carbs, but for the life of me, I don't know how in the hell they do it. I saw one diet that called for eating fewer than twenty-five grams of carbs each day. How is that possible? I eat a banana every morning, and that would be enough for one day. No way. Besides, bananas are healthy, and I need my potassium. At least that's what I tell myself. They say drinking alone is a sign you're an alcoholic, so I guess stuffing my face at a table for one makes me a carboholic. I'll be in a food coma tomorrow, but that's okay. It's worth it.

But just like drinking, it only makes me forget for a little while.

THE FLIGHT BACK to Savannah is hell. My mind is spinning, and no amount of deep breathing helps. I've never been so thankful to get off an airplane in my life. I need to pace, to do something besides be strapped to a chair.

I go through the Savannah airport and feel trapped in slow motion, everyone hustling around me. My eyes land on one person standing still, looking at me with her strong blue eyes. Poppy must've called her. Layla tilts her head, opening up her arms.

"I can't talk about it," I say.

"Talk about what?" she says, but I know she knows. "I'm kidnapping you for a ladies night out."

Layla tells me the plan, and it's a doozy. The kidnapping will involve pole dancing, which was on my list. It's apparently a great workout, and a great way to get in touch with your inner diva. I don't buy the inner diva bullshit, but I know it's their way of helping me forget everything else, and Layla promises Mexican food afterwards, so what's to lose? I can work all the carbs out of my system and then fill it up again.

Layla's got a gym bag and everything I'll need for the class. I like to be prepared, so I spend the drive over combing the internet for instructional videos—anything to keep my mind off my other situation. I find numerous YouTube videos highlighting some legendary wipeouts, most all of them in sexy stripper heels.

I opt to go barefoot, but not even that saves me. I was attempting to do what I was told was a basic spin move. I was supposed to hold onto the pole with my inside arm, walking around it, then hook my inside leg around the pole, and do a little spin. Instead, I fell flat on my ass, my foot twisted around the pole.

One trip to the after-hours emergency clinic, coming right up.

"You'll need a few x-rays," the nurse says then asks, "Could you be pregnant?" I wasn't expecting that question, although I probably should've.

I feel Layla's eyes on me. "It's possible," I say softly.

The nurse hands me a little specimen cup and points me towards the bathroom. Am I the only one that hates the instructions on how to get a "clean" urine sample? I've been wiping myself for forty years—do I really need directions? It's completely embarrassing to hand her the cup, still warm, and to think my entire future is contained in a batch of pee. Hobbling back to the bed, I lay back down to wait. I don't feel pregnant. I craved Pringles when I was pregnant with both the boys, and I couldn't get enough roast beef with Ava. Right now, the only thing I want is my pillow—and some dignity.

Layla suddenly busts out laughing. It's unlike her to laugh inappropriately. She turns her phone to me, where I see that Poppy is promising to dye half her hair blue and the other half pink in a show of solidarity if I'm pregnant. Poppy used some filter to show us what it would look like. She looks like a cross between the Joker and Harley Quinn. Psychotic is putting it mildly. Then she used the same filter on pictures of Layla and me.

The nurse appears and says, "Let's get you to x-ray."

I sit straight up. "Does that mean I'm not pregnant?"

She flips a paper over. "Your test was negative."

Damn, she could've led with that. The relief that floods my body sends chills over my skin. There's not one cell in my body that is sad. I thank God many times over, promising not to mess up again. I can work on my sex bucket list, but I have to be smart about it. I can't screw anything that moves, and I need some reliable birth control. Instead of shopping for vaginal steaming, I should've made an appointment to get an IUD. That's going on the top of my list now.

I'VE LOST TRACK of how long we've been in the clinic. No other business can keep you waiting as long as doctors can. "You're lucky you didn't break anything," Layla says.

Hard lesson to learn—not every woman can work a pole. I dislocated my big toe. Honestly, who dislocates a toe? It hurt like a mother when the doctor popped it back into place. At least my doctor was cute, but unfortunately, she was also a woman. I guess it doesn't matter because sex with a doctor isn't on my bucket list, anyway.

I look down at my swollen foot, at the lovely shades of purple and black. "Are you alright?" I hear Ryan's voice and look up, seeing him in the doorway.

"What are you doing here?" I ask.

"Gage called me."

"I'm going to kill him," Layla says. "I'm so sorry, Emerson. I called him to let him know I'd be late because of the baby's feedings. I didn't know he'd call Ryan."

Layla and Ryan don't really know each other. My divorce was well underway by the time Layla and Gage got together. They've met a few times at functions for the kids.

"What happened?" Ryan asks me. "Gage said you got hurt working out."

"She's fine," Layla says. "I'll take care of her."

I have to smile. My girl has my back. She'll pick my ass up after a pole dancing injury, no questions asked. Don't think I can say the same for my ex-husband. I'm sure he'll have some judgment.

"What should I tell the kids?" he asks.

"Tell them I tripped on my computer cord and dislocated my toe," I say. "They'll believe that. I tripped on that damn thing last week."

"Okay," he says. "But what's the truth?"

"I fell in my pole dancing class."

Surprisingly, he doesn't laugh or sneer or anything else, so credit to him for that. "Could we talk for a minute alone?" he asks me. "Maybe I could drive you home. Ava and Jacob are watching Conner. I can stay."

"Go home, Ryan," I say, unsure why he's even here in the first place. It wasn't until this very moment, seeing him again, that I realize how truly hurt I am that he's ignored me after we had sex. I'd been telling myself it was just goodbye sex, but it wasn't—it clearly was more, at least to me. It never could be *just sex* with Ryan. And it hurt that I was *just sex* to him. Still, it's my fault for letting it happen in the first place. "I'm not your problem anymore."

"So damn dramatic," he mumbles.

Layla steps in front of him. "Emerson is the least dramatic person I know."

"It's alright," I say. "It's nothing I haven't heard before. It *barely* even hurts anymore."

Ryan's eyes lock on mine. He caught that word. "Emerson, I never meant to hurt you. Not the other day and certainly not tonight."

"Don't flatter yourself, Ryan," I say, scooting up on the bed. "You were merely on the list."

"What list?"

"Don't," Layla says, grabbing my hand.

"My sex bucket list," I say, glaring at him. "Having sex with an ex was number 26."

He looks at me with a twinge of sadness, and without a word, barges out of the room. A flood of guilt hits me. I don't feel better for chiding him. I feel worse. It even makes my toe feel worse.

"There isn't a number 26," Layla says softly.

My lips in a tight line, I shake my head and close my eyes. I feel shitty, but I will not cry over that man. I will not. At least not right now. I've shed so many tears over him, but for some reason, I'm still not out. How is that possible? I always thought you only had so many tears you could shed per person, but Ryan's well just keeps getting filled up again.

CHAPTER SIX
ORGASM MEDITATION

So that's it. I hurt Ryan, he hurt me, I hurt him. I've got to get off this carousel. It's making me sick. Not even remembering flirting with Mateo can lift my mood. Plus, I'm extra emotional because I finally got my period. This time of the month always makes me feel vulnerable and insecure. But make no mistake, I'm very thankful my little romp with Ryan won't have any reminders.

Still, I don't feel myself. So like a little girl, I run to the one place, the one person who always makes things better. "Mom?" I call out, heading inside her stately mansion and tossing my purse on her couch.

My mom doesn't need to know about my list, of course, but sometimes a daughter just needs a hug from her mother, no matter how old she is. "Emerson, honey is that you?" a muffled call comes from upstairs.

Walking up, I let my fingers gently roam the banister. I didn't grow up in this house, but it was the last place my dad lived. He and Mom bought it after the airline struck it big. He loved this place, and everything from the wood tones to the roses in the backyard make me think of him.

I call out for my mother again, finding her in her bedroom, pulling boxes and boxes out of her old cedar chest that has sat at the end of her bed for as long as I can remember. She's in her late sixties, but she doesn't seem to know it. "What on Earth are you doing?"

"Found it," she says, a huge smile on her face.

God, I hope I age like she has. She's still got a figure on her, and the wrinkles on her face just seem to make her eyes stand out more. Her hair is all gray, but not in a dry, crinkly way. No, her hair shines. She's beautiful to me, even if I'm just seeing her through a devoted daughter's eyes.

She hugs me tightly, and I bury my head in her hair. My mom has the best smell. I've tried for years to figure out what it is, but I've yet to put my finger on it. As a young girl, I used to smell her goodbye. I wanted to breathe her in and hold her close. If she walked up the stairs before me or by my room, I always knew she was there.

"Look," she says, taking my hand. "I found Gage's baptismal gown. I thought they'd like to have it for Greer."

I try hard not to laugh. Gage in a dress, even as a baby, is great ammunition. "I'm not sure Gage will love it, but Layla will."

The baptism is only a couple weeks away, and afterwards, my mom is having a party at her house. I usually help plan these types of things, but I've definitely dropped the ball on this one.

"How's your toe?" my mom asks. "Did you do something about that computer cord?"

"Yes, and I'm fine."

I don't like that my mom got fed a lie, but I didn't want her knowing I was on a stripper pole. As for my toe, it's not really fine. It's a lovely mix of blues, yellows, and purples. I'm glad it didn't happen during winter, because I can't get a real shoe on to save my life. I'm hoping the swelling goes down enough before I have to go into the office; otherwise, I'll be showing up in flip-flops.

Despite my assurance, my mom knows I'm not myself. She takes my hand, sitting me on the bed, then wraps one arm around me, urging my head to her small shoulder. I don't talk about my feelings much, but she knows just what I need. She hums a little and squeezes my hand. I'm five years old again, and for those five minutes, it feels incredible.

No one tells you, one of the hardest things about divorce is that no one holds you anymore. I mean, your kids rush in and out, and then occasionally—if you're real lucky—they might throw you a quick hug, probably a sideways one. So it's nice to have someone hold me close when I'm feeling blah.

I wonder if my mom feels like that. Dad died about a year before my divorce. "Momma," I whisper.

That's the only word I need to say. "Oh baby girl, you're doing good." My head starts to shake, and she holds my cheeks in her hands. "Really good. I couldn't be prouder." Mom's words are like magic, and my heart flutters inside.

"Are you ever lonely?" I ask. She gives me a curious look. "With Dad gone, I mean. You and he were so affectionate."

"You and Gage used to hate that," she says, smiling.

"Now I realize how nice it was. You must miss it."

Her head tilts, a sparkle in her eye. "Why do you think I got massages every week for the first couple years after he passed away?" she says. "I craved someone's touch."

"I never realized that. I just thought you were treating yourself."

"I saw on the television the other day about people whose jobs are professional cuddlers," she says. "I never hired one of those, but it speaks to our need to be loved and touched."

"Why don't you go anymore?" I ask. She releases a deep breath. And I know the look in her eyes. It's the one I have every time I think about bringing a new man into my kids' lives. Straight up terror. "Are you dating?"

"I don't know if I'd call it dating."

I fly to my feet. "Mom, don't tell me you have a fuck buddy?"

"Emerson, don't you talk to me that way!"

She hasn't lost her mom voice, that's for sure, and I haven't lost my little girl vision of my parents. My daddy slapping my momma's butt every chance he got. There isn't room for another man in that story. I sit back down, sheepishly. "I'm sorry, but what about Daddy?"

She pats my knee. "Your father is the only man I've ever loved. He's the only man I've ever shared my bed with. You know that."

"But you're seeing other men?"

"There's one man. We met at a church thing. He's around my age and a widow. We go to some events together. He's my partner for the senior dancing club. We're friends."

"Friends who cuddle?" I ask, raising an eyebrow.

"It's about companionship, nothing more."

I look down at her hand on my knee, her wedding ring still on her finger. "And you feel less lonely?" She nods. "Should I meet him?"

"If you want," she says, laughing. "I'm not hiding him from you. I am, however, hiding him from your brother." We both start giggling. "I'm not looking for love. Your father gave me enough to last ten lifetimes."

Nodding, I think I grasp what she's telling me. The man is a friend. He's not going to be my stepdad. He's not coming into our family. Time to change the topic. "So tell me, what do you have in mind for the baptism?" I ask.

We spend the next hour going over the menu, cake, flowers. The church service will only be family, but my mom is hosting a larger reception at her house after. With their hands full with their daughter, Layla and Gage are grateful that Mom is handling all the planning.

"Layla's only request is that there be no chocolate. It gives the baby terrible gas, and she says she can't be tempted," Mom laughs out.

My phone rings in my purse. I know it's Ava from the sound. She programmed a special ring tone just for her, and I can't figure out how to change it. For the past few months, I've been stuck listening to the latest boy band singing so high, it's obvious their balls haven't dropped yet.

The next few minutes are complete teenage girl drama. Translated, that means she and Ryan are fighting because she was invited by one of her friends to the country club. She wants to wear a bikini, and Ryan is not having it. So she needs me to bring her a tankini. Why this has become my problem, I have no idea.

But I do what most moms would. I drop what I'm doing and run to her aid.

✧ ✧ ✧

Between the end of my pole dancing career, the pregnancy scare, and running interference between Ava and her dad, I'm making virtually no progress on my sex bucket list, unless you count going to the gynecologist for birth control. I'm a doer, a planner. I set my sights on things and tackle them. It's what I do. It's in my DNA. It bums me out I'm not making progress. Sure, I've had some opportunities, but nothing's felt right.

I find myself alone and restless working from home. With the kids gone, I decide to head into the Atlanta office before Ryan brings them home tomorrow. I've got meetings and paperwork for days, and it's easier just to knock it all out in the office. Besides, I haven't been in at all since I hurt my foot. Between that and my period, I didn't really feel like traveling. This is a perk of it being my family's company. But my period is over, and I'm starting to go crazy. Time to get my butt into the office.

No shoe was covering my swollen foot, so I'm in flip-flops. They're cute, Kate Spade, and stolen out of my daughter's closet. They're also completely inappropriate for work, but I have no choice. When I arrive, the main receptionist informs me that the elevators are down so I will have to take the stairs.

Eight stories.

Blowing out a deep breath, I silently tell myself I've got this. And I'm thankful I'm late arriving. No one will see me struggle up the stairs. I'll just take my time, one step at a time, just looking ahead. After a few floors, I adjust my purse and the satchel I carry my work stuff in. I love the satchel. I actually lust over it sometimes. It's this really cool distressed red leather, so much prettier than a briefcase, which looks so corporate.

A rough voice calls out my name, booming through the stairwell. Glancing up a few steps, a new lust settles in. The man's tan skin contrasts with the white walls, his broad shoulders seemingly blocking the whole staircase.

"Where you off to, Mateo?"

"I'm meeting a guy about some equipment downstairs," he says then notices my gimp. "What happened to your foot?" He steps to me and offers his arm. I don't need it, but I take it anyway. The muscles in his forearm flex under my fingertips. I tell him it's fine, that it happened while working out. "Does it hurt?"

"No, it's really fine." His head does the cute tilt, the corner of his mouth curving up. "Actually, it does hurt."

"I don't like to think of you in pain," he says quietly.

I squeeze his arm and find his eyes, flirting, "A little pain can sometimes be a good thing."

"You being in pain could never be a good thing," he says quietly, his eyes finding mine.

His hands grasp my waist, pulling me close to his broad, muscular chest and shoulders. "I thought you had a meeting," I say.

He leans down, his mouth inches from mine. "It can wait," he breathes out, "until I have you taken care of." Then he takes my satchel and purse from my arm and scoops me up in his arms, carrying me up the last few flights of stairs. This is light years beyond anything on my list.

"Oh my God, you picked me up!" I say, half in shock and half laughing. I look down at the floor quickly moving under me. "You're carrying me!"

"Don't you remember what I told you in the hallway outside Poppy's office about me taking care of you?"

"Well . . . I . . . um . . ." Apparently I'm incapable of stringing two words together.

"It starts now."

The intensity in the atmosphere shoots up—his words, my hands on his arm, the way he's looking at me. It's overwhelming, and I'm grateful when we arrive on the eighth floor landing. "I can take it from here," I say.

He puts me down, opens the stairwell door, and follows me to my office to make sure I get there safe and secure. As I turn the knob on my office door, I hear him call out my secretary's name. I peek my head out and see her nodding, making notes, mouthing "Yes, sir."

She glances my way. I'm sure she's wondering why Mateo is suddenly so interested in me. I'm kind of wondering the same thing myself. But I'm kind of loving it, too.

"YOU DO A disservice to pole dancers everywhere," Poppy laughs out.

"Some of us weren't born with your skill," I say.

"Your secretary asked me to bring you this," she says, handing me a takeout container of salad.

This is Mateo's doing. "That's sweet," I say, as Poppy hands me another sack. "What's this?"

Poppy shrugs as I reach inside and find a pair of fluffy slippers. This is Mateo's doing, too.

"Did Layla do that?" she wonders.

"I don't know," I lie.

"I'm sure it was her. She makes me look bad."

I'm not sure how to thank him. Well, my dirty mind has a few ideas. We could spend some more time in the stairwell. I could knock some things off my list. But let's face it, knowing me, I'll end up writing him a thank you note and leaving it on his desk.

"By the way," Poppy says, "why didn't you tell me right after you slept with Ryan?"

"Honestly, it was so terrible that I just wanted to forget it happened."

"That bastard didn't make you come, did he?"

"Shh!" I say, half giggling. "Maybe it's me."

"Maybe you should go to an orgasm class. There are workshops you can take to teach you how to orgasm." Part of me wants to know if she's been, but I can't bear to ask. "There's also orgasm meditation."

"Is that why people chant *Om*—for orgasm meditation?" I ask, laughing.

She rolls her eyes. "No, you go there to get your pussy stroked."

No more laughing. She's dead serious. "You do that with a

stranger?" I ask.

"Yeah, the man stays dressed. It's all about you."

"Nothing is all about me."

"That's why you should go."

"I can do that at home for free."

CHAPTER SEVEN
PUBLIC DISPLAY

IT'S BEEN A long day. Maybe I should try Poppy's orgasm meditation to reenergize myself. That girl is hilarious, and she does make the workplace a lot more entertaining. Sitting in my office, I take my list from my purse and lay it flat on my desk. Looking at it, I wish I'd made more progress. My cell phone rings and I roll my eyes, thinking this is exactly why I haven't got more stuff checked off. Something always pulls me away. This time it's my brother Gage. He needs me to bring some file back to Savannah. He tells me where I can find it in his office, and I head down the hall.

I don't know why he just doesn't have it faxed or scanned, but I don't bitch too much about it because I know he's feeling torn between work and family. I fetch the file, hang up, then walk back to my office. I step inside to find Mateo standing in front of my desk, his fingers on the list.

"Oh God!" I cry out and cover my face with my phone, quickly trying to come up with an explanation, or *lie*, about what he's holding—it's just a joke, it belongs to a friend, it's from the internet, it's Poppy's fault.

Suddenly, he's right in front of me, taking my phone and placing it on my desk. Then he pushes the door closed and pulls me into his body. I have no time to explain, let alone think before his lips crash into mine, his tongue claiming me.

Our kiss is hard and rough, and it has my legs clenching together. His hands go to my ass, pulling my dress up slightly, lifting me up onto the edge of my desk, grinding against me. Wearing a wrap dress today was a good call. I usually wear wrap dresses because they are no fuss, add a nice cinch to my waist, and feel like pajamas. Easy access wasn't one of the reasons, but I'm thankful for it now.

Wrestling with his shirt, I yank it out of his pants, desperate to feel his skin under my fingertips. His tongue finds my neck, and he kisses a path along my collarbone. I thrust against every hard inch of him. He pulls on the tie of my dress, and I wrap my legs around his waist. Picking me up, he pushes me up against the floor-to-ceiling window.

I can't remember the last time a guy banged me up against a wall, or a window, for that matter. This is a perk of being with a younger man. Am I really going to do this? In my office? In the middle of the day? He must feel my hesitation because he lowers my legs to the ground, flipping me towards the window, his hard dick pushing up against my ass, his warm breath tickling my neck.

He whispers in my ear, "Number 19. Orgasm in a public place. I'm saying this counts." I look down the few stories to the busy Atlanta street, the neighboring building. Roughly, he forces my legs apart with his foot then reaches his hand between my legs and pushes my panties to the side. "Your list belongs to me," he says, his voice hard.

"Yes," I say as his finger invades me.

I want to cry out with each thrust, but I know I can't—not here in my office, with the walls and floors so thin, and because I think the passersby outside would hear me, too. I bite down on my tongue, my lip, my cheeks, trying not to make a sound. But Mateo's making it almost impossible. Pushing against me, he's got me so needy, his finger thrusting in and out of me, over and over again.

I can't believe this is happening. We've been flirty with each other for a while, but I never thought this would happen. Honestly, I thought most of the flirting was only in my head. I was wrong, so very wrong.

He clearly knows I'm about ready to explode and starts moving faster, deeper. I'm almost there, digging my nails into the window, and he grips my ass hard. A few more thrusts, and I clench around his finger and push back against his hand.

"Hey, Emerson, can you . . . Oh shit!" My office door slams shut, with Poppy inside.

"Fuck," Mateo curses, shielding me.

"Poppy, get out," I cry, struggling to get my dress tied back.

"Uh, we have a meeting in here to go over the layout for the new ad campaign," Poppy says. "There's like three people outside the door waiting right now."

"Take them to the conference room," I say, motioning with my hand. Poppy winks at Mateo before opening the door just wide enough to slip out.

Frantic and frustrated, I straighten my dress then search for my glasses and notes for the meeting, trying not to make eye contact with Mateo—my employee, my brother's friend, the man who almost made me orgasm. He captures my hand, slowing me down, gliding me back into his arms.

"I have to go," I whisper, pulling away.

He cocks a little grin and swipes the list from my desk. "I'm keeping this."

THE MEETING SHOULD'VE been done in an hour, but with my mind in a faraway place, it took twice as long. When it's finally over, Poppy follows me back to my office and stops outside my door. "You've totally been holding out on me."

"Not now," I say, unable to make sense of it myself. I'm not ready to talk about it. Besides, it's late, and I need to head home. I tell her good night then open my door to grab my stuff.

I gasp at the sight of Mateo sitting with his feet propped on my desk, and I quickly close the door behind me. "Have you been waiting in here the whole time?" I ask.

He nods, then gets to his feet, towering over me. "We've got some unfinished business, wouldn't you say?"

"I . . ."

"Relax," he says, taking my hand. "I just meant we should talk."

This must be the first time in the history of the universe a man ever suggested a *talk*. "We should," I say breathlessly. "But I need to catch my flight to Savannah."

"Stay over," he says. He must see the look of shock on my face, because he clarifies. "I'm sure Layla and Gage wouldn't mind you crashing at their place here in Atlanta."

Ryan has the kids until tomorrow. There's nothing stopping me from staying, but something inside tells me not to. "Gage needs a file," I say, grabbing it off my desk and starting for the door.

He doesn't try to block me, but instead gently says, "Emerson." There's a certain magic in his voice. He says my name so sweetly that I stop in my tracks. Any man can control with his actions—a real man dominates with his heart.

I feel him come up behind me, his fingers lightly combing through my hair. It's a light touch, but it makes me feel safe, calm. Turning to face him, he cups my cheeks in his hands, and my eyes are drawn to his.

I may be seeing things, but he looks worried, even a little sad. "Thank you for my slippers and lunch today," I say.

A soft smile graces his perfect lips. He's got the best lips, full and soft, and when he kissed me, it made me feel things. And I'm much better at thinking than I am at feeling. Feelings get me hurt every damn time.

"I won't be back in Atlanta for a few days," I whisper. "Call me."

I DIDN'T EXPECT Mateo to call that night, but he did—a FaceTime call, no less. Why would he do that? That really ups the stakes. Still, he timed it perfectly, just when I'm crawling into bed. I don't want to answer too quickly and seem desperate. But I don't want to wait too long and risk him hanging up. Three rings seem the right number, and his handsome face appears on the screen. He's in a blue t-shirt, but it's his brown eyes that light up the darkness.

"You're not supposed to FaceTime a woman without warning," I playfully scold him.

"You look beautiful," he says, and I squeeze my eyes shut. I can't help it. It's strange to have a smoking hot guy compliment me.

"Open your eyes," he says again, but I squeeze them tighter. "I want you to look at me when I tell you how sexy you are."

With that, I toss the phone on the bed like it's going to burn me, and I make sure it's facing down. Compliments are a dangerous thing. If you hear them too much, you take them for granted. And if they ever stop coming, it can really hurt. I've known that hurt.

I hear a muffled laugh coming from the phone, Mateo chuckling out my name. Carefully, I pick up the phone and ask, "What's so funny?"

"How can a woman with a sex 'to do' list get so embarrassed?"

"You don't understand the list," I say.

"Explain it to me."

"One night Poppy and . . ."

"I knew she had to be involved."

I give him the background on the origin of the list. "I didn't make the list because I felt sexy. I made it because I didn't."

For a second, I wish I could take those words back. I really shouldn't open my mouth sometimes. And now Mateo's not saying anything.

But then I see his finger on the screen, as if he's trying to reach out to me, touch me, soothe me. Relieved, my heart twinges with a little pain—not bad, not sad, almost like a growing pain, a hurt with a purpose. I snuggle down into my pillow and flirt, "Are you looking to be on my list?"

"I *own* that list," he says.

How he manages to make cocky sound sexy is beyond me, but it's working for him. He can be my list master. "I'm just getting started with it," I say.

"I only see one thing checked off. What have you done?"

"There was sort of foreplay to the list," I say.

"Like?"

Shouldn't a woman have some mystery? Something tells me

Mateo isn't going to settle for intrigue. He wants the nitty gritty. "I started how most women start new phases in their lives—with a little shopping. This time for lingerie."

"When will women learn guys don't care if your bra and panties match? I mean, it's nice, but not a deal breaker."

"When will men learn that women wear sexy things for themselves sometimes and that everything is not about them?"

"Point taken. Did you make any other purchases just for you?"

Oh God, did I give him an opening to ask that question? What can of worms did I open? Here's the thing—if I'm trying to recharge my sex life, I guess I just have to own it. I'll just be honest. I mean, what's the point of holding back when the man had his hands all over me a few hours ago? "A vibrator."

I'm not sure how he's going to take this news. Some men would like it, thinking it's hot and a little kinky for a woman to control her own orgasms. Other men might feel threatened, like they aren't needed anymore. Still others, like Ryan, might be relieved. It takes the pressure off their performance.

The sparkle in his brown eyes looks almost proud. He's definitely in the category that finds it hot and kinky. "Does the color match your lingerie?"

I start laughing. "Hey, don't make fun. I did a lot of research."

"Of course you did," he says, laughing.

"What's that supposed to mean?"

"I know you. You make a list for everything. Case in point, you made a sex list. So of course you'd do research on a vibrator."

"Well, you'd be surprised how many kinds there are. They even make one that's disguised as a necklace."

"Wonder if it could get through TSA?"

"You're head of security," I say. "You should know these things."

"I'll have a full report for you next week," he says and gives me a wonderful smile.

"Mateo," I whisper, "thanks for not judging me about the list." He doesn't say a word. His smile turns to something wickedly dirty.

"What's that look about?"

"I'm thinking about all the things I could add to it."

"Really?" I ask, my voice low. "What did you come up with?"

"It's not my list. This is about you. You tell me what you want."

My body tingles. "I want to go back to my office, the window, your fingers and hands."

"Let's go back to that moment," he says. "I want to watch you come."

On instinct, I hesitate. I can't do that. I'm too shy. I'm not dressed in sexy lingerie. I'm on camera. And what does he want me to do anyway? Stick the phone between my legs? My excuses are endless. Besides, this isn't on my sex bucket list.

But maybe it should be. "Your face," he says, "Make sure I can see your face." Ah, sweetness in the middle of my upcoming porn moment. How refreshing. He cares about me. He wants to see the real me. I reach to my nightstand and grab my new toy. Holy hell, I can't believe I'm actually going to do this!

I place the phone on my pillow. Part of me wants to pretend he's not watching, but a bigger part of me wants to watch him, pretend it's him under me. That's what I'm going to go with. As soon as I turn it on, all bets are off.

It feels too damn good to worry about how I look, what he's thinking or doing. I swear my body is trained to get turned on just by the buzzing sound. Plus, I'm still frustrated from earlier. Either way, I'm getting off in under a minute.

I collapse down on my pillow, waiting for my breath to slow. When I finally open my eyes, I see his face right in front of me, his eyes lowered, his hand pulling slightly at his hair. He doesn't look happy. I cover myself with the pillow, as my lip starts to quiver. Then his eyes dart up, shooting at me through the screen. "I've got to go," I say, my finger going for the hang-up button.

"No," he says, and even though it's a mere whisper, he commands me. "I should've thought this through more. I want to be there holding you, kissing you, feeling your warm skin. Watching isn't enough. It could never be enough."

FaceTime fucking turns mushy, and my heart doesn't fare much better. He continues to sweetly talk to me, and my eyes close, pretending he's beside me. This is the best pillow talk ever.

When I drift off to sleep, I know he's watching. Though we're hundreds of miles apart, sleeping with a man has never felt better.

"ANSWER YOUR PHONE!" Poppy's voice screeches through my answering machine.

Grabbing my home phone, I sit up with a jolt. "What's wrong?"

"I've been calling your cell for hours."

The sleepy morning fog rolls off of me, and I reach for my cell. It's completely dead. Never has a dead phone battery made a woman so happy. I wonder how long he watched me sleep, how long it was before he fell asleep.

"Are you listening?" Poppy shrieks. "I tried to jump Dash last night, and he shrugged me off. He went to bed at nine! What grown man goes to bed at nine?"

"Maybe the kind that have flights at five in the morning," I say.

"No, we always have sex before he flies. Always. It's our thing."

"Pop, maybe he was tired or not feeling well."

"Remember when I had that root canal? We still fucked before he flew," she says. "I'm losing him!"

Being as good a friend as I can so early in the morning, I try to talk her off the ledge, promising her that she and Dash will get through this, that sex can dwindle the longer two people are together. I go on to support her decision not to have kids if she doesn't want them and encourage her to have a frank discussion with Dash about her fears of having a family.

So basically I'm the AM version of Dr. Phil. And my charms seem to be working, because after a few minutes, she's not quite as hysterical and opts to change the subject. "You want to tell me what I walked in on yesterday at work?" she asks.

"I think you know what you walked in on."

She laughs. "Is it serious or are you just playing?"

CHAPTER EIGHT
NAUGHTY PICS

POPPY'S QUESTION HAUNTS me. I've never been the casual sex type. Can I just work through my list with him and not get attached? And what are his thoughts about all this? Is this typical for him? Has he even given me another thought?

Like a lot of women, I can drive myself crazy thinking too much, so to regulate myself, I spend the rest of the day doing what most moms do—cleaning and cooking. I'm not a great cook, but I do like to bake. I always have batches and batches of cookie dough in my freezer, so I put some cookies in the oven and turn to cleaning.

I wish cleaning was as enjoyable as eating raw cookie dough, but it's not. I even bought these cute rubber gloves that look like something Audrey Hepburn would wear in *Breakfast at Tiffany's*, but cleaning still sucks. The only thing that gets me through is blasting my music and dancing as I go. Thank goodness, my toe is feeling better.

I hit the kids' bathroom, and even Pitbull can't save me. My sons have the worst aim. When they were little, I'd put Cheerios in the toilet and tell them to sink them. That was the only way I could get them to aim, so I know they know where the toilet bowl is. But now it seems they're intentionally trying not to pee in the toilet. I mean, there's pee on the side of the toilet, around the toilet, near the tub, on the wall. It's disgusting. What in holy hell is wrong with my boys?

I brave the bathroom then turn to the laundry. Usually, each kid does their own, but since they've been gone a bunch lately, they don't have much to clean, so I put it away for them. Conner's still little enough that he wants cartoon underwear. Ava has started insisting her undergarments match. In my mind, that means only one thing: someone is seeing them, but she denies it. I'm inclined to believe her because no boys, including Justin, have been calling lately.

Jacob is a whole different story. That boy is giving me a run for my money these days. At only fourteen, I've already caught him looking at porn. Ryan and Gage both tried to tell me how "normal" that is, but no—my son looking at skin flicks is not normal. Never will be. And it seems no matter how many times I lecture him that those women are someone's wife, mom, or daughter, he doesn't seem to care. I'm scared to go in his room these days. I'm not sure what I might find, and I absolutely refuse to touch his sheets, not even with my cute rubber gloves.

I put his clothes away and straighten a few things, although he'll insist I messed it up. He's got all kinds of video game magazines strewn across his floor, and I start putting them in a pile when I find a book. Jacob has dyslexia. He hates reading, so the fact that he has a book is surprising. Even more surprising is that it's from the public library. I didn't think he knew where that even was, much less that he'd have an interest in photography. I flip it over and realize why—boudoir photography. Good God, please give me the strength not to pop this boy over the head as soon as he walks in the house later.

Plopping down on his floor, I start flipping through it. Well, at least it's not trashy. Maybe there's hope for him yet, or maybe this was all he could get his hands on after I blocked the internet access from his phone and changed the passcode on the computer.

As I move through the pages, I see women of every shape and size, every age, every ethnicity, some dressed in men's shirts, others totally bare. It's the most beautiful thing. Every single one of these women are owning and working their sexuality. They aren't worried about their wrinkles, stretch marks, or pimples. I bet everything on their sex bucket lists is scratched off already. I carefully place the book back where I found it. If my son is going to look at naked women, at least he's looking at real women with real bodies. So, I'll overlook this.

Before I know it, the kids are home, and I hug and kiss them before they run upstairs. Strangely, Ryan follows them inside. "How's your toe?" he asks.

"Fine."

"Do you really have a sex bucket list?"

My eyes dart to his. How dare he! It's none of his damn business. He steps close to me, his hands finding my waist. "What's on it? I mean, we were pretty adventurous, if I remember correctly."

I step away, his hands no longer feeling natural. "Obviously, sleeping together was a big mistake. We don't work anymore."

"Chemistry was never our problem, Emerson," he says, taking hold of me again.

"The kids are here," I snap.

"They were last time, too."

"A mistake," I say, and he releases me. "And if we had so much chemistry, why was there so little sex the last few years of our marriage?"

He shrugs. "We got too comfortable, too busy. I regret that."

"Fuck!" I say, pulling at my hair. "You're seeing someone else. Did it occur to you that you cheated on her with me?"

"I told you it's not serious with her."

"Where is this coming from all of a sudden? You left me!"

"I fucking hate the idea of you with someone else," he says. "When I walked in here that morning and thought you weren't alone, I don't know. I just lost it. And now I find out you've got some list that you plan on fucking your way through."

"So?"

"So I was your only. I'm supposed to be your only." He releases a deep breath. "Guess I took that for granted."

"Did you think I'd spend the rest of my life mourning you? Because I've done that for two years, and I just can't anymore."

"I know," he says. "I just didn't expect it to hurt."

"What are you saying?"

"Nothing," he says. "But I'm going to keep my distance for a little bit. I just wanted you to know why." He opens up the front door, glancing back but not exactly at me, more at the house, the life he left behind, and his eyes catch mine. "Please don't run through some dick just to prove something to yourself. You're better than that." Then he's gone.

What the hell? Typical man—he doesn't want me; he just doesn't want anyone else to have me. That keeps me pretty ticked off the rest of the night. I try to fake it for the kids. I'm the queen of faking it. I was so good at it, I convinced Ryan for years. I drove that happy train until it derailed in the most gloriously awful way possible.

I start dinner in an effort to busy my mind. In a lame attempt to cut out some carbs, I decide to make spaghetti squash, which has only about seven carbs compared to the whopping forty in pasta noodles. Supposedly, spaghetti squash looks very similar to angel hair pasta when grated. Well, that turns out to be a crock of shit. They look nothing like it, and drenching it in red sauce won't fool my snotty little detectives.

Ava calls out from upstairs, "Mom, the doorbell's ringing."

The groan from me rivals that of a wild bear. "Well, answer it, honey."

"I'm doing . . ."

My ears tune out whatever the hell she's saying. I've heard it all before from her and the other kids. *I'm in the bathroom, Jacob's closer, I'm not dressed, I'm eating, I'm on the phone, I'm tired.* Blah, blah, blah. The list of excuses is a mile long. I've managed to answer the door partially nude with a donut in my mouth while on the phone and doing the laundry. But apparently, my children did not inherit my supernatural ability to answer the damn door.

Yanking the door open, a clipboard and pen are shoved in my face. "Sign." Without looking, I scribble my name, take the small package addressed to me, and toss it aside. I call up the stairs for the kids to come to dinner.

"What is this?" Connor asks, his little nose wrinkled up so high it's almost on his forehead.

"Spaghetti squash," I say on a wish and a prayer.

Without a word, Jacob gets up and goes to the pantry. "What are you doing?"

"Making myself chili," he says.

"Sit down," I bark. "It took me a long time to make this, and we are going to sit as a family and enjoy it."

"You didn't work today, did you?" Ava says.

I want to strangle her. "Yes, in fact, I did, Ava. It's called being your mother. Believe me, that is a lot of work."

"I'll eat it, Mommy," Connor says.

"Kiss ass," Jacob mutters.

"Everyone, be quiet," I say. "We are all going to sit at the table and eat as a family. I don't care how long it takes!"

I swore I'd never do this to my kids—make them eat nasty-looking food, make them sit at the table all night—but I'm fed up. Somewhat surprisingly, they each sit down, one more leery than the next, and begin to move their dinner around with their forks.

Connor is the first to take a bite, and he takes a big one. His lips purse together as he swallows it all down, his little eyes watering. His tears only increase my level of aggravation. Ava goes next, cutting the smallest little piece. Her bird bite makes me want to pull my hair out. And Jacob just crosses his arms and stares at me, hard. That boy, I swear—his essence makes me mad.

Rather than explode, I decide to lead by example. "How bad can it be?" I ask, taking my first bite. Not a second later, I begin to gag and spit that shit into my napkin as all three kids heartily laugh at me. I swallow my pride. "Okay, Jacob, order a pizza."

"And garlic knots," Connor begs.

We spend the rest of the night binge eating and binge watching shows on Netflix. It was a perfect night. I watch my three babies all heading up to bed. It's quiet. They're safe, healthy, and happy. And that's all any mom wants.

Jacob goes to bed with his one word: "Night." Connor goes to bed with me reading to him for fifteen minutes. Ava, however, is suddenly more quiet than she's been since birth. My mom radar goes up, but after several attempts to get her to talk, I tuck myself into bed, reach for my glasses, and open up my laptop, checking my social media pages.

I find the vibrator inventor lady accepted my friend request. I check out what she's posting and take a look through her bio. She's a Southern girl like me, born and raised in a small town in south Alabama. Wonder what made her decide on that career path? I mean, what's your major in college to end up in the sex toy industry? It looks like she lives in New York now. There aren't any personal photos, and I understand why when I see a few hateful comments on her page condemning masturbation as a sin. Damn, guess I'm burning in hell.

Then I click on Ava's page to spy on her a little bit—any new friends, anybody deleted, perhaps a change in status. Nothing. A soft knock comes on my door, like she knows I'm stalking her.

"Mommy." Oh Lord, she called me *Mommy* in a sweet voice—not a good sign. Something's wrong. I pat the bed, and she cuddles beside me. Stroking her hair, I wait and wait. Ava is a lot like me; she doesn't volunteer much about herself. It takes her a good while to process. Maybe I should ask Layla if she knows anything. She and Ava have always been close.

Finally, she speaks. "Justin and I broke up a few weeks ago."

"I figured," I say. Justin has been her boyfriend for close to two years, even when she wasn't allowed to have one. I wonder if this is the reason for her attitude lately. "Want to tell me why?"

"Sex," she whispers.

Don't freak. Don't cry. Don't kill him. Don't threaten her. Don't judge. But so help me God, if she slept with him and then he dumped her, I'll hunt him down. "What it is, honey? Ava, you can talk to me."

"He was at a party, playing some drinking game, and ended up having sex with some random."

"Oh, sweetheart. I'm so sorry."

"I loved him."

I don't tell her it's puppy love. I don't tell her there will be others. She's hurt, and none of that will help.

"I think he slept with her because I wouldn't."

Hurray! Thank you, Jesus!

"If I would've . . ."

"No, baby," I say. "If he cared for you the way you cared for him, he wouldn't have done that, so you made the right decision." I don't feel the least bit hypocritical saying that to my daughter. I know what I did after boot camp class was bad, but I never slept with anyone else. I add, "Your first time should be special."

"Like you and Daddy?"

"Yes."

"It's humiliating," she says.

"This reflects poorly on him, not you."

She rolls her eyes. "Justin seems more popular now. No other boy is going to want to go out with me. They think I'm a prude."

"Assholes," I say, and she laughs. "There's still a double standard when it comes to men and women and sex. It's not right, but it exists. Do you know the girl?"

She shakes her head. "She goes to a different school. But rumor is, she didn't know about me. Justin didn't tell her he had a girlfriend." Then she flashes me a big grin. "Asshole."

"Exactly."

She cuddles down into my bed. "Can I sleep in here with you tonight?"

"Sure, baby." I flick off the light and hug her tightly, hearing my phone starting to buzz. It rang around this time last night, but I'm not answering now. Mateo and my list have to take a backseat tonight.

Ava suddenly leans up on her elbow, looking so serious, so much like Ryan. "I think since Daddy's dating again, you should, too. You're so pretty and smart and . . ."

She continues to talk, and I absorb every word. I'm sure the first sentence was pretty hard for her. My little girl is trying to be so grown up. And I realize she feels about me exactly how I feel about my mom. It's one of those breathtaking, full circle moments. And I also realize that I don't see myself the way others see me.

As Ava gets quiet and drifts off to sleep, my mind flashes back to Jacob's library book. It's high time to see the real me. First thing in the morning, I'm finding a boudoir photographer.

CHAPTER NINE
SELFISH SEX

DRAGGING MYSELF TO the kitchen to start breakfast before the kids wake up, I see the package from yesterday. I had totally forgotten about it. I don't recognize the return address or the name of the place it's from. I open it up, and my jaw drops. There's no note, but I immediately know who it's from.

Dangling from a long silver chain is a sleek silver pendant—a vibrating one. I'm not sure how he pulled this off within a day, but the vibrator necklace must have intrigued Mateo enough to make it happen. Does it make me crazy to think about flying to Atlanta just to try it out with him? Everyone needs a little crazy, right?

So I drop the kids off at school, make sure my new necklace is all charged up, and head off to the airport. I can see Mateo and be home for carpool. As much as I fly, I really ought to get one of those TSA pre-checks. You'd think as an airline employee I'd automatically be given one, but nope. I add that to my list of things to do that will probably never get done, like cleaning out the attic or going to confession.

Glancing down at the silver bullet dangling perfectly between my boobs, I thank God for the miracle that is the push up bra. They actually look pretty good in my white button down blouse, several of the top buttons undone. Perhaps I should've waited to unbutton until I got to Atlanta?

This has got to be the longest booty call in the history of booty calls—right under two hundred and seventy miles. The line moves up. With no carry-on luggage, I'm next in line for the full body scanner, and my mind goes back to something Mateo said. Will the necklace make it through security?

Starting to sweat, I step into the booth, lining my feet with the outline on the floor and raise my arms in the air. Every time I do this, I'm reminded of my mom, who always gives a double middle finger during the scan. That lady is something else. She likes security but hates government intrusion. I hope I can be as kick ass as her one day.

"Ma'am, please step aside," a bearded, muscular TSA hunk tells me. Shit, the necklace! What am I going to do? Still, I drool a little—if I wasn't on my way to see one sexy man, I'd admire this guy and let him search me wherever. He's got the whole rough sex look about him. "Did you empty your pockets?"

Trying to look innocent, I shake my head and smile, "Don't have any."

"Any piercings, pacemaker?" he asks. Looking guilty as sin, I shake my head. "I'll need to use the wand."

I close my eyes in horror, as he bends down with the metal detector thing, starting at my feet.

Silence.

Up my legs, across my belly—nothing.

Over my arms—quiet.

Here it comes, towards my neck—the thing starts beeping like a defective house alarm. Sure enough, his eyes land on my necklace, and he lowers the wand. Our eyes meet, a realization between us. He knows. He can completely humiliate me if he wants. There must be some code among pervs because he grins.

"Pleasure trip?" he asks.

"Boyfriend," I say, trying to normalize this behavior.

"Lucky guy," he says, holding his arm open for me to pass.

It's not until I board the plane that I start breathing again. I spend the forty-five minute flight planning my attack. Mateo doesn't know what he's in for. I beam with pride. This is the new me, the independent me, the MILF, the woman who proudly wears her vibrator around her neck. I remember something on my list about being completely selfish in bed. Taking what I want and heading out the door. Guys do that shit all the time. Well, it's my turn. I'm ready to play.

I get to Mateo's office and head inside. He's not there, which is good. I prop my freshly lotioned legs up on his desk and unbutton my shirt some more, until it's almost completely undone, the vibrator nestled in my cleavage. After a few minutes, he opens the door, surprised to see me there, but immediately knowing what I want.

I hear him lock the door behind him, his dark eyes piercing, probably replaying the other night, in pleasure and in the peace of sleep. I get to my feet as he approaches. Somehow he seems even bigger than before, more dominating. He gives a wry smile at the sight of the necklace then begins to toy with it, his fingers grazing the smooth flesh of the top of my breasts.

Pressing the button once, a soft hum fills the room, and an anticipatory wetness follows. My body knows the sound of pleasure, and it sure is impatient. He stretches the chain, letting it buzz my nipples through the lace of my bra. He doesn't take his eyes off me as he lifts the chain over my head, lowering it to the skin of my outer thighs.

"You came here to get off?" he asks, his voice a low growl.

I refuse to apologize for wanting him to service me. Holding his eyes, I say, "Yes."

Without any hesitation, he flips me over his desk, forcing my legs to spread wide. I can feel him pressing against me, his erection begging to come out. The vibrating noise gets louder. He leans over, his warm breath rolling off my hot skin.

The cold steel slips inside. "Oh!"

"Quiet."

My head nods frantically. "Please, please."

"You don't ever have to beg," he whispers in my ear. "All you have to do is ask."

Asking? Begging? Pleading? I'll do it all to have this moment.

"This is nothing compared to the way I'm going to fuck you," he says. "How good my cock is going to feel in that sweet, tight pussy."

Three kids do not a tight pussy make. And suddenly, this little three-inch device inside me, about the size of a tampon, isn't doing it for me. I need more. Pushing against his hand, I cry, "Mateo, please. I need to finish."

Because the man is a sex god, he somehow knows what I need, what I've needed this whole time to get me over the edge. In one smooth motion, he shifts the necklace from inside to outside. I'm a clit girl. There, I've said it. My eyes clench and my hands grab the side of his desk as my legs tighten, and I release a mountain of sexual frustration.

I lay there a few minutes, bent over, skirt hiked up sans panties. I know I'm supposed to just walk out of here satisfied and sexually empowered, celebrating my new liberation and all, but my resolve is weakening. "Um . . . I guess . . . Should I thank you or something?"

His eyes grow huge. "You're leaving?"

I shouldn't smile, but I do. "Well, yeah. Got what I needed."

Another guy may be offended, but not Mateo. He likes our little game. He glances down at the bulge in his pants, grimacing. "Number 8?" he asks.

Giving him a flirty smile, I nod and say, "Selfish sex, otherwise known as 'how boys screw'."

"You could've warned me," he chuckles, capturing me in his arms and for the first time today, he kisses me, long and slow, our tongues gently exploring each other. We haven't done this nearly enough. We pull apart, and he looks at me gently.

"How long did you watch me sleep?" I ask.

"Until the phone died."

Smiling, I turn for the door, but he catches me by my hips. "Your necklace?"

"Keep it. It was a bitch to get through security," I tease then disappear, leaving him with his mouth on the floor.

CHAPTER TEN
COUGAR DENIED

"I KNOW, BABY. I know," I say, opening the door to my brother's condo.

This is what I get for being selfish with Mateo. The sex gods—and perhaps the real God, too—have punished me by grounding all flights out of Atlanta due to a horrible thunderstorm. I can't get home. I had to call my mom to pick the kids up from school, completely lying to her about why I was out of town at the office. My mom will keep the kids overnight. I wasn't about to call Ryan to help. It's not his week, and he asked for distance.

Gage and Layla don't mind me crashing at their place in Atlanta since they're at their house in Savannah with the baby. I feel bad, though—not about staying at their place. I feel bad because Connor is sad that I missed his Cub Scout troop's pinewood car derby. He worked so hard on his car, and I'm not there to see him win.

There's no good excuse. *Mommy was horny, honey. You understand, right?* That just won't work. I feel the burden of mommy guilt. I could call Poppy to come over, but I don't feel like explaining my presence in Atlanta on a day I'm not supposed to be here.

So instead, I call the reason for my visit. Maybe it's time for me not to be so selfish. Unfortunately, he doesn't answer. My message to him resembles that of a crazy person, something out of a stream of consciousness novel—making no sense at all, not even to me. I think I asked him to come over or maybe it was just to call me back, or maybe both.

I've got no clothes, no toothbrush, no vibrator. I shouldn't have left that with Mateo. It's going to be a long night. Layla told me to borrow whatever I need from her closet, apologized for the little food in the fridge, and told me where I could find extra toiletries. But all of that can wait.

My brother has the best flat screen television I've ever seen. The thing looks like a movie screen. Layla, the bookworm that she is, hates it. So Gage has it in what's supposed to be his office, but looks more like a man cave with its dark brown Chesterfield sofa and deep wood tones.

I decide to pop some popcorn and watch a movie. Popcorn is my weakness. I have it most every night. Is popcorn a carb? If so, that would make total sense. And I don't like that microwave stuff, either. It has to be popped the old-fashioned way on the stove with just a touch of real melted butter and just a dash of popcorn salt. Warm popcorn is my friend.

I get the kernels poured in the oil when the phone rings. It's the downstairs security guy. My brother and Layla live in the penthouse condo, and somebody's trying to come up. Apparently, I have a visitor. I guess I did ask Mateo to come over. He must be good at translating Emerson into English.

The next two minutes should be a mad dash to get myself together. The younger me would run around the condo like a maniac, applying lipstick and lotion, checking my hair, adjusting my boobs, but who has the energy for that? I answer the door with my shoes off, my hair loose and wild, and a smile on my face trying to cover how nervous I am.

He gives me a little smirk. "Popcorn time?"

"How did you know?" Right about then, I smell the burning kernels. "Oh no," I cry out, waving him to come on in before I burn the place down.

Nothing smells worse than burned popcorn. It's rancid. And because my brother's place is in a high rise, I really don't want to set off the fire alarm. Grabbing the pot with an oven mitt, I yank it off the stove, holding my nose.

Mateo wrinkles up his face, clearly both hating the smell and trying not to laugh at me. He grabs the trash can while I dump the kernels inside, then he carries it through the living room out onto the balcony, where we will pollute and poison all of downtown Atlanta with our popcorn stench.

Frantically, I wave my arms around, trying to move the stink through the air. Why does Gage not have any ceiling fans? Mateo takes hold of me, tightly wrapping his arms all the way around me, and I pout my lip at him. "You hungry?" he asks.

"I was. There's not much to eat," I say. "But there's a liquor cabinet."

Lining up two shot glasses, I say, "You know, I always tell my daughter it's a bad idea to drink, especially with a boy. Could lead to all kinds of trouble."

"What kind of trouble?" he asks, leaning into my neck.

That should be sexy, but because I'm such a mom, I think of kid drama. "Cheating." Mateo leans back like he's been tasered. Releasing a deep huff, I say, "My daughter, Ava, her ex-boyfriend was playing some drinking game, and he ended up cheating on her. She's been pretty upset."

"I bet you're pretty upset, too," he says sweetly.

His fingers lightly stroke my arm. Something about the way he touches and talks to me, it makes me want to open up to him—and not just my legs. When Ryan stopped touching me, something shifted, like my heart just sealed itself off. When Mateo touches me, it's as if he's unlocking my heart. And he does it with such ease. I've found it's easy for me to be distant and aloof when a guy isn't close; but when he is, when he's affectionate with me, all my defenses break down. And I don't always like it, feeling vulnerable.

"Why don't we play?" I say, filling each glass.

"What's the game?"

"Two truths and a lie. You ever play?"

"I know the rules."

Don't think I didn't notice he dodged the question. Basically, you're supposed to tell two truths and one lie. If Mateo knows which is the lie, then I have to drink. If he's wrong, then he drinks.

"Ladies first," he says.

Biting my lip, I consider how far I want to go, things I'd like or not like to know about him, things I'd like or not like him to know about me, maybe things that aren't already on my list. "One: I'm a member of the mile high club." Since my family owns an airline, I figure he'd believe that one is pretty obviously true. "Two: I lost my virginity in a car." It was actually outside. "Three: I've only had sex outside once." I don't recommend losing one's virginity outside. It's awkward and uncomfortable, and I don't think the woodland creatures will ever be the same.

"Number two is the lie," he says simply, pushing my shot glass towards me.

Wow, I think. I'm in big trouble here. It was clearly a mistake to play with a man who does security for a living. He's probably trained in the art of lying. I down the shot of whiskey like a pro. "Your turn."

Mateo leans back, his arms outstretched on the sofa. He recites his two truths and a lie without a moment of pause. "I beat off in my office after you left me today. I wore a thong swimsuit when I lost a bet in college. And every time I've played this game, I've never had to take a shot."

My eyes pop out of my head. The third one has to be the lie, right? Otherwise he's not human. But the thong can't be true? I'm kind of hoping the beat off is true. Would he do that in the office building my family owns? Fine by me after what he's done for me. Ugh, I'm confused by this game. He's good. "Number three is a lie."

His head shakes slowly, his eyes on my glass. "The thong."

"Damn." This time the whiskey doesn't go down so easy. Another round of play leads to another round of shots for me. I'm going down fast. If I'm going to have any chance in hell, I'm going to have to cheat. "Rim jobs are my favorite sex act. I always have multiple orgasms. And I once had sex for one hundred and seventeen straight days."

He busts out laughing. "All lies."

"How did you know?" I ask in the middle of slamming down my shot. I wobble a bit and feel the room start to spin. Then I giggle a few times for no apparent reason. "I think I lost this whole game."

"You're drunk," he says and strokes my hair off my face.

"A little." Smiling, I straddle his lap, my skirt rising up, barely covering my ass. He squeezes me, forcing me tighter into his body. "I think I want to find some trouble," I say, kissing his neck.

He quickly gets to his feet, my legs around his waist, and carries me down the hallway towards the bedroom. Feeling his hardness between my legs, I swear he must live with an erection. He lays me down on the bed and stands over me. Damn, he looks so good. I can't wait for him to have his way with me.

"Sleep," he says.

"What?" I ask.

"You need to sleep."

I stick out my bottom lip. "No."

"Not like this," he says, kneeling down beside me.

"But I just got an IUD. You don't have to worry. You can fuck me and . . ."

He gives me a sweet kiss and says, "Get some rest."

I suddenly feel my face getting red, my insides churning. I'm not sure if it's just me, but alcohol always seems to heighten my emotions. "You're turning me down. Oh my God, I'm throwing myself at you. And you're saying no."

True or not, this is how I'm feeling. Tears start rolling down my cheeks, his rejection bringing back all the times Ryan turned me down, all the nights I snuck into the bathroom to cry, wondering what was wrong with me, all the times when I'd flirt with him and we'd make plans to have sex that night, and then within five minutes, we'd end up fighting about something dumb and the plans were quickly shattered. Was he fighting with me on purpose? To avoid being intimate with me? Was it subconscious or was he fully aware what he was doing?

Mateo reaches out to soothe me, and I smack at him, only I just hit the air. He whispers, "Emerson." He's so in control at work—firm, bossy, direct. I'm not used to his gentle side. The side that makes my heart flutter with a simple whisper.

But more tears come. "You don't want me!"

He cups my face. "I do want you. And I want you to remember it the next morning, the soreness from me burying myself deep inside, the feel of my cock slipping in and out, the orgasms I plan on giving you, the way I'm going to kiss every damn inch of your body. I don't want you numb with alcohol. I want you tingling with need."

I've got nothing to say to that. But the sting of his rejection and my embarrassment cause fresh tears to fall. Sniffling, I close my eyes, his fingers gently combing through my hair, lulling me to sleep, and a peace settles over me.

But there's nothing peaceful about the bombs going off in my head and stomach when I wake up the next morning. I feel like death warmed over. Why can't I drink anymore? In my college years, I wouldn't have felt this crappy. Something happens with age. Maybe it's the metabolism slowing down so the alcohol stays in your system longer. I don't know, but it sucks. For all the advances in modern science, why has no one come up with a hangover cure?

I sit up in bed and try to focus my eyes. I could really use my glasses, but there's no telling where I've left them. But it doesn't matter. I can make out his handsome face anyway.

I find Mateo asleep in a chair in the corner of the room. A twinge of embarrassment hits me hard. I can't believe I said the things I did and cried in front of him like that. But something inside tells me it's all going to be okay. If he was an asshole, he would've taken advantage of me last night. But he didn't.

Mateo's a good man. A man I just might want to keep.

CHAPTER ELEVEN
PANTIES TO A STRANGER

IT DIDN'T TAKE me as long to get the appointment as I thought. I guess not every forty-something single mom is as excited as I am to get naked in front of a total stranger, but sex bucket list challenge accepted.

Number 15: Take naughty pictures of yourself.

I'm technically not taking the pictures, and I'm not sure anyone but me will ever see them, but I'm counting this. If I'm getting naked in front of a stranger, it counts. And if the whole idea isn't strange enough, after my boudoir photo shoot, I'm going to Greer's baptism.

With the kids at my mom's house helping set up for the baptism, I spend the morning getting my hair and makeup done. I don't know why I bothered. It seems like every time someone else does my makeup, it doesn't turn out right. I told the girl I didn't want black eyeliner, but she just ignored me and turned me into a goth clown. It took asking her three times to remove some before I didn't look like I'd been in a fistfight. She kept trying to convince me I needed high-definition makeup, whatever that is.

By the time I get to my house, I'm not feeling very sexy, and the photographer's arriving any minute. I line up my many outfit changes and throw on my robe, feeling myself start to panic. *I'm going to be naked in front of a total stranger.* That's the only thought pounding in my head. Right as I'm about to invade my liquor cabinet, the doorbell rings. Thank God, she's early. And thank God, she looks like a normal woman, not some supermodel type.

I spend a few minutes showing her the house and my outfits. We decide to start in my bedroom with my most conservative black and pink bra and panty set. She turns on my television and sets it to the music channel. I take a deep breath and step out of my robe. Mercifully, there's not one ounce of judgment showing in her eyes. She poses me modestly at first and makes some small talk. An Enrique Iglesias song comes on, and she comments how sexy he is. I agree, thinking he and Mateo could be brothers. She snaps the photo, and I start to relax.

Two hours later, I'm completely nude. If I'm going to do this, I'm going all the way. Besides, I think my new vagina is still shiny, so I'm going to show it off. Just kidding, I kept it classy. When we're done, she lets me scan the photos on her fancy camera. I'm actually amazed it's me. It's like I'm looking at someone else.

"Every woman has something sexy about her," she says. "It's waiting to be found. For you, it's the curve of your waist and your booty."

This woman is a saint. I love her. And I think I look good. Don't get me wrong, some of the pictures are horrible, but I think I actually look good in a number of them. I almost die when my ass comes up on her screen, full on, in my cute little panties. I ask her not to retouch anything. I want to know the pictures were of me, not a Photoshopped version. She promises to get me proofs soon, and I start walking her to the door then realize I'm still stark naked. That's how comfortable I'd become in just two hours.

She leaves, and I lean against my front door, giddy as a schoolgirl. Taking these pictures has done more for my self-esteem than ten years of therapy ever could. Feeling like a new woman, I dash to my bedroom to get dressed for the baptism, wishing I didn't have to put clothes back on. I feel so liberated. Heck, I want to do the photo shoot all over again. Maybe I missed my calling as a nudist.

"Please talk to Layla," my brother begs Poppy and me. "She's refusing to come out."

We aren't sure what the problem is. The service at the church was sweet and beautiful, and everything seemed to go well, but Layla's been hiding in my mom's spare bathroom since getting to the party.

"What did you do?" Poppy teases him.

"Nothing," Gage says. "It's something about her boobs. I don't know."

I lightly knock on the bathroom door and call out to her. "Layla, it's Emerson and Poppy," I say, waiting until I hear the lock unlatch, then open the door. Layla's sitting on the edge of the tub hunched over in tears, her cardigan sweater in the sink. Poppy and I kneel in front of her, and her tears come out harder.

"What is this about?" Poppy asks.

"I'm a dairy cow," Layla says.

"A cow?" Poppy cries. "You're one of those bitches that came home from the hospital in your damn skinny jeans. You've even got the elusive ITG going on."

Let me just state for the record that the inner thigh gap, or ITG, is the most ridiculous body standard to date. Whichever male sexist pig came up with that should be strung up by his balls.

"Greer spit up all over my cardigan," Layla says. "And I don't have anything to change into."

I say, "You still have on your camisole."

"Look at me!" Layla snaps and straightens her posture. "My boobs are so huge, it's obscene. I can't go out there like this."

Layla makes a good point. Her breasts are so big it looks like her chin is resting on them. And like Poppy said, she's a skinny little thing, so she does look very top heavy.

Layla goes on, "Emerson, do you know what your stupid brother told me? He told me I look sexy!"

"He just wants to take those babies for a test drive," Poppy says. "It's his only chance to have some big ones to play with."

In normal circumstances, Layla would laugh at that, but not today. I know what it's like to be a new mom—hormones all over the place, unsure of yourself, scared you won't ever feel normal again. I start to slip my shirt off. "Here, let's switch. This top is really big and flowing, so your breasts should fit."

"What if I leak on it?" Layla asks.

"Then I'll have an excuse to go shopping," I say.

"You're so sweet. Are you sure?"

"Of course," I say, and Layla puts on my shirt. It fits her perfectly. Her camisole on me is another story. It's pretty tight, but I won't let on that it bothers me. I just took naked pictures. What's a little cleavage?

Everything now under control, the three of us step out of my mom's spare bathroom looking like the badass women we are, like Charlie's Angels, like gals who are not to be messed with. We find Gage leaning against the wall, waiting. He pulls Layla into his arms and mouths "thank you" to me and Poppy.

"Since Poppy's in town," he says, "why don't the three of you go out tonight? I can watch Greer."

Poppy and Dash are staying the night at my house, so she offers up Dash to watch my kids. "Great," I say. "I guess I'm free. Layla?"

Gage can sense Layla is hesitant, guilty about leaving the baby. "I really think you need some time away," he tells her. "Will be good for you, Layla—just no urgent care trips this time."

"No guarantees," I laugh out.

"Come on, Layla," Poppy says. "We'll just go for a few hours. We'll work around your milking schedule."

Giving Layla a little nod, I say, "The best moms know when they need a break."

Layla nods, and Poppy and I walk downstairs, giving her and Gage a moment. As soon as we hit the bottom step, Poppy's eyes fly to Dash, standing with little Greer, a huge grin on his face. I look down at Poppy, a look of concern on her face. "I'm going to lose him over this," she says.

Based on the way he's loving on that little girl, she may be right. But Poppy has a right to her feelings, too. I don't believe a woman has to have children to be fulfilled in life, and she shouldn't be made to feel that way or ashamed because she doesn't want kids. "You need to have a real conversation with him about this," I say, walking over to steal my niece from him, hoping she and her boyfriend will finally talk.

Greer is a beautiful baby. How could she not be? Her parents look like they walked out of the pages of *Southern Living*. I so love babies, everything about them, really, even though I was scared shitless when I thought I might be pregnant again. I take in Greer's little face, that new baby smell. Some of the happiest times in my life were when my kids were babies, and I loved being pregnant. Call me a freak, but I loved every second of it. I never felt sexier than when I was big and round and full of curves that mattered. Now my curves typically serve no purpose other than annoying me.

I walk past my mom's living room and see Connor playing on the floor. He's growing up too fast. Not so long ago, he was consumed with his imaginary friend, a crocodile that walked on two feet. It drove me a little nuts at the time, but now I miss it.

Greer starts to fuss a little. Whenever my kids fussed, I'd take them outside. It always seemed to settle them. I open up the door to my mom's picture perfect Savannah backyard, complete with the rose bushes my dad planted for her. Everyone who knows our family knows the story of the rose bushes, how my dad planted them when he was dying, wanting my mom to be surrounded by his love even when they were apart. I know he'd be happy his roses were surrounding Greer now. It makes my heart hurt that she'll never know him.

"Hey," he says from beside the outdoor bar, placed for the occasion.

"Mateo," I say, my voice a little too high.

Maybe because I was consumed with the photo shoot this morning, or because the church service was only for family, I didn't give any thought to him being here today. My mom was in charge of invitations, so she must've invited him to the party. I shouldn't be surprised he's here, though. He's become one of Gage's best friends, aside from Dash.

We haven't seen each other since my drunken attempt to mount him at my brother's condo. He called, but I was with the kids and couldn't answer. I should've called him back, but I was still embarrassed by my behavior, even if he wouldn't hold it against me.

His eyes slip down my borrowed camisole, clearly displaying too much skin for the occasion, my bra straps showing. There's no telling what he's thinking, but I'm not going to offer an explanation for my clothes. Better to keep him guessing. And from the look on his face, his imagination is working overtime.

Feeling myself starting to sweat and motioning to the gift under his arm, I ask, "What did you get for the baby?"

If I didn't know better, I'd think he just blushed. "A picture frame." His nose wrinkles up. "It's lame, huh? Do people even print pictures anymore? Ah, hell."

I start to giggle. It's the first time I've ever seen the man unsure of himself. Leave it to a little seven-pound baby girl to shake up a two hundred pound man. "People do print their baby pictures. I'm sure they'll love it."

"My mom suggested it," he says, giving Greer's tummy a little tickle.

That's sweet. He told his mom about my niece's baptism. She was even involved in the gift. He must have a good relationship with her. Wow, his hotness level just increased by ten.

"Did you fly in just for this?" I ask.

"Yeah, and I've got to fly back later tonight. With Gage out so much, I've been slammed."

"Me, too," I say. "So how have you been?"

He raises an eyebrow at me, as if to ask "Is this how you want to play it? All casual?"

"I've missed you," he says.

Looking around to make sure no one but Greer is within earshot, I say, "I think maybe now's not the best time."

"Maybe you need to think a little less and feel a little more," he says, running a finger along my arm.

"Mom!" Connor screams. "Jacob just hit me."

Grabbing Connor, I tousle his hair. He's met Mateo before, but only briefly. "Little snitch," Jacob says, joining us. "I knew you'd run straight to mom."

I hate for Mateo to see this, but this is my life, who I am. "Why'd you hit your brother?"

As usual, all I get from Jacob is radio silence. "I caught him sneaking a beer," Connor says.

"Fucking little snitch."

"Jacob!" I whisper shout, not wanting to upset the baby.

"Hey, Connor," Mateo says. "You like convertible sports cars?" Connor nods excitedly. "Come see the rental car they gave me at the airport. If your mom says it's alright, I'll drive you around the block."

Of course, I let Connor go and thank Mateo while trying not to strangle Jacob. I know he's a teenage boy, still angry about the divorce, but my patience is running thin with him these days. I spend the next several minutes trying to talk to him—not lecture, just talk—but I get nothing from him—just grunts, shrugs, rolled eyes, stares. And I know this is something I need to bring Ryan in the loop about.

I'M NOT SURE how it happened, but our girls night out turned into the guys hanging out at my house. Gage came over, and Dash is supposedly watching my kids. They are both good guys. They know you don't get in the middle of women and their girlfriends. We get crazy about that shit. It's sacred time. Before we head out, Layla's on my bed nursing Greer for the last time while Poppy's helping me pick out something to wear that's not "mom attire."

"Every moment is an opportunity to scratch something off your list!" Poppy says, rummaging through my closet, tossing things around like we're in a tsunami, before finally throwing a few items into my arms.

"What's this?"

"Go change."

I peek through, seeing some black high-waist shorts I last wore before Ava was born and a black lacy bra. "Jesus, is there a matching strap-on, too?"

"Relax, I'm not asking you to go pegging some dude."

Layla starts laughing. "I'm glad we're all together. I feel so much better already."

"I'm sure that's why Gage suggested this little night out. He's hoping to get laid when you get home," Poppy says.

"Stop it!" I cry. "That's my brother. Layla, please come up with some code word when talking about sex with my brother. You'll need it now anyway."

"Code word?" Poppy asks.

"All parents have them," I say. "You use it when the kids are around to indicate you want a quickie or sex later. Hey, honey, can you help me with that *paperwork* for a second? Or, kids, we're going to go take a little *nap*. A code word."

"You know I don't want kids, but if I ever have them, I'm going to be honest and just say, 'Mommy needs Daddy to fuck her hard right now so she doesn't wring your little necks'."

I must get drunk on the laughter, because when I check myself out in the mirror, the outfit is not looking so bad on me. Poppy tosses me a see-through black blouse before taking off her thigh-high black boots and passing them to me. Good thing my foot is all better, and we're a similar size. "This completes the look," she says.

Poppy's very creative and has great fashion sense, but I'm not sure a forty-something should be wearing this outfit. Granted, nothing is skin tight except the boots, and I'm not showing much skin, just a couple inches of my thighs, so everything is mostly covered. But you can see through my shirt to my bra. "I think maybe I'm too old to wear this."

"You look hot as fuck," Poppy says.

"She's right," Layla says.

I think my kids are going to freak when they see their mom going out like this. Poppy tosses me a pair of panties. "For the sex bucket list challenge. Give your panties to a stranger."

"You need to do that tonight," Layla says and unlatches the baby from her breast. "Okay, let's go."

We head downstairs together, and I yell a "goodbye" to my kids, and they do the same back to me. While Layla creates a diversion handing off the baby to Gage, and Poppy gives Dash some final instructions for the night, I manage to sneak out the front door before anyone glimpses my outfit.

Poppy and Layla quickly follow me out, and I lock the door behind us. Then I hear Poppy say in a singsong voice, "Hi, Mateo." My head whips around, finding him still in his suit from the baptism, minus the coat, his sleeves rolled up, showing off his tan skin.

"Ladies," he says, but his eyes stay on me, meandering down my body.

Poppy bumps me with her hip. "We'll go wait in the car," she says and walks down the front path with Layla. They glance back at us, flashing me a look that says they both expect details.

"I thought you were flying back," I say.

"Not until later. I hope you don't mind. Gage and Dash told me to come by and hang out until my flight."

I'm not sure if it's wishful thinking, but he sounds disappointed I'm heading out. Was he hoping I'd be home? Was it me he wanted to see? "I don't mind. My kids and Greer are inside, too."

"Looks like you'll be having more fun," he says.

"That's the plan," I flirt.

For a half second, I consider handing him my panties, but think it best to stick to the list, which requires giving them to a stranger. Besides, if Mateo ever gets my panties, I want it to be because I got in his. Not his panties, of course, cause that would be just weird. I silently wonder if he's a boxer or boxer briefs kind of guy. Flashing him my best smile, I strut past him, walking away, feeling his eyes on me, knowing he's watching, hoping he's liking and wanting what he sees.

CHAPTER TWELVE
PORN AND BEER

I'M TRYING TO respect Ryan's need for distance, but I need to talk to him about kid stuff. So like a complete chicken, I decide just to text him, not call. He calls me back within a few minutes, and I suggest dropping the kids off at his place instead of him picking them up from mine.

I find myself nervous driving to his house. I know where he lives—I've seen it from the outside—but I've never stepped foot inside. I've never had the kids spy on Ryan, never pumped them for information. I'm more than a little curious what it's like in his house, but I don't plan to go inside this time, either.

We stop in front of the single story brick ranch house. Ryan is a professor at SCAD, Savannah College of Art and Design, and teaches urban design and dabbles in historical preservation, so I know he must hate living in a place with so little character.

When we divorced, he insisted I keep our house. It was the only home our kids had ever known, but I think the real reason was that he couldn't afford it on his own.

Getting out of the car, the kids and I head up the driveway, ring the doorbell, and wait on the front porch for their father. He greets them all with hugs and smiles and holds the door wide open. Jacob and Ava head inside.

"Come see my room," Connor tells me and tugs at my hand. My feet frozen on the porch, I hesitate. I didn't plan to go inside, and Ryan hasn't invited me in. Then Connor yanks my hand a bit more.

"Come on, Mom." He clearly loves his dad's house. That's the way it should be.

I awkwardly look up at Ryan, and he nods for me to come in. I carefully step inside, unsure what awaits me in this unknown other world in which my kids live half their lives. It's kind of sad, but true. The house is small but updated, and I don't see a trace of another woman anywhere.

The kids' rooms are like something out of a magazine. Connor and Jacob share a room with a flat screen television, and every plush pillow and throw blanket imaginable are in Ava's pretty room. The rest of the house is nice, but I can tell that Ryan's spent most of his time and money on the kids' rooms.

After the kids settle in their rooms, Ryan says, "I was glad you reached out. What did you want to talk about?"

"Is there someplace private?" I ask.

He motions towards the French doors that lead to the small backyard, a bistro table and chairs on the patio. "I wanted to talk to you about Ava," he says.

"I wanted to talk to you about her, too. About what happened with Justin?" I ask.

His eyes widen, and he shakes his head. So I fill him in on what a douchebag Justin is, how he hurt our daughter, how he cheated with some random—which I'm sure strikes a particular nerve with Ryan. I go on to say that she'll be okay, that she's been talking to me, that she'll get through it even though there's some shitty gossip.

"I want to kill him," he says. "And I want to take my time doing it."

"I know," I say. "So what's your news about Ava?"

"I want to buy her a car." He must see my reaction because he immediately goes into argument mode. "I know we said not until she's seventeen, but I really want to do this for her. She's obviously been going through a lot lately. And I want it to be from me." He reaches out, but doesn't take my hand. "I know it's huge. But I worry about her and the boys being without a car when you're in Atlanta."

"My mom is five minutes away. And Gage and Layla are usually in town now, too."

"Relax," he says. "I'm not insinuating you're doing anything wrong."

"It felt like you were."

"Emerson, I think you're a great mom. The best. If you ever think I'm saying otherwise, that's coming from inside you, not me."

Even though we're divorced, that still means a lot to me. "You know I think you're a good dad, too."

He flashes me a smile, his dimple popping out. "So we agree we're awesome. How about the car?"

"I don't know." I always tell the kids a car's a weapon. When you hand them the keys, you are handing them the ability to kill themselves or someone else with a two thousand pound missile. Maybe Ryan's right, I am dramatic.

He pulls out his phone. "Look, I've got a picture."

"Wait, you have it picked out?" I ask.

He shows me a blue Fiat. It's completely adorable, and Ava would look adorable in it. "It's got good ratings for safety and gets good gas mileage."

"How long have you been thinking about this?"

"Not long. It belonged to the daughter of one of the professors at school, and she's going to NYU for college and can't take it. It's a good deal."

"You know if you do this, the boys will expect you to buy them cars at sixteen, too?"

"Is that a yes?" he asks.

I can see the excitement all over his face. He really wants to do this for her. I suppose it's okay. We spend the next few minutes working out the details for insurance and maintenance and how we expect Ava to contribute. Then it's time for something else.

"I hate to damper the fun, but I need to talk to you about Jacob. He's drinking."

He nods like he's known. "Last time they were over here, I swear I had four beers in the fridge, but then there were only three. I thought maybe it was him, but I was hoping I was just getting old and forgetful."

"What are we going to do?" I ask.

Ryan gets up, opens up the French door, and calls for Jacob. After a moment, our son appears and says, "What?"

I'm so sick of the one-word answers from Jacob, and "what" is not the way you respond when an adult calls for you. I raised him better than that. Ryan and I both did.

"Grab me a beer and come out here," Ryan says.

Jacob's eyes dart to me. "You told him!"

At least we got three words. Ryan's stance gets a little taller. "Get the beer and get out here, Jacob. Now."

Jacob does as he's told and Ryan motions for him to sit. "First porn and now beer, huh?"

"You drink, Dad!" Jacob says. "You trying to tell me you never watched porn?"

"Only with your mother," Ryan says with a straight face.

"Gross," Jacob says. Playing along with my ex, I smile and nod my head. Then Ryan pops the top on the can and slides it in front of Jacob, whose eyes grow to the size of baseballs. "Is this a trick?"

"Nope," Ryan says, and I'm suddenly wishing we'd discussed this first. "I get that you're curious. But rather than you sneak around and do something stupid, I'd prefer you be stupid with me and your mom here."

Jacob looks at me, and though I'm not sure how I feel, I motion for him to drink up. Unity is the only way to parent. If a kid thinks mom and dad aren't united, the kid will play that for all it's worth. "This is crap," Jacob says before pushing away the beer and storming back inside.

"That went well," I say.

"Now he knows you and I don't keep secrets, divorced or not."

"And that we used to watch porn together?" I tease before picking up the beer and taking a long swig.

Then, from out of nowhere, Ryan asks, "Want to stay for dinner?" I give him a confused look, which prompts him to awkwardly add, "I mean, I can't let you drink and drive."

I put down the beer. "It was only a sip."

"Still, why don't you stay?"

"It's not a good idea," I say, getting to my feet.

"Yeah, it might confuse the kids."

"It confuses me," I quickly whisper.

He gently takes my hand. "We shouldn't have slept together. It was a mistake."

His last word lingers in the air. I'm a *mistake*. I know I said the same thing to him. But hearing him say it really hurts, even after all this time. Tears start falling from my eyes. I wipe my face and try to keep more from falling, but I can't. They keep coming. I don't want the kids to see me, so I scurry away around the side yard towards the front of the house.

"Stop," he says, coming up behind me and grabbing me by the waist. "I just meant it confused me, too."

"What's that supposed to mean?"

"You were always the one that held us all together. It's just that when you told me about that boot camp guy, I . . . "

He can't finish the thought. Even after all this time, he can't talk about it. "Let's not relive things," I say.

"I fell apart without you. I was so angry, and I held on to that like some sort of weapon, like a reminder of why we weren't together, telling myself not to forget that pain."

I pull away from him. "I get it. Seems pretty certain how you feel. You don't seem confused."

"But I am," he says. "Despite everything, I think you'll always be the love of my life."

His words hit me hard, and my knees buckle a little. Wondering if this is real, I lean against the side of his house for support. I prayed and begged God for this moment for so long, and at times gave up hope that it would ever come, especially when we signed the divorce papers. "What are you saying?" I ask carefully.

"I don't know," he says. "That's why I wanted some time."

Time, I think. I've been spending my time lately on my sex bucket list. And it's not time spent on sexual freedom or experimentation, but on finding myself again, feeling worthy of love again, loving myself again. And it's been time well spent, and a far cry from the waning years of my marriage.

Ryan and I were really good at the business of being married. We could coordinate a schedule with the best of them. We were also really good at being friends. But towards the end, we really sucked at the lovers part. I never stopped wanting him, desiring him. Even after almost twenty years, I still got excited when he was coming home from work.

But somewhere along the way, he stopped feeling that way about me. He'd say it wasn't true. But that's the way I felt, so it was true for me. It was my reality. And the fact that we could go weeks without so much as a kiss was all the proof I needed. Maybe it's something that happens with all men. As soon as they marry us, they forget how to date us.

I think most women feel that way from time to time. But year after year, it took a toll.

It wasn't an intentional thing on his part. I don't think he was doing it to be cruel. We were just moving past each other, away from each other. We weren't connecting anymore. And it made me wonder whether it was my saggy boobs, stretch marks, the extra pounds I carried after birthing three children, or even the one weird stray hair that grows by my left nipple that perhaps I forgot to pluck out one day and he happened to glimpse it.

Perhaps other women wouldn't be bothered by a lack of affection from their husband. Perhaps they'd even welcome it, but it did a number on me. I'm ashamed to admit that. I wish it didn't. I wish my self-esteem were invincible, but it's not. Being married to a man that doesn't show his desire for you hurts. Even two years later, I still find myself trying to recover from it.

Talk about wasted time. And I'll be damned if I waste any more. The next man that comes my way is going to want me with a passion so great that neither one of us will be able to see straight. Could that be Mateo?

"That's just not good enough, Ryan," I say. "I want a man who knows he wants me. Not one who needs to think about it."

Truer words have never been spoken. Right then, I know I've finally forgiven myself for that kiss. And for the first time since Ryan left me, I'm not going to look back, only ahead.

CHAPTER THIRTEEN
LIST EMERGENCY

MATEO AND I haven't spent any real time together since our drinking game, so I march over to his office, feeling strong and confident. It's like everything is right with the world. My bra and panties match. My toe is healed. I'm sporting some killer stilettos, and my black skirt looks good. Granted, it's probably too short for the office, but I just don't give a fuck.

I knock on his door then barge right inside, finding Mateo dressed in a white dress shirt sitting at his desk. His deep, dark eyes hold a look of shock. I close the door behind me and throw my hand on my hip, needing some answers.

"Why now?" I ask. I know he knows what I'm talking about, but he also seems entertained by my little show. "Why are you interested in me now, after knowing me for two years? Is it just about the list?"

"The list is fun, but no."

"Then what changed?" I ask.

"You," he says.

"I'm exactly the same," I say and stiffen my spine. "I'm still your boss. I'm still your friend's sister. Nothing is different now than it was a year ago."

"Things are very different," he says and walks around his desk, leaning against it. "You weren't ready a year ago."

"You expect me to believe that?"

"Believe it or not," he says. "I've been waiting for you."

I open my mouth to speak, but nothing comes out.

"I will not just be some checkmark on your list," he says sweetly then closes the distance between us, his fingers gently lining my face. "Because once I have you, I'm not letting you go." He leans in to kiss me, our mouths mere inches apart.

There's risk in hoping. It's much easier to just be happy with the status quo. It's when you start hoping for more that disappointment can happen. Mateo's right, I haven't been ready to take that risk until now. But we've got some obstacles. "Since my family owns the company, technically, I'm your boss."

"I won't sue for sexual harassment," he teases.

"Still, people might talk," I whisper.

"Does that bother you?" he asks, his hands starting to roam the curves of my body.

"I don't know, maybe, not really, but . . ." I stop babbling when he leans forward to give my lip a little nibble. My legs start wobbling. There's something so sexual about this man. You know how some people are cute or handsome, like the boy next-door type? Then there are people that are sexy, hot. Something about them just oozes sex. Mateo is the latter.

"I don't care what people think."

"What if it doesn't work out?" I breathe out, running my fingers down his hard back. "Then we're stuck seeing each other every day."

He pulls back and looks me straight in the eye. "Then I'll quit."

"You'd do that? Just so I'm not uncomfortable?"

He inches closer. "I'd have to quit. There's no way I could see you everyday, and not kiss you, touch you."

"Mateo," I whisper, my voice coming out hot and needy.

His lips land on mine with a sweet little kiss. "It feels to me like it's going to work out," he says, grinning a little.

"I've got three kids," I say. "I'm not like other women. You have to understand, I'm not going to always be available."

"The nights you don't have your kids, you can be with me here."

"At your place?" I ask, my throat dry.

He tilts his head, a cute little smirk on his face. "This is beginning to feel like a business negotiation."

"I tend to overthink things."

"I know." He takes me by the waist. "Emerson, I know you're a mom. I know you have many things pulling you in so many directions. I'm okay with all that. I know I won't be able to see you every time I want. But it's better than not having you at all."

My heart melts at the thought. This time it's me who kisses him, and I want to do much more. But then another thing hits me. "What about Gage?"

"He knows."

"What?" I cry.

"I told him I wanted to ask you out."

"You did? What did he say?"

"He was cool about it."

"He was? When did you talk to him?"

"I don't know," he says, wrinkling up his nose like he's trying hard to remember. "Maybe a year ago?"

"A year ago!"

Mateo laughs, and it's gorgeous. "Yeah, when he and I started talking about me working here, one condition I had was that it wouldn't prevent me from being with you. I told you I've been waiting for you to be ready."

He makes it sound so simple, like a sniper waiting for his moment. Maybe that's where Mateo's patience comes from, his security background? "This is crazy!"

"Why?" he asks.

"I don't know. It just is." The truth is, I know why. It's because Mateo is a great guy, handsome as hell with a perfect body, and can have any woman he wants. But he wants me, and has wanted me enough to wait for me. Is there anything sexier than that? I don't think so. "What have the past few weeks been about, then? All the flirting, the fooling around. It didn't seem like you wanted more than that."

"You know how much I love your list," he says, throwing a flirty smile my way.

"But the whole time, you wanted more than that?"

"How could I not?" he asks, wrapping his arms around my waist. "I was waiting for you to figure out that you wanted more. I figured I had one shot to get this right. I knew if I pushed too hard, if you weren't ready, then you'd find every excuse in the book."

He's right. I feel like I'm ready, and still I just threw a ton of excuses at him.

"I find it hard to believe you just sat around waiting for me, crying in your beer."

"I never cry," he says. "And I don't pine for women, either. I wanted you, and I waited for my shot, that's it."

I HAVE A date. Tonight.

After Mateo and I talked, he insisted he finally take me out. I guess it's official. Mateo and I are dating. God, that's so weird. They really need to invent some new words for grown-ups who are dating. Boyfriend? Girlfriend? It all sounds so juvenile. My significant other—too old. My special someone—too corny. My lover—too French. My plus-one—too formal. My beau—too old fashioned. And if I start calling him my *bae*, just shoot me. Who invented that stupid word?

I'm dressed cute for work, but want something special for tonight. So, I sneak out of the office to buy something new to wear, preferably something to knock his socks off. Perhaps his pants, too. Atlanta has some great shopping close to the office, and the first store I come upon has some amazing stuff. That's how you know it's going to be a good shopping day, when the first store you go to just works.

And the first thing I try on actually fits. It's a lace black blouse with a scoop back. I'll have to buy some sort of backless bra, maybe one of those adhesive ones. They don't do much to support the girls, and I'll be paranoid about them peeling off all night, but it will be worth it. Of course, if things go beyond second base, then Mateo would see it. Maybe our relationship is too new for that.

I decide to reach out to Layla to see what she thinks. I mean, this is important. My sex bucket list challenge may hinge on this decision. I don't want to call her in case the baby is sleeping, so a one-word text should do it. *Help!* My cell phone rings a couple seconds later. "Thank God," I say, "I've got no idea what to do. I need your help."

"Emerson!" I hear my brother's voice. "Layla and Greer are sleeping. Are you alright?"

"Yeah, I'm fine," I say, composing myself. "Just a wardrobe question."

Gage exhales into the phone. "You scared the piss out of me."

"Sorry," I say. "I have a date and didn't know what to wear."

"I can have Layla call you," he says.

"I'm going to dinner with Mateo. I understand you gave him your blessing."

He chuckles a little. "He told you?"

"Why didn't *you* tell me?" I ask playfully.

"He told me the same day Layla told me she was pregnant. I totally forgot about it until just now," he says, adding, "I think I hear Layla now. She's awake. I'll see you in an hour or so. I'm flying in for the night."

He hands off to Layla, and I go through my wardrobe dilemma for the next thirty minutes. FaceTime can be very useful when needing a girlfriend's opinion. I walk around the store with my phone out like I'm starring in an old episode of *Lifestyles of the Rich and Famous*. Layla's got great taste. She always manages to look great without looking like she put forth any effort. I need that superpower. By the time we hang up, I have a couple of cute new date outfits picked out.

I'm waiting to pay when my cell phone rings. It's Mateo. I glance at my watch. I've been out of the office too long. "Missing me?"

"Emerson, one of our planes is in trouble."

I look down at my phone, another call coming in, this one from Poppy. Without purchasing a thing, I hand the clothes to the young girl at the register. "Mateo, who's the pilot?"

✧ ✧ ✧

RUNNING IN HIGH heels is not for the faint of heart. By the time I make it the few blocks back to the office, the building is on lockdown, unsure whether the plane is having some mechanical trouble or is the target of some attack. It's a bitch trying to get through security. I'm flashing my badge at everyone in my line of sight, but my eyes are focused on Poppy pacing back and forth in the lobby.

"Let her through," Poppy yells, smacking the security guys over the shoulders.

"Poppy, stop!" Mateo barks then grabs my hand and pulls me through.

"What do we know?" I ask.

"Dash is the pilot," Mateo says.

"Shit!" Poppy screams.

My stomach drops, but I keep my composure. It won't help if I freak out, too. "Any word from the plane?"

"I don't have full details yet."

"Fuck!" Poppy screams.

"Let's go," he says, pulling Poppy into his arms as we head into the elevators up to his office. He sits her down on his sofa as his computer is dinging with emails, and his phone starts ringing off the hook.

"Gage is flying in now," I say. "I'm not sure he even knows."

"Flights are grounded until we know if . . ." Mateo says.

"If what?" Poppy asks.

"Gage left at least forty-five minutes ago," I say. "He should be landing soon."

"If what?" Poppy screams.

I motion for Mateo to get to work. He's not a therapist. He's not here to comfort Poppy or deal with me right now. He needs to be on his game. This is what we pay him for.

"Poppy," I say softly. "Let me see what I can find out." I pull out my phone, and Poppy stands up and begins to pace.

As the head of PR, I don't have much security clearance, but since it's my family's business, I've got a little pull. I make a few calls to see what I can find out. Unfortunately, it's not much. Plus, it's just hard to get much information about what's going on in a plane several thousand feet in the air. I keep reminding Poppy that whatever is going on, air travel is very safe, that planes can fly safely even when an engine fails, that there are fire extinguishers if that's necessary, and that there are so many back-up systems it's unbelievable. Human error is always possible, but Dash is one of the best.

Mateo looks at his computer and then takes yet another call. He hangs up quickly, and I can tell by the look in his eye we need to sit down. "It's not mechanical. The plane is fine."

"Thank God," Poppy says.

Mateo sits down next to her on the sofa, placing his hand on her shoulder. "There was some sort of incident on the plane."

"Terrorism?" I ask.

"They don't think so," he says. "I don't have the whole story, but it seems a man and his wife were fighting. He was drinking, and he punched her. The flight attendants tried to intervene, and things got out of control."

Poppy looks up. "Dash left the cockpit, didn't he?"

"All I know is that a pilot is injured," Mateo says.

"I know it's him!" Poppy cries, and I can't console her. "Is he okay? How bad is it?"

"I'm trying to find out more," he says.

"The plane will land here?" I ask.

"Yes," Mateo says. "Soon."

The next fifteen minutes are a complete zoo. Poppy wants to go to the runway and meet the plane. My brother just landed, was briefed on the incident, and is now trying to get to the office. And my dinner date is trying to manage the situation.

Once Mateo confirms the injured pilot is indeed Dash, there's no stopping Poppy. I do some quick thinking and call one of my contacts, who tells me which hospital the ambulance will head to once the plane lands.

I manage to convince Poppy to head there rather than put up with the police and TV crews descending on the airport. And within about twenty minutes, she and I are standing at the entrance to the emergency room, waiting for Dash to arrive, watching passenger accounts of the event on our phones.

The man was drunk, out of control, and abusive. There were no air marshals on the plane. The flight attendants were overwhelmed, and a few passengers intervened. Dash exited the cockpit and ultimately restrained the man, though in the process, he pulled a small knife from his pocket and stabbed Dash in the neck. It's unknown how the knife got through security. Dash's status is also unknown. There's a lot that's unknown. But everyone's saying Dash is a hero.

Gage and Mateo are at the hospital with us. Their phones won't stop ringing. They should really be at the office, but Dash is their friend. And the security issue is over; it will now just take time to sort out how the knife got on the plane and what happened in the air. So it's fine the guys are both here. In fact, from a PR standpoint, I like that Gage, as head of the company, is checking on an injured pilot. He's clearly worried about Dash, pinching the bridge of his nose so hard that I fear he'll leave a permanent indention. Our dad used to do the same thing when stressed. As for Layla, she's a mess and keeps calling me, but she can't leave Greer and get here. My mom isn't faring much better. I've talked to Ryan, and he, too, is upset. So are our kids. Dash is like an uncle to them.

Mateo is the only one holding it together. Hell, I think he's holding all of us together. He's listened to Gage, talked to my mom, consoled Poppy, brought everyone food. And ever so often, he gives me a little smile or a simple brush of his hand to mine. We never got our first date, and I'm not sure when we will, but he waited before and that's his way of letting me know he'll wait again.

Where is the damn ambulance? Poppy hasn't said a word since we confirmed the injured pilot was Dash. She either cries quietly or looks like she's in a daze, pulling out her hair extensions one by one. At times, I see her trembling a bit. I've asked a million times if I can do anything for her, and she just shakes her head each time. The waiting is killing her. I know she needs to see Dash, to know the extent of his injuries.

After I ask again if there's something I can do, she takes my hand and finally speaks. "Stop wasting time, Emerson. Go to Mateo. That's what I need you to do."

I get to my feet, catching Mateo's eyes, knowing he'll follow me. All the crazy stuff on my sex bucket list is great, but a simple hug and kiss would be perfect about now. I head outside to get some fresh air, looking up into the afternoon sun. Is it really not nighttime yet? Nothing about the past few hours makes any sense. How could this have happened? How can I help my friend?

"Have you eaten anything all day?" Mateo asks.

I turn around, and a soft smile appears on his face, but it doesn't hold happiness. It's a worried smile. "I can't eat," I say. His phone rings again. Pulling it out, he moves the switch to vibrate. "Mateo, you can't . . ."

"Two minutes," he says, holding out his hand to me. "Me and you for two minutes."

I fall into his arms and hold him tightly. He strokes my hair as I cling to him. I haven't had a man hold me, just hold me, in years. And for those one hundred and twenty seconds, I hold on as tightly as I can, knowing how quickly it can be taken away.

Now it's the buzzing of my phone that forces us apart. I have to answer; it's Ava. I console her on the phone as best I can, and then Jacob, too. I tell them I wish I could be there to comfort them. I know they need me. I don't think my littlest one knows what's going on, which is good. I feel so torn between my kids and everything else—Gage, Poppy, Dash, my work, and so on. Such a typical mom feeling. I promise them as soon as Dash arrives at the hospital and is stable, I'll head home.

I step out of Mateo's arms and we go back inside. There's been no update, so I take a seat next to Poppy—and wait.

Waiting is the worst. I was absent the day God handed out patience in heaven. I suppose waiting is a little better when you're with someone, when it's a team sport. The mind goes to dark, scary places when you're alone with your fear and worry. I heard a priest say in a homily once that fear is bad, but being scared while you're alone is intolerable.

Glancing up, I find Mateo's brown eyes fixed on me. He looks so strong, so sure, like he's been here before, like he's in this for the long haul, no matter how long it takes. Maybe I won't ever have to worry alone again.

I HATE I had to fly home. It's Ryan's week with the kids, but they need me. He brought them to my house for the night, thinking they'd be more comfortable in their regular rooms. He was right, and I don't mind. He hangs around a little while to let me collect my thoughts, hug and talk to the kids, and clean up a bit. I keep my shower short because I start to think too much. And checking my phone every thirty seconds isn't helping, either.

Dash is fine, for the most part. The knife didn't go in too deep, and it missed the carotid artery and whatever other important veins and nerves there are. He was alert and stable when I left the hospital. But the adrenaline coursing through my veins hasn't settled. I haven't heard from anyone since I left. I don't know how Poppy's holding up, or whether Dash was released. And I know I need to be handling PR for this episode.

Putting on my most comfortable pajamas, I hear the doorbell ring and come out of my bedroom, finding Ryan at the door taking a couple sacks of food. "You ordered?" I ask him.

"No, I thought you did. The guy said it was paid for already."

I smile, knowing exactly who did this. Then I take out my phone to send a thank you text. I know I should call, but don't feel like I can with Ryan here.

Mateo's response is immediate. *I'm keeping our dinner date.*

"It's from that Italian place you like," Ryan says. "Should we call and tell them it's a mistake?"

I smile and shake my head. Did I tell Mateo my favorite place at some point? If not, how did he know? I'm not too hard to figure out. I'm a total carb whore—pasta and garlic bread are my biggest turn-ons. My food porn pictures would be anything made from dough.

I take the sacks from him. "Think I'll keep it. I need the carbs."

I kneel down and start to unload the sacks on the coffee table in the den, feeling it's wrong to share any of this with Ryan.

Taking a knee beside me and eyeing the cartons, he says, "Weird. It's all your favorite stuff."

I shrug. "By the way, thanks for helping with the kids. You don't need to stay."

Ryan places his hand on mine. "You shouldn't be alone."

I slip my hand out from beneath his and get up. "I'm flying back in the morning. I think the kids will be alright now."

"They will be. Are you alright?" he asks but doesn't get to his feet. "I can stay the night."

"I'm fine."

"I'll sleep on the sofa."

"I said I'm *fine*. Go home."

"I know what you said," he says, getting to his feet. "But . . ."

"It's been a day from hell. You said you wanted distance. So go home."

"Emerson," he says softly, "let me be here for you."

"I can't."

"It doesn't have to mean anything."

"I can't."

"Why not?"

"Because my . . ." My phone rings, stopping me from blurting out I'm finally moving on. Mateo's name lights up my screen. I doubt that's any sort of red flag to Ryan. He knows that we work together and that Mateo is at the hospital. Quickly grabbing my phone, I motion for Ryan to leave, but he doesn't.

"I want to know if there's any update," Ryan says, and whether I like it or not, that's a pretty good excuse for him to hang around.

I answer the phone. "Hi, Mateo. Have you seen Dash?"

Listening to Mateo, I nod to Ryan. Mateo goes on, and I learn that Dash is being discharged from the hospital soon, but he's being grounded until the investigation concludes.

"How's Poppy?" I ask.

"She's strong, hanging in."

"Tell her I'm flying back in the morning."

"I will."

I glance over at Ryan, now plopped down on my sofa. "How about you?" I ask.

"Just keeping an eye on Poppy and your brother."

"You're a really good friend," I say then bite my tongue, hating the way that came out. "I mean, thank you."

"You're welcome," he says. "Did you eat?"

"Thank you for doing that," I say. "You've got so much going on. I can't believe you took the time to do this."

"Emerson," Ryan blurts out, "you want the spaghetti or the lasagna?"

"Is that Ryan?" Mateo asks.

I gnash my teeth, plotting various ways to murder my ex-husband, then lower the phone to my chest. "I want them both," I snap. "That's all mine." Ryan holds up his hands in peace, and I bring the phone back to my ear, to a laughing Mateo. I move from the den into the kitchen to get some privacy. "Sorry about that. Ryan was watching the kids. That's why he's here."

"I'm glad he's there."

I scrunch my face. "Really?"

"I was worried when you left. I hated the idea of you by yourself."

"I'm used to it," I say. "I thought it might bother you that Ryan is here."

"Don't worry about me," he says. "Plus, if you and I are going to work, it'd be best if he and I got along."

"That's so mature. I was worried that . . ."

"How about you stop worrying about everyone all the time? And let me worry about you for a change?"

"I'm a mom, worrying is a prerequisite for the job."

"My mom says the same thing," he says.

"I'm so tired."

"Eat and try to sleep," he says. "I'll see you in the morning."

I hang up, walk into the living room, and find Ryan asleep on my sofa. Is this his idea of being there for me? Rolling my eyes, I grab the takeout and head to my room, looking forward to a long, deep carb coma.

CHAPTER FOURTEEN
UNSELFISH SEX

I MAKE MY way to Atlanta and continue to monitor the news. Lucky for us, all the accounts are showing Dash went above and beyond his duties to ensure the safety of our passengers. That's a blessing. It makes my life easier. Still, the media has questions, and I'm the one providing the narrative.

Walking into the corporate headquarters, I never realized that buildings had moods until today. I can feel the worry and sadness. It's as if the very walls, the very bricks have absorbed the emotions of our employees. Even with good news swirling about Dash, it will take a few days if not weeks for everyone to feel "normal" again. From the looks of my brother, it might take even longer than that.

I step off the elevator and look through the open door of his office, seeing his head resting in his hands, and just for the briefest moment, he looks like our father. Then Mateo appears in my line of sight, his back to me. I can't hear them, but I know the stress has them both on edge. Gage glances up, catching my stare. And the big sister in me kicks right in.

I step into his office and shut the door behind me, as Gage stands up. I move to him and wrap my arms around him. Ten years older than he is, Gage will always be my baby brother. It doesn't matter that he's the boss, that he towers over me, that he's now married with his own baby.

He releases me, probably embarrassed in front of Mateo. "You've handled the media brilliantly," Gage says.

I nod my thanks. "Any word on how he got the knife onboard?"

"TSA error," Mateo says. "Nothing on our end. Apparently, the guy has a history of domestic violence."

"I checked on his wife this morning," I say. "Doctors checked her out. She's fine. I offered her counseling on our dime." Gage nods in response. I should've asked him first, but I knew he'd be fine with it.

The three of us catch up on the details of the past day until we are all on the same page. But in the quiet pauses, I feel the tension between Mateo and me building, both of us anxious to check on each other, to have a proper hello, and a moment alone. This is why it's hard to be involved with someone at work.

Gage thanks Mateo, indicating he wants a minute alone with me. I'm really hoping he isn't going to lecture me about something. His face looks so serious. Mateo's eyes catch mine over his shoulder, as he closes the door behind him. He's obviously concerned, too. Alone together, Gage paces back and forth in front of his desk a few times, pinching the bridge of his nose.

"You're freaking me out," I say.

"I'm not sure how to start this conversation."

"Is it about me and Mateo?"

He shakes his head. "I need your opinion."

"This is a first."

He grabs some papers off his desk and hands them to me. I pull my glasses out of my purse, and my eyes scan over the pages. "You're selling now?" I ask. He's had offers before, but was never serious about them.

"I've thought about it before. And after what just happened, maybe it's a sign."

I continue to look over the document. "It's an extremely good offer."

"Half would be yours."

My eyes shoot up. "Dad left the company in your hands."

"We were both his kids."

"Gage, I've worked part-time mostly. You've really run things, grown the company. What it's become is built on your hard work, not mine."

"Well, I won't sell without your blessing and Mom's. And I won't sell unless you're taken care of."

"Half is too much."

"So you're okay with me selling?"

"Let me think about it," I say. "But don't rush into something because of Dash."

"Layla said the same thing. But it's more than that. I'm married now with a kid. I can't go back to eighty-hour work weeks."

"Have you talked to Mom?"

"Not yet. I wanted to talk to you first."

We go on to talk about options, negotiating tactics, his concern for our employees, whether everyone would keep their jobs at their present pay. It's a lot to consider, but nothing needs to be decided now.

"I plan on talking to Mom tonight," Gage says. "I've asked her to fly in. I'd like you to be there when I talk to her."

I agree, of course, but my heart sinks for purely selfish reasons. I may never get to have dinner with Mateo. Forget the damn sex bucket list—right now I'd settle for a bucket of chicken and him.

I make my way to my office, tending to a pile of papers on my desk and answering a few emails and calls. Looking up from my desk, I find Mateo standing in my doorway. I wonder how long he's been watching me. The smile on my face is enough to invite him inside. "That looked serious back there," he says and closes the door. "What's up?"

Another reason not to date an employee: some things I really can't discuss. Just because I know what an amazing kisser the man is doesn't change my position in the company or over him. *Over him?* That would be nice. "Just company stuff," I say, tossing my glasses on my desk and walking to him.

He cocks a cute little smirk. "You mean, *boss* stuff."

"Yes," I say and try to hold his gaze. The man always looks like he's ready to devour me. It's hot but unsettling. It's been a long time since a man looked at me like that. Casting my eyes down, I notice his clothes, the same suit he was wearing yesterday. "Did you not go home last night?"

He shakes his head. "Worked all night."

I step to him, my fingers lightly touching the stubble on his face. "You must be exhausted."

He shrugs, as if forty-eight hours without sleep is completely normal. Maybe it is for him. I guess if you work security, you probably don't get naptime.

"I'll cut out a little early today if I can. Don't tell the boss," he teases.

"I may do the same," I say.

He reaches for my hand, and my heart beats faster. "Why don't we sneak out together? Maybe a long afternoon nap?"

Turning away from him, I collapse down on the sofa in my office and release a deep breath. "Gage needs me tonight for work, so I can't. I'm sorry."

"You don't ever have to apologize to me for being a hard worker or a mom. I happen to love those things about you."

He said the word *love*. I'm such a girl. He didn't say he loved me, but hearing him say it in any connotation peaks the teenage girl inside me.

He sits beside me and slips an arm around my shoulders, helping me relax back into his hard chest. "Soon," he says.

"I promise. The kids get out of school in a few days, and then Ryan's taking them on vacation. And I'll have some time."

He doesn't say anything, but he squeezes me a little tighter, just holding me like he did at the hospital yesterday. This should've been on my list. Just have a man hold you without expectations. Usually a man only cuddles to try to get in your pants or after he's already gotten in them. This is nice. There seems to be no ulterior motives, and if there are, he's hiding them well.

Fortunately for him, I've got some motives of my own. I slide away from him, walking towards the door.

"You leaving?" he asks.

I lock the door then turn back towards him. And God, the smile on his face almost kills me. I love this side of him, playful and cute. He gets to his feet, cups my cheeks, and tilts his head, his eyes roaming over my face and hair, admiring me, but it's me that drops to my knees. Unbuckling his belt, I look up at him, and he caresses my hair. I can't believe I'm fooling around at work again. It seems like the corporate office is becoming my personal sex parlor.

I slide down his pants and run my hands up his thighs to his tight ass, his body tightening under my fingertips, then I slip his boxer briefs down. As a general rule, I don't think the penis is a particularly pretty body part. Don't get me wrong, I like dick as much as the next girl, but I'm not going to get all poetic about the way it looks. Mateo's dick, however, is an entirely different subject.

He gives my hair a little yank, and I expect him to guide my mouth to his dick, but he doesn't. I glance up at him and pull my bottom lip between my teeth, giving him a naughty smile. Then I grip his ass and take him deep into my mouth. The groan he releases shoots a power through me. He may have tried to muffle it, but anyone passing outside the door definitely heard. It's been years since I did this, but it's coming back to me. Ryan never finished this way. It always gave me a huge complex, like I'm a blowjob failure.

Holding his ass, I encourage him to move. He starts slowly, like I knew he would. "Mmm," I moan, letting him know I'm enjoying this almost as much as he is. I love feeling him come undone at my doing. I slide my hand to his dick, and I start to move faster. He pulls my hair up, holding it like a ponytail, so he can watch.

"I'm so fucking close," he says.

So I go harder and faster. And then it occurs to me: swallow or not? Like I said, Ryan never finished this way, so it was never an issue. A hint of saltiness hits my tongue. There's no time for decisions. I can't have a mess in my office. Okay, I got this.

"Fuck!" he groans.

Okay, I might not have this. Poppy told me in one of her sex rants that the average man only releases about a teaspoon of semen, but I beg to differ. Whoever did that study had not met Mateo. Still, it doesn't taste as bad as I thought, though I'm not going to start craving it like carbs.

I look up at Mateo, finding him content and relaxed, and a certain pride hits me. I'm a blowjob failure no more! And I can mark unselfish sex off my list. I lift up his boxer briefs and pants, then he falls to his knees, joining me on the floor, pulling me to him, cradling my head to his chest. "That was unexpected," he pants out.

"It was on the list," I say, playing it cool. "But I can't remember which number because you stole it."

"I told you I own that list," he says, chuckling. "And there was nothing about you on your knees. I would definitely have remembered that."

"How am I supposed to keep track? What if you lose it? Or it falls into the wrong hands?"

"Don't worry," he teases. "It's in a safe place."

WITH MY NEWFOUND energy, I push through the rest of the day and visit Poppy and Dash. I take her a little snack package—power bars, tiny bottles of wine, caramel popcorn. You know, the essential girl's comfort food pack. She thanks me over and over again for the stuff. I let them know that the company will continue paying her salary in addition to Dash's salary while she takes care of him. They're both extremely grateful, but it's so unnecessary. He was hurt on the job. It's the least we can do.

I head over to Gage and Layla's penthouse and barely make it there in time to talk to my mom. I wasn't sure what to expect from the conversation, but found myself surprised at my mom's openness to selling the company. She'd watched my dad build Southern Wings from one small aircraft with one route, to a full-fledge commuter airline. Then she watched Gage turn it into something my dad only dreamed of, a major player in the industry, serving parts far and wide.

My brother's done such a good job with the company that I suppose it makes sense she left the decision in his hands with her full blessing. I'm frankly not sure what he'll do. Part of me thinks this is just a reaction to what happened with Dash, but Gage doesn't usually act on emotion unless Layla or Greer are involved.

Staying at my brother's place tonight, I call the kids to say goodnight, catch up on their days, and give them an update on Dash. According to Poppy, he's milking his injury for all it's worth; he apparently claims he won't be able to do any chores around the house for like three months. The kids get a good laugh out of that.

After hanging up, I lay down in bed. Usually this is the time when I replay the day in my head, all the things I didn't get done, could've done better. Worry is my bedmate. But Mateo's hard body, and replaying what we did in my office earlier, is filling my mind right now. Grabbing my cell, I see a text from the man himself, and my heart does a little leap.

Mateo: Checked the list, twice!
Me: Are you Santa?

I hit send before I realize he may not get the reference to the Christmas song. After all, Mateo doesn't have kids. He may not have heard that song in decades.

Mateo: I definitely know who's been naughty and nice!
Me: Which do you prefer? Naughty or nice?

This is so much better than worrying myself to sleep. Some people call it sexting, but I think *textual relations* has a nice ring to it. Either way, it's good for the soul.

CHAPTER FIFTEEN
REVERSE COWGIRL

RYAN IS BRINGING the car over any second. I'm doing my best mom impression not to spoil the surprise. All three kids are sitting at the kitchen island, sandwiches in front of them. Sandwiches say nothing special is happening today. Connor hasn't touched his. I only have to say his name for a few tears to roll down his cheeks. To my surprise, it's Jacob who reaches over and pats his back.

"What's going on?" I ask. All three of them stare down at their plates. "I promise you guys Dash is fine."

"It's not that," Ava says then nudges Connor a little. "Tell her."

He looks up at me with those big blue eyes of his, filled with tears. "I don't want to go on vacation with Daddy next week."

Shooting glances at Ava and Jacob, I ask, "Why not? You love the beach."

"It's too far away," Connor says, the tears coming faster.

Again, it's Jacob who places an arm around him. "It's the same amount of time you usually spend with your dad."

"It's too far," Connor cries. "I Googled it. It's almost an hour from here. And if you're at work in Atlanta, it's super far."

"Connor," I say gently, "you're used to me going to Atlanta for work. It's never bothered you before."

"That's when I'm here. This is different. What if I need you?"

"Did you forget your Uncle G owns an airline? I'll hop on a plane."

"No, you won't," he cries.

"Connor, of course I would."

"Maybe for something big," he says. "But not if I just scrape my knee or want to show you something cool."

I reach for his hand as Jacob still holds him. "You're right. Not for those things. But you can FaceTime me and show me."

"It's not the same," he says.

"I know," I say, and divorce guilt settles hard and heavy on my chest. I fucking hate this for my kids, especially Connor. He barely remembers his dad and me together, and probably doesn't ever remember us being happy.

"You can show me," Jacob says.

I nearly fall down in shock—that my teenage son is comforting his little brother, that his voice is so deep, that he didn't just grunt and actually completed a sentence.

"You hate playing with me," Connor says.

Jacob shrugs. "Only on vacation."

"Really?"

Jacob answers by fist bumping his brother. That's as good as a signed contract.

"And I'll fix any skinned knees," Ava says. "I know just how Mom does it."

I nearly fall down in shock again. I love these rare occasions when the kids support each other, when we're all pulling in the same direction. But at the same time, I feel a sense of sadness, that they have to make do without me around. It's unfair to them. I turn away and walk out of the kitchen before completely losing it. Will this ever get easier?

The doorbell rings. It's time to put on a happy face, but Ryan knows me too well. I open the door, and he greets me with a question.

"What's going on?" he asks and opens his arms.

I take a step back. "Talk later," I say, wiping my face. I peek out the front window and see a huge bow on the top of the car like you see in the commercials. "Kids!" I call out. "Come here for a second."

Jacob and Connor are the first to appear. Jacob's hand is on his little brother's shoulder. Ryan glances at me, seeing Connor's little red eyes, and I just shake my head. "Daddy, what are you doing here?" Connor asks.

"It's a surprise," he says, bending down a little. "You okay, buddy?"

"Can Mommy come on vacation with us?" Connor asks. "Like a real family."

Ryan winces a little. I've only seen that look in his eye one other time. The other time I watched his heart break. "Mommy has to work, buddy."

"Uncle G would let her off," Connor says, his little voice gaining hope with each word. "I know he would."

Ava walks in, fiddling on her phone, giving her dad a distracted hello. She's going to regret that in a minute. "Let's talk about it later," Ryan says to Connor then gets to his feet. "Ava, I forgot something in the car. Could you go get it for me?"

Still looking at her phone, Ava opens up the front door. Jacob sees it first, but we motion for him to stay quiet. When Ava reaches the front steps, she's forced to look up, and then she screeches so loudly. Ryan jiggles the keys in front of her. She quickly grabs them and races towards the car, doing a 360-degree sprint around it before running back into her dad's arms, thanking him over and over again.

"Your mom, too," Ryan says, which is sweet because it was all him.

"I want to sit in the front seat," Connor says.

Ava gives me a huge hug then motions for her brothers to follow her, and they all crawl into the car. She starts the engine, and we hear the radio turned up, and the windows start going up and down. She can't drive off because the bow is in her way, but it doesn't matter. They're all having a good time checking out the features.

I'm not sure why, but Ryan drapes his arm over my shoulder. I reach up and squeeze his hand a little then step away. "Want to tell me what I walked in on this morning?" he asks.

"Connor doesn't want to go to the beach. He doesn't want to be so far away from me."

"We talked about it for months. He was so excited."

"I guess now that it's so close, he's nervous." Ryan releases a deep breath looking back at our three kids, all happy, all getting along, such a rare moment to experience. "I should be taking some pictures," I say, turning to go get my phone.

"You could come with us," Ryan says quietly.

"Huh?" I say and whip around so fast, pain shoots through my neck.

"It's not unheard of for divorced couples to travel together. It's on those reality shows Ava makes me watch all the time."

"I can't," I say.

"Why?" He steps a little closer. "It might be good for us."

"Us ended when you left," I snap.

He barks back, "It actually ended when you kissed . . ."

"Can I take it for a drive?" Ava calls out to Ryan and me, as Jacob is pulling the bow off.

"Sure, honey," Ryan says.

"But remember, Ava," I say, "you can only drive one of your brothers at a time."

Jacob lets Connor go first and plops down by the sidewalk, waiting his turn. I love how the kids are cooperating today, but Ryan has me some kind of pissed off right now. Why can't everything ever be good at the same time? I turn to go inside, and Ryan follows me into the foyer, grabbing my elbow.

"Emerson, I'm sorry."

"Go fuck yourself, Ryan," I say. "I don't need you to forgive me anymore. For a long time, I waited for that, hoped for it. But you know what? I finally forgave myself, so I don't give a damn if you do or not. I may have made the mistake, but I was ready to fight for us. You never were. I would've never given up, but you did."

"What if I'm ready to fight now?" he asks.

"Too late. I'm seeing someone," I bark, hating that the words came out like a weapon.

"Oh." He pushes on his eyes a little. "Is it serious?"

"It could be."

"Do the kids know?"

"I'll let you know when that happens." Notice I said *when* instead of *if*. I'm hoping Ryan caught that.

"Who is he?"

"None of your business."

His eyes bore into me. "My kids, my business."

"Don't be childish."

"Who is it?" he demands.

A quick pro-con list goes through my head—all the reasons to tell him the truth, all the reasons to lie. Maybe the best route is to dodge. Or maybe I'll just say nothing. I don't like Ryan's tone; he doesn't deserve an answer from me. We glare at each other for a moment before I see a shift in his eyes.

"The Italian food," he says like he just found a clue.

I don't respond, except to fold my arms. Ever the professor, he thinks he's such a smart guy, a true detective. I see more wheels turning in his head.

"The phone call after the food was delivered," he says.

He's getting warm. He'll put it together soon. Who gives a fuck?

"Mateo!" he cries, so proud that he figured it out, then rattles off five minutes of reasons why the man's no good for me, everything from his age to his occupation. "You can't be this stupid. The man is a glorified security guard."

"He is not," I cry out. "Besides, I don't care what he does for a living."

"Please, he's just using you for your money."

All the air leaves my chest. He might as well have slapped me across the face. It would've been quicker and less painful. I guess the only way Ryan thinks a younger, hot man would be interested in me is for money. Fuck him!

"It's my family's money, not mine. You know that."

Ryan rolls his eyes. "Please. You stand to inherit a shitload. You don't think Mateo knows that?"

I will not let Ryan make me second-guess things. I've known Mateo for two years. I know who he is—the kind of man he is.

Ryan's just playing head games with me. Well, I can play right back. "I guess you know that, too, then," I bite back. "Maybe that's why you slept with me. Maybe living a couple years without my family's money has made *you* second-guess things."

"I can't believe you'd say something like that to me," he shouts.

"Well, I can't believe you'd think the only way Mateo is interested in me is for money."

"Oh, I forgot," he barks. "He's helping you with that list of yours!"

My hand whips across the side of his face. I've never hit anyone before in my life, and I'm not sure I did it right, because my palm is stinging like a bitch. Ryan's hand flies to his cheek, which is bright red.

Connor comes running inside. Ryan and I spring into action and fake that things are fine. He turns away the red side of his face and scoops up our son. "Guess what, buddy?" he says. "Mommy's coming on vacation with us."

He did not just do that!

"That's the best thing ever!" Connor screams.

"I know," Ryan says, grinning from ear to ear.

Connor jumps down and wraps his little arms around me, kissing and thanking me then taking off upstairs to his bedroom.

"How's that for fighting for you?" Ryan says before walking out the door and slamming it behind him.

WHAT THE FUCK? What the fuck? What the fuck? Yes, that completely deserves three WTFs. We have never, ever used the kids against each other. How dare he do that! My mind starts racing. If I don't go on vacation, what will I tell Connor? If I do go, what will I tell Mateo? Better question—where will I sleep? Oh, what am I thinking? Come hell or high water, I'm not going on vacation with that man.

I just don't know how to get out of it. I've got to figure something out. I debate calling Layla or Poppy, but they have their hands full with other issues, like a baby and an injured boyfriend. And I don't want to dump on them. I feel like I've been so full of drama lately. I need to get things under control. Time to woman-up and make the call I've avoided all day. As soon as I hear Mateo's voice, I launch into what happened.

"So he wants you back?" Mateo asks.

"He left me."

"Not what I asked. Is he still in love with you?"

I really don't want to talk about this with Mateo. No woman wants to talk about her ex with the new man in her life. Just when I'd made a decision to move on and never look back and live my life and focus on my list, Ryan worms his way back in. But the fact is, Ryan will always be in my life. Mateo has to understand and accept that. But I also want to make sure he knows that Ryan isn't a threat to what we are starting.

Just because Mateo and I have known each other and been friends doesn't mean he knows what went wrong in my marriage. It's time I explain a few things. So I spend the next few minutes telling him the details of my divorce—the fighting, how unhappy I was, the kiss, how Ryan couldn't forgive me. All of it.

Thankfully, we're not on FaceTime so he can't see me, but I'm sure he can hear the shame in my voice. Tears roll down my cheeks. I can't help it.

"They say 'once a cheater always a cheater,' but I promise I'm not like that. I was faithful all those years," I say before stupidly adding, "Ryan is the only man I've ever been with and . . ." Oh holy shit, that did not just come out of my mouth, but that's not where his focus is.

"I hate hearing you cry," he says softly. "Especially when I'm not with you."

"I don't know what to do. Now he has Connor's hopes up. I can't believe he did that. I'm so pissed off."

"Well, if he wants to act like reality-star royalty, then let's give it to him."

"What does that mean?" I ask.

Before I know what's happening, Mateo proceeds to dial a number and quickly has us on a three-way call. I have to say, when I put a threesome on my sex bucket list, I didn't have this in mind. After a few rings, Ryan picks up, and I stay quiet and let Mateo talk.

"You have some fucking nerve calling me," Ryan says.

"I wanted you to hear it from me," Mateo says, his voice cold and calm.

"Hear what?"

"Well, since you ambushed Emerson the way you did today, I wanted to let you know I'll be coming on vacation with her. We can be one big, modern day family," Mateo snarks.

Never in a million years did I think Mateo would pull something like this. The man is cunning and protective in the best possible way.

"I don't think so," Ryan says with a laugh. "My kids don't even know about you and Emerson."

"Well, I thought it would be nice if the three of us told them together. You know, so they can see we have your blessing."

"Son of a bitch," Ryan snaps.

"Remember, Ryan, you started this by using your son," Mateo says. "Trust me, I can play harder and dirtier than you can ever imagine. Hurt Emerson again, and you'll find out just how hard I hit."

Holding my breath, I wait for Ryan to respond. Would he really go toe-to-toe against Mateo? Finally, Ryan says, "Tell Emerson I'll talk to Connor," a heavy guilt coming through the phone, and then his line goes dead.

"Emerson, you hear that?" Mateo asks.

I wipe a few tears, saying, "Yeah, I can't believe you did that, protecting me from Ryan like that."

"That's my role as the man in your life. To guard your heart."

Oh my! I'm not sure which takes my breath away more—the fact that he called himself the man in my life or his desire to guard my heart. My heart couldn't have a better man protecting it.

"No one will hurt you again. Not on my watch."

"I wish you were here."

"Me, too," he whispers.

✧ ✧ ✧

I KNOW I should go to sleep, but it's impossible. The day's drama is eating at me. Looking over at my clock, I see it's nearly one in the morning. I'm going to regret this tomorrow, but I grab my remote. The list of television shows I need to catch up on is a mile long. Scrolling through my TV channels, I hear a noise, a clicking sound.

I pause the television and sit straight up. This was always Ryan's job. If I heard something strange in the night, he investigated it. And it was always nothing. Usually, it was the damn smoke detector chirping. Those things always seem to decide their batteries need changing in the middle of the night.

It's probably something stupid like that. Besides, I have a house alarm and am faithful about arming it. I look towards the panel in my bedroom. It's now green. I know it was red and armed before I went to bed. Shit!

The kids are all upstairs. I'm the only thing between them and potential danger. Maybe I just forgot to set the alarm in all the chaos with Ryan, the joy with Mateo. I grab the phone and hit the number nine then one and keep my finger over the one, in case I need to hit it quickly.

I've got no bat, no golf club, nothing. If somebody's inside, maybe I could clang him over the head with my vibrator? I get up and move towards my bedroom door, hearing the unmistakable squeak of shoes on the hardwood floors outside my bedroom.

Moving like lightening, I reach for the lock, but the door starts to open. Oddly, I'm not scared. I feel a sense of calm as my mind goes to Sandra Bullock's character in *Miss Congeniality*, when she does the SING self-defense sequence for her talent—Solar plexus, Instep, Nose, Groin.

I toss the phone, drop to the floor, and punch hard and up, my fist landing right between the motherfucker's legs. A muffled curse word fills the room. I expected it to be louder, but it's like he's trying to be quiet. I look up and see Mateo, holding his nuts, his teeth clenched together.

I just punched my sex bucket list partner in the balls. This would happen to no one else but me.

"Oh my God," I cry. "I'm so sorry." I have no idea what to do, my hands hovering over his genitals, not knowing if I should offer to kiss and make it better or get him an ice pack. I take his arm, helping him inside my bedroom, then shut and lock the door.

Grimacing, he makes his way to my bed. "Guess you don't like surprises."

"I feel horrible. What can I do?" I ask, stretching out his legs.

"I'm okay," he says, his face looking anything but.

"What are you doing here?" I ask.

"You said you wished I was here," he says, smiling at me.

Remember when I said Mateo was the real deal, the one that I could be serious with? You understand why now. "How'd you get in here? The alarm? The kids?"

"I'm head of security. You don't think I can bypass an alarm?"

"Creeper!" I tease.

"I only use my skills for good," he says, moving around a little. Hopefully, the pain is subsiding.

"You're crazy. How did you get here?" I ask, sitting down beside him.

"Drove," he says, pushing my hair back from my face.

"You drove over four hours in the middle of the night?"

A naughty look in his eye, I know he was hoping I'd reward him for his chivalry. Instead, I gave him a fist to the nuts. "Only took me three and a half. Number 11 had me motivated."

I bite my lip, trying to remember. "Was that the reverse cowgirl or . . ."

"That's the one," he says, chuckling.

Damn, I really screwed this up. So I say again, "I'm sorry."

Gently, he kisses my lips. "I had to see you."

"When do you have to go back?" I whisper.

"It's Sunday, so as long as I'm back for work tomorrow morning, I can stay."

"My kids are here."

"Does that mean you're a screamer?" he teases. I bust out laughing, quickly covering my mouth. He pulls me to him, my back to his front. "I'll sneak out before they wake up."

Sitting between his legs, he hands me the remote. "What were you watching?"

"Nothing," I say. He nuzzles deeper into my bed, cuddling me close, motioning for me to start it. I hit play, and his arms tighten around me. It feels nice and normal. Is this what life with Mateo would be like? "You didn't come all this way to watch TV with me," I say.

His mouth lands on neck, causing delicious little tingles to radiate down my spine. "You've never watched TV with me."

Gently, he continues to plant little kisses on my neck, causing an ache between my legs. Turning my head to him, he finds my lips. With each stroke of his tongue across mine, I can feel how much he wants me, how hard waiting is. "Not with my kids here," I say between pants.

"I know," he says, his hand drifting between my legs.

Wish I could say I was wearing something sexy, but I'm in an old college t-shirt and plain ole cotton bikini panties. His hand massages my thigh as it moves upward. My wax was weeks ago. Damn, I should've had another.

But as soon as his finger touches the edge of my panties, I don't care anymore. I've thought about him touching me like this again for weeks, since that day in my office. That's a lie. I've thought about it since I laid eyes on him. He's the one I think of when I take out my new toy. He's the name I cry into my pillow when I orgasm. But none of that compares to having his warm body next to me, his finger teasing me.

Something happened when Ryan and I got married. I think I first noticed it around year seven. Sex became only sex. The fun foreplay tapered off until it was almost non-existent. I'm not sure if it's because we were always in a hurry with the kids or what, but he almost never took me to orgasm with his fingers or mouth anymore. And I'm not one of those women that can climax just through penetration, so I was left high and dry a lot. I should've said something, but I never did, not wanting to bruise his ego, telling myself it was nice just to be close to him, that I didn't need the orgasm. I was a damn fool.

"Faster," I breathe out, pushing against his finger hard.

I need to ask Poppy what this move is called. He's got one finger inside me, and one on my sweet spot. I'm sure she'd know the name, but I'm calling it the "dynamic duo" for now. I wonder if this is what they do in those orgasm classes she was telling me about. If so, I might need to reconsider signing up. Mateo continues to stroke me over and over again. And this time, when I cry out his name, he's right here beside me, my cries muffled by his shirt instead of my pillow.

He slips his warm hand out from under my stretched-out panties but doesn't remove it. Instead, he just lets it rest on my inner thigh. Watching TV is going to mean something totally different to me now. I can't help the little giggle that escapes.

"What are you thinking?" Mateo asks, grinning down at me.

"Just something Poppy and Layla and I talked about after Layla had Greer. Every couple with kids has a code word they use for sex. Something you say so the kids won't bother you for a few minutes. I was just thinking we found ours."

He smiles, "Watching TV."

I giggle again, and he nuzzles my nose with his. "I can't believe you did this," I whisper, turning my head and kissing him softly before glancing down at his crotch. "I'm sorry," I whisper.

He nuzzles my nose a little. "It's alright. It was worth it."

"But I already did the selfish sex thing."

Burying his head in my hair, he chuckles, pulling me tighter to him and smiling down at me, his arms coiled around me. "Right now, this is enough."

But what I hear is: *I'm enough*.

CHAPTER SIXTEEN
WHY ME?

When I open my eyes, he's gone. It was like some beautiful, wonderful dream, only very real. His good morning text proves it.

Don't ever make me leave again. It's too fucking hard.

Before I can even respond, I hear the front door opening. Maybe that's him. Maybe I can catch him before he goes. Hurrying out of my bedroom, I see Ava's back. "It's six in the morning," I say. "Where do you think you're going?"

She freezes, the door still open. My eyes land on her reason for leaving: Justin.

"Don't freak out, Mom," she says. "It's not what you think."

I'm standing in my t-shirt and panties, so I grab a coat out of the closet. I'm not about to go fetch my bathrobe. I won't take my eyes off these two. I head outside, with Ava clinging to my arm. "Please, Mom."

"You have some nerve showing up here," I shout at the punk-ass boy.

"*Mom!*"

"I did not raise you to let some boy mistreat you. You are better than him, Ava."

"I don't want to get Ava into trouble," he says. "I just heard about her new car and . . ."

"And saw a chance to weasel back into her life."

"Mom, you're overreacting," Ava says. "Justin heard about the car from some of our friends. He texted me to say congrats and cool.

That's it."

"Then why is he here? Why are you sneaking out to meet him?" Her eyes fall to her feet. "How long have you been seeing him again?"

"I'm not."

"Don't lie to me."

She glances up at Justin. "I asked Ava to forgive me," he says. "We've just been talking for a few days. This is the first time we've seen each other except for at school and stuff."

I look at my daughter, and she nods. "Ava, he cheated on you."

"You're one to talk. I saw Mateo sneaking out of your room this morning."

Oh fuck! Some stealth security guy he is. "Go home, Justin," I say, taking Ava by her hand. "In the house now, young lady."

As soon as the door closes, I fire off a text to Mateo. On top of my daughter, now I'm pissed at him, too. *Ava saw you!* That's enough for him to know what kind of state I'm in.

"I'm calling Daddy," she cries.

I've never stopped the kids from calling their father whenever they wanted, but this is different. "No, you're not. You and I are going to have a serious conversation about *that* boy."

"Mateo or Justin," she says.

"Last I checked, I am the adult in this household. My relationships are not your business," I say, and she rolls her eyes at me. "Ava, who I date doesn't concern you."

"He could end up being my stepfather!"

"If I ever choose to bring someone into your life, then we can discuss it. Right now, we are talking about you and your poor judgment."

"You mean like fucking your boyfriend with your three kids upstairs?"

It takes every ounce of self-control not to smack her smart mouth. "You told me to start dating, remember?"

She glares at me. "And you told me that sex should only happen when you're married."

The only thing that saves her this time is a soft knock on the front door. "Does that boy not know when to quit?" I bark, barreling for the door, ready to rip his nuts off for thinking my daughter will be his next conquest—and he'd probably want to do it in her new car. Ava's right on my heels, probably ready to defend this boy like they're Romeo and Juliet. I fling open the door, ready to fight, and my body comes to a grinding halt. "Mateo?"

Ava doesn't miss a beat. "Stepdad?"

"Want to grab some breakfast, Ava?" Mateo asks.

She laughs right in his face. "You're completely crazy if you think I'm going anywhere with you."

"There was this boy I passed on my way here," he says. "Justin, I think. He asked me to give you a message."

Mateo is really good. Though he doesn't have kids, I have to admire his parental manipulation techniques. Still, my admiration doesn't squelch my pissy mood, or Ava's for that matter.

"What did he say?" Ava asks.

"Breakfast first," Mateo counters.

Steam is coming out of my daughter's ears. Mateo better not be bluffing, and he better fucking tell me what that boy said. Ava looks at me, and I give her a shrug. "Fine," she says, "but I'm buying my own breakfast. I pick the place. And I'm driving."

"Deal," Mateo says, giving me a little smile. "Bring you back something?"

I shake by head. No way can I eat anything, not even carbs can make this situation better.

Watching my teenage daughter and my new man get into her car together is the weirdest fucking sight. Ryan would go ape shit if he knew. Nothing can distract me while they're gone—not a shower, getting dressed, doing my hair, checking my emails. Not even a response from my vibrator inventor gets my mind off what the hell they could possibly be talking about. Is Ava being a brat? Is she crying or upset? How is Mateo dealing with an emotional teenage girl? Where did they go? How long will they be gone? The questions are endless. And I'm worried the boys will wake up, too. Ava may know I'm dating, but I don't want the boys to know, especially Connor.

After seventy-three minutes, I finally hear a car door and bolt out onto the porch, finding Ava walking up the steps. "Everything okay?"

She glances back at Mateo standing in the driveway. "I know what I said about you dating, but it hurts to see you with someone other than Daddy."

"I know. And I'm sorry it hurts you. But please don't tell your brothers. They need to hear it from me."

She nods. "He's waiting to talk to you."

I start towards him then stop, turning back to ask, "Justin?"

She just shakes her head. "Later, okay?"

I give a little nod, watching her disappear through the front door, then turn back to Mateo, who meets me halfway up the path to my house. "How dare you show up here like that?"

He looks surprised by my bark. "Figured she knew and I could help."

"There's nothing for you to do. The damage is done."

"Emerson," he says. "I feel horrible that I wasn't more careful when I left. But I didn't expect her to be sneaking out so early."

"I need to go back inside. I can't have the boys wake up and see us."

"Emerson," he says, taking my hand.

"I've hurt them so much. I don't want them to hurt anymore."

"Neither do I."

Shaking my head, I ask, "What did you say to Ava?"

"Not a whole lot. Mostly she cried," Mateo says, softly. "Freaked me the fuck out."

I'm smiling before I even realize it. "What did you do?"

"I poured more syrup on her pancakes," he says, grinning. "My mom used to feed us when we were upset, so I just kept putting food in front of her."

"I'm not sure that works on girls."

"Well, it got her laughing at me, which was better than the tears," he says. "It got so bad the waitress asked if she was alright, probably thinking I kidnapped her."

"How'd things end?"

He shrugs. "I told her she has a dad, and that's not my job. I told her my job is to make her mom happy."

"That's very sweet."

"Look," he says, taking my hand again. "I don't expect your kids to welcome me with open arms. I know it's going to take time."

Mateo's managed to handle my ex-husband and eldest child all before breakfast. He's getting served a big heaping bowl of my crazy. And yet he keeps coming back.

"Why me?" I ask.

I asked him before "why now," but not what it was about me. Don't get me wrong, I've got some things going for me—I'm an executive, and I don't look like a troll—but there's also the stretch marks, mom boobs, three kids who love trying my nerves. Why the hell would he choose *this*, when he can have any woman he wants?

"Are you fucking kidding me with that question?"

"No."

Ava opens the front door, sticking her head out. "Mom, Connor just woke up."

Without another word, I hustle back inside, wondering what his answer would've been.

IN MY HOUSE, we avoid doing any and all homework on Saturdays, so Sundays are complete chaos. And this week is final exam week, so lucky me. Why can't this be Ryan's week? Ava is pretty self-sufficient, but Jacob is a different story. Even with accommodations for his dyslexia, it's still rough. Thankfully, Connor doesn't have exams yet, so he's just gearing up for his end of the school year party. Between that and final exams, I'm not going back to Atlanta for over a week. As soon as they finish up next Friday, I'll be packing them up and getting them ready for their vacation with their dad. It's a lot to handle.

Summer won't be much easier—Ava has a job at the library and volunteers at Hope Cottage, which is Layla and Gage's charity project; Connor's camp schedule is insane; and as for Jacob, I'm not sure how I'm going to keep him busy and out of trouble. He's too old for camp, but not old enough to work a summer job. Poor baby, typical middle child problems. I'm feeling overwhelmed at the thought of running everyone here and there and trying to work at the same time.

Pushing all that out of my mind, I hustle around, wrangling the kids to get ready for Sunday Mass. Ava doesn't complain too much. Connor likes that we go to family lunch after, but Jacob hates it altogether. He tells me he doesn't believe in God. I tell him that's between him and God, but as long as he lives with me, he'll give an hour to Jesus every Sunday morning.

I push them all through the doors of the church, the opening hymnal already playing. We are late again. Every freaking Sunday. We slide in the pew next to my mother, who's always early. Thank God, she saves us seats. And she's kind enough to always sit towards the back, so we don't raise too many eyebrows with our late arrivals.

Connor immediately finds a bulletin and starts to read it. I should probably make him listen, but at least he's still and quiet. Jacob sits with a scowl on his face. And Ava fakes like she's listening but usually is too busy fiddling with her clothes, hair, or nails. My mom gives me a little smile down the pew, seemingly impressed that somehow we at least made it here, as we always do when I have the kids.

Ryan doesn't go to Mass at this church, even though we did when we were married. It's not like we decided that in the divorce decree—who gets which church or Mass time—but it just sort of worked out that way. I have to admit, it's hard to sit in these pews some Sundays. Divorce is frowned upon in the Catholic Church, so much so that in the eyes of the Church, I'm still married because we never got an annulment. So, if I ever want to remarry, I can't do it in the Catholic Church unless I first have my marriage to Ryan annulled. I'm not sure how I feel about any of that.

My mom's fingers tap the hard wood of the pew, startling me. She's old school, completely quiet and reverent during Mass. She never even uses the restroom. Jacob uses the church restroom like it's recess or something. I look up, and her eyes catch mine. Then she scans across the church, her head motioning several pews in front of us and to the side. I follow her line of sight. I can barely make out his profile through the crowd, but it's him.

Mateo.

It looks like he's alone on one side of the pew. A family of four is sitting on the other end. He's facing forward, not singing the current hymn being played. Giving my mom a little shrug, like I don't know what he's doing here, I study his handsome face. I haven't had the chance to do this in a long time. I used to admire him discreetly at the office, but it was always so brief. I was afraid someone would notice. Or worse yet, he'd notice. Now's my chance to really watch him.

He doesn't seem to have a clue that I'm here or that my eyes are glued on him, but I know when we walk up to take Communion, we'll have to walk right past him. Never has Mass gone by so fast before. I spent the whole time watching his every move, or lack thereof. He stays still, almost too still, his eyes always focused on the altar or lowered to his lap. He recites the prayers when appropriate, but never sings.

He is quite possibly the most beautiful man I've ever seen. The man who drove all night just to see me. The man I left abruptly this morning. The man I owe an apology.

My heart is pounding louder and faster as Communion approaches. I watch him walk to the front to take the body and blood, or bread and wine to you non-Catholics. He is quiet, solemn. When he gets back in his pew, he kneels down, making the sign of the cross again, his head lowered, eyes closed.

Our pew stands. My mother is the first one out, then Ava, Jacob, Connor, and me. There is no way he won't notice us when we walk by. Especially when my mom places her hand on his shoulder. His head darts up, a surprised smile on his face. He may know my favorite restaurant and how to bypass my house alarm, but clearly, he didn't know this was my church or that I'd be here. As my mom takes a step forward, he sees Ava, but only for a second, because he flips around knowing I'm not far behind. Connor gives him a little wave as he passes.

The line pauses with me standing right to the opening of his pew. A tear rolls down my cheek, and he slyly places his hand out of the pew, letting his finger just barely graze the back of my knee. It's so quick, so subtle, that no one but he and I know he did it. Then the line moves up again. Quickly, I wipe the tear away, not wanting my family to see. I'm sure the priest sees all kinds of emotions at Communion, so I'm not worried about what he thinks.

I take the body, but not the blood. I never take the wine. Seriously, how many people have had their mouth on that chalice before it's my turn? Sure, they wipe it and it's supposed to be blessed, but that's not stopping the possible backwash.

I sense Mateo's eyes are following me the whole way. When I turn to go back to my pew, I glance at him, a little smile on my lips. I want him to know I'm sorry. He doesn't turn around to see where we are sitting, but he's knows I'm there. I notice his body is a bit more relaxed, and there's a little smile on his face.

Ava gives me a look, and I shake my head that I had no idea. Honestly, I would've thought he was on the road by now. And I didn't even know he was Catholic. When Mass ends, we're usually the first ones to head out. Connor is always starving, and Jacob and Ava can't wait to check their phones. This time is no different. Connor is begging to go to a certain place to eat, and Ava is saying the place is gross.

I'm not even listening. I see my mom waving at Mateo, motioning for him to meet us out front. Mateo walks right up to my mom, and she thanks him for all his help with the situation with Dash. "What on Earth are you doing here?" my mom asks.

"Gage and I had some business, so I came in," he says. "I was going to drive back this morning, but thought I'd come to Mass before I head back to Atlanta."

He is a good liar, but my mom is better. I know she's not buying that for a minute. "Why don't you join us for lunch before making that long drive back?" she asks. Ava looks up from her phone, her eyes wide.

Mateo smiles politely. "Maybe another time."

A quick goodbye, and he walks away. And I'm left second-guessing. Did he refuse because he's mad? Or because it was awkward with my mom? My mom places her arm around me. "How about I pick up some pizza and soda and we make that lunch? I know you kids have a lot of studying to do."

Of course, the kids love that idea. Pizza and grandma are the perfect combination.

JACOB'S WITH HIS tutor. Ava's studying in her room. And Connor is playing some computer game. As for me, I'm trying to make cleaning up pizza look like a hard task. Yes, I'm avoiding my mother. She takes a seat at my kitchen island, prepared to wait as long as it takes. Tossing my cleaning wipe down on the counter, I say, "Go ahead. Let's get this over with."

"I like Mateo," she says. "Good choice."

"I'm terrible at this," I say. "Then add in living in different cities and the kids. It's proving to be impossible."

"Make it work," she says, and my eyes bulge out of my head. "It's time you let someone love you again. I know you can do things on your own. And you're doing a heck of a job, but we all need love and affection."

"There are so many issues, Mom. You don't even know. Just when I think things will work out, another roadblock gets thrown up." I look up. "Ava knows about Mateo."

"Why is it a secret?"

"Because the kids don't need me bringing different men into their lives."

"The kids should know you have a life outside of them."

"Ava didn't handle it well."

"I wouldn't expect her to. You haven't gotten them used to the idea."

She's right. I haven't prepared them at all. That's on me. "Ryan went ballistic when he found out."

"No surprise there. He still loves you."

"I don't know if it's that."

"Please, Emerson," she says and waves me off. "You can still love someone that hurt you. Ryan chose hurt over love. He's regretting that now."

Ava walks in, her eyes red. "What's wrong?" I ask, and she shakes her head a little. "If it's school pressure, please don't let that stress you out."

"It's Justin," she says, glancing at her grandmother.

My mom quickly gathers her purse and gives us both a hug, whispering in my ear that she loves me. And just like that, I go from a daughter seeking advice to a mother who's supposed to know how to dole it out. Leading Ava to the sofa, we sit down together.

"I know I should let go of him," Ava says, "but I'm having a hard time doing that."

"That happens. Your head knows one thing, but your heart feels another way. School's almost over. You won't be seeing him everyday. That should help."

"Mom," she says, her wet eyes looking up at me, "I need to tell you something."

My stomach flips. "It's okay, honey. Whatever it is, I will always love you. Nothing changes that."

She takes a deep breath and begins. "Like I said, I know I should move on, but my heart is telling me to give him another chance. I always wished you and Daddy would've done that."

"Your dad and I tried very hard."

"I want to get back together with Justin, but I know you're going to be mad."

Damn right I am. I'm fucking furious. "Let's make a deal. How about you get through exams, through your vacation with your dad, then when you get back, if you still feel the same way, I'll allow him to come over here to see you. But only here, and only when I'm home."

"And you won't be mean?"

"I won't be mean." I look into her eyes. "I trust you, Ava. Even though I don't agree with you letting him back into your life, I'm trusting your judgment. Don't make me regret it."

"I won't," she says, hugging me. "One more thing."

"What?"

"Could you go over chemistry with me? Please!"

WHAT'S THE DIFFERENCE between mixtures and solutions, acids and bases? Four hours of the periodic table and the afternoon is shot. I'd much rather be working on my list, but instead, I spent the day working chemistry formulas. Then it's dinner and baths and laundry and more studying, trying to fit in some actual quality time with each kid. Next thing I know, it's after ten at night.

When did getting ready for bed turn into a whole damn routine? Used to be, you brushed your teeth, said your prayers, and that was it. Now I've got to lotion every inch of my body, comb through my hair, floss and brush. And don't even get me started on the facial regime. I mean, there are serums and cleansers, moisturizers and better moisturizers. Then there are special gadgets to wash our faces, special ones to zap pimples or wrinkles. I swear it takes forever. That's why I don't think I'll ever get contacts, no matter how bad my eyes get. It's just one more thing to have to do. Men have it so easy. Whenever Ryan and I would come home after a night out, he'd be ready for bed before I even got my eye makeup off.

Throwing a little extra anti-aging cream on my forehead, I lift my hair, folding it under, trying to imagine what I'd look like with bangs. I haven't had bangs in over two decades, but maybe it's time. Last time I went to the dermatologist, she told me one day soon I'd have to choose between Botox and bangs. Bangs are a whole lot cheaper, so I probably should lean that way, but my forehead is looking okay so far.

After the marathon anti-aging regime, I grab my phone, put my glasses on, and crawl into bed. I don't know if you're like me, but I hate when the little number shows up next to an app. I can't leave it. I have to update it immediately or check the message. Somehow I've gotten over fifty emails today, and there's one text sitting there, too. One extremely important text.

Mateo—Since I took your sex bucket list, I thought I'd replace it with a new list. The "why you" list.

Number one: Have you looked at your ass lately? Well, I can guarantee that every man in the office has. Number two: You are loyal to those you love. You literally gave Layla the shirt off your back. You didn't think I noticed that, but I did. Which brings me to number three. You have no idea how amazing you are. Number four: The curve of your waist between your breasts and hips. When I hold you, my arms fit perfectly there. Number five: This is going to sound unsexy, but your work ethic. You don't do anything half-ass, not your job, not being a mom, not when you kiss me.

His list continues for a couple more text screens. With each word, my heart pumps a little harder in a weird mix of excitement and fear. It's almost like being on the top of the roller coaster right before you start to fall. This deserves more than a text back. I dial his number, but it just rings—once, twice, three times, four. Finally, his voicemail clicks on.

I leave him a message, telling him how touched I am, how sorry I am, how I hope we're okay, and that I'm sad I won't see him for a week. I hang up, knowing I'll be up all night waiting for a response, but none comes.

I'M OLD SCHOOL. I always tell Ava she's not to text a boy first, and if she texts him and he doesn't respond, she's not to text him again. But it's noon on Monday, and I haven't heard from Mateo, and I'm now fighting against my own rules. Sitting in carpool line, the temptation to call him is great. The kids only have school a half-day because of exams, so they won't be out for another fifteen minutes.

I push the buttons on the stereo in my SUV, hoping for a song to sing. Why is Justin Bieber always on during carpool hours? It never fucking fails. Every single day, it's Justin Bieber. Frustrated, I turn to AM, maybe some talk radio. I know there's some guy who talks food and restaurants, but what channel is it?

The one good thing about not sleeping is it gives you a lot of time to think. I did my fill last night, and something became very clear. I've tried to keep everything in a category. Work, play, mom, girlfriend—everything had a place. But that approach to life is not working. I'm all of those things, and I need to be all of those things at the same time. Mateo understands that, so it's time I cut him in.

A knock on my window startles me. There's a security guard on duty at the school, a short man with a big attitude. He starts yelling and motioning for me to move up, complaining that I'm holding up the line. Nodding and trying to quickly put the car in drive, my phone rings, and I hit my Bluetooth phone connection, seeing Mateo's name. "I was starting to worry," I say.

"No, you weren't," he says. "You started to worry like twelve hours ago."

"If you know that, then why didn't you call me back?"

"I crashed when I got back to Atlanta. Long drive, no sleep the night before. Long days working with the Dash thing. I guess it all just caught up to me."

The dismissal bell rings. "I'm at pick-up. The kids will be getting in the car any minute, so I don't have long to talk. But I've made a decision. I want the kids to know we're seeing each other."

"Okay, when?"

"You're sure you want to do this?"

"Yep."

Laughing, I toss my hands up. "You're a man of few words today."

"You said you only had a minute," he teases me. "I think this is a good step. It will make it easier for us to see each other. No sneaking around. Right now, I can't even send you flowers because they might see the card or ask who they're from. I hate that."

"You've wanted to send me flowers?"

"Lots of times," he says. "So tell me the plan. I know you have one."

"When exams are done. Maybe Saturday, before the kids go out of town with Ryan?" He quickly agrees without a moment to even consider his schedule, flight times, drive times. "So I'll see you then."

"Emerson," he says, "while the kids are gone next week, I want you to stay with me."

"All week?"

"All week."

My answer is simple. "Yes."

CHAPTER SEVENTEEN
THE TALK

MENTAL NOTE—NEVER TELL your ex-husband that you're going to tell your kids that you're dating. That conversation did not go well. He repeatedly asked me to wait—but it's my decision, and Mateo supports it, and that's all I need.

Exams are done. It's officially summer break. Mom guilt tells me I shouldn't jeopardize their first night off school with my own news, but there will always be some reason not to tell them. Maybe the pizza I ordered will soften the blow. I mean, I sprung for the cheesy bread and everything.

The kids and I sit down at the kitchen island. We don't even bother with paper plates. The pizza box is open, and everyone's attacking it. Poor Connor eats so slowly, he may not get a second slice.

"Kids, I need to talk to you about something important," I say.

Ava looks up mid-bite. She knows what's coming. "Are we getting a dog?" Connor asks.

"No," I say and take his hand in mine. "I've started seeing someone. I'm dating." Jacob looks at Ava, who's picking the cheese off her pizza.

Connor's whole body slumps. I move closer to him and hug him from the side, feeling him start to cry. "I'm the only kid in my class whose parents are divorced," Connor says. "Why can't you date Daddy?" he asks.

I look up at the older two. I know Ava's thinking the same thing.

Jacob's staring at his plate; I never know what he's thinking. "Your dad and I love each other, but we are better as friends."

"I'm going to bed," Ava says and stands up, clearly still uncomfortable with everything, and needing more time to process.

"So tomorrow," I say, "Mateo is coming over and . . ."

"Mateo?" Connor says, looking up at me, freezing Ava by her chair. "Why's he coming over? I like him. Is he bringing that cool car?"

Jacob rolls his eyes and exhales. "Mom's dating Mateo, moron."

I narrow my eyes at Jacob then say, "Mateo and I, we'd like to spend some time with you guys. He wants to get to know you better."

"I don't like Mateo anymore!" Connor screams with wet eyes then runs off, with Ava following after him.

Jacob takes another slice of pizza. "Would you like to scream or cry now?" I ask him.

"Middle child always goes last," he says with half a grin.

I playfully bang my head against the countertop then turn to look at him. "I really need to know how you feel about this."

"I'm okay."

"Okay is not a feeling."

"Can I let you know later?" Jacob asks. "I want to talk to Mateo first."

"You want to talk to him?"

"Yeah. You're my mom," he says. "When Dad left, he told me that I was the man of the house. He told me to take care of you."

I watch my fourteen year old take another bite, so proud he feels protective of me. It's as close to an "I love you" as I'll get from him, and I'll take it for sure. I kiss the top of my boy's head, making a mental note to warn Mateo.

I HATE PACKING. The toiletries are the worst. I can throw my clothes in pretty quickly, but it takes forever to remember all the lotions, makeup, and hair stuff I use daily. Then it's the medicine. As a mom,

I've learned to pack for anything. We've been struck with strep throat on vacation, sinus infections, stomach bugs. Hell, once Ryan even got a chicken bone stuck between his teeth. So now I pack my whole first aid kit and medicine cabinet. There's also extra pressure for this trip because I won't be there. Yes, there are stores. Yes, Ryan will be there. But still I want them to have their own things. Plus, I'm trying to pack my stuff for my week with Mateo without anyone noticing. Talk about pressure.

But it's all a big distraction anyway, trying to avoid thinking about Mateo's visit today. And he'll be here any minute. There's really nothing you can do to prepare for this situation. I haven't been a nail biter since high school. The SAT really stressed me out. Now my nail beds are suffering again. As for the kids, Ava refused to stay, telling me she already talked to him and didn't need to stick around. Connor turned on Minecraft when he woke up and has not left the computer since. Jacob actually woke up early for his meet up with Mateo; the phrase "the talk" has taken on new meaning in my house.

The bell rings, and I hustle to answer. Mateo's dressed casually in jeans and a t-shirt, and I wonder if he gave that any thought. Probably not, but I know if the roles were reversed, I would've emptied my closet looking for the right outfit. I motion for him to come in. He leans in to kiss my cheek. I'm pretty sure he gave that greeting some thought—sweet without being sexy. "I missed you," he says.

It's been a while since we've seen each other. It's been a while since I—or we—have focused on my list. Life is always getting in the way. And now's not the time to be checking things off. "You ready for this?" I ask. "Because I'm so nervous."

He gently places a little kiss on my lips. I take his hand and lead him towards the kitchen for a drink, wanting to keep this casual. I don't want this to be some big production, but Jacob clearly has other ideas. He corners us at the kitchen island, as Mateo takes a seat on a stool.

"That's the one my dad always used," Jacob says.

"Jacob!" I snap.

"What? It's weird for him to sit there."

Mateo holds up his hand to me. "Jacob, would you like me to move?"

Jacob starts pointing, saying, "Ava sits there, then Connor, then me. And that was Dad's stool. Mom's always standing. There are no other seats. So I guess there's no room for you." I know this is hard for Jacob, but he could try to handle this better. Out of the corner of my eye, I see Mateo just smiling at him.

"Maybe we'll have to start eating in the dining room," Mateo says. "There are more chairs in there."

A bit thrown by the idea, Jacob takes his own seat and cuts to the chase. "Don't hurt my mom."

"I won't," Mateo says, staring into his eyes, like this is a real man-to-man conversation, like they are equals in some way.

Then I move beside Mateo, careful not to touch him. Still, I want to show some solidarity. "Mateo's not here to replace your dad."

"I have an idea," Mateo says. "Why don't you and I do something your dad doesn't like? That way I'm not stepping on his toes."

That's a decent idea, but I know the mischievous look in my son's eyes. "Dad doesn't like the movies I watch."

That seems harmless enough, but I'm sure he's up to something. He's never this agreeable. Mateo shrugs and says, "Okay, what kind do you like? Comedy? Action? Science Fiction?"

"Porn," Jacob says flatly.

"Jacob!" I yell, steam coming out of my ears, then look over at Mateo, who's stifling a laugh, his hand covering his mouth. I can see it in his eyes. He likes my smartass son. "Your dad and I do not want you looking at a woman's . . ." I'm so flustered that I can't even think of the right words. "Sexy bits." Mateo and Jacob bust out laughing. Clearly, I'm spending too much time with Poppy.

"Gross, Mom!" Jacob says. "Don't ever use that phrase."

"I should just take the TV away all together," I say.

"Don't do that," Mateo says with a straight face. "I know how much you love watching TV."

I feel my face flush, remembering our code word for sex.

✦ ✦ ✦

I THOUGHT CONNOR was going to be the easy one, but I was dead wrong. He refused to eat lunch with us, even though I had his favorite chips. No amount of love, tenderness, threats, or bribes could convince him to even glance away from his computer screen. And when I unplugged it from the wall, he simply stared at the blackness. He loves his dad a lot, and I fear the only way Connor will ever accept Mateo is if Ryan does. Needless to say, I'm not feeling very optimistic at this point. As for Ava, she did come home in time to say hello to Mateo and tell me about some new flip-flops she just has to have. All and all, it wasn't a disaster.

CHAPTER EIGHTEEN
NO THREESOMES

THIS AFTERNOON, RYAN'S leaving with the kids to drive to the beach. My flight to Atlanta leaves around dinnertime. Mateo doesn't know that. He thinks I'm coming in tomorrow, and we'll leave together after work. After a long week, and the drama of him formally meeting my kids, I figure he could use a little surprise. My suitcase is packed. My mail is on hold. And my home phone is being directed to my cell. That took some figuring out, but I didn't want to have to tell Ryan to make sure to call my cell. Yep, this is the new sneaky me—the one who's dead set on making progress on my sex bucket list.

Checking my suitcase one more time, I've packed so much it feels a little bit like I'm moving in with him. With all the starts and stops, waiting and wondering, I feel like it's taken forever to get to this point. But this feels *big*—spending a whole week together—24/7. Not even Ryan and I did that unless we were on vacation. So this is a huge step for us.

Closing and locking my front door, one of my neighbors runs up the front walk holding a package. "I'm so glad I caught you. This was delivered to my house by accident," she says.

I thank her, taking the package, and say a quick thank you to God that the package is discreet and she didn't open it. I stuff it in my suitcase, not wanting to be late to the airport. It's a short flight between Atlanta and Savannah, and a lengthy cab ride to his place. He lives in a hip and trendy area of the city, his building sleek and modern, the complete opposite of my charming old Savannah home.

His apartment is on one of the upper floors, so I know he'll have a great view. I put my suitcase at my feet, wanting to have my arms free when he opens up the door. Then I ring the bell. I suddenly hear a woman's voice calling out. My heart drops.

The door opens. Her brown eyes slide up and down my body, landing on my suitcase. She looks like a model: perfect, exotic, beautiful, young. "I take it you're not here to deliver the dry cleaning," she whispers.

My head shakes slightly, and hers does, too, muttering something in Spanish under her breath. Dammit, why did I take French? I've never even been to France, or French-speaking Canada, for that matter.

"Emerson," I hear Mateo say from behind the gorgeous woman.

I throw my hand towards my suitcase. "I was trying to surprise you."

Thank God, he smiles. "Celia," he says in a voice almost begging, one I've never heard him use before.

She rolls her eyes. "Okay, but you owe me, Mateo." Then she takes my suitcase, turns around in time for him to drop some keys in her hands, and disappears into the elevator. He steps into the hallway, shutting the door behind him, his hands slipping around my waist. I motion towards the elevator. "Um, she took my suitcase."

"She's putting it in the trunk of my car."

"Did I miss that part of the conversation?"

He laughs. "She's my twin sister. We just kind of know that stuff without having to say it."

"Twin?"

"Yeah, I'm older."

I can't help but laugh that this thirty-something buff man felt the need to make that point. "Still, why is she taking my suitcase?"

"My mom and dad are inside, along with Celia's husband and kids," he says. "My parents are old school. I mean, I'm sure they know I'm not saving myself for marriage, but I don't want to rub it in their faces."

"Should I go?" I ask.

"Not at all," he says, playing with a few strands of my hair. "My mom was disappointed you weren't here. She wants to meet you."

"You told them about me?"

"Yeah. We're close."

"Do they know I'm divorced with kids?"

"Of course."

The door flies open, another beautiful woman appearing, an older version of Celia. This must be their mother. Clearly, sexy is in his gene pool. "Mateo," she says, the slightest hint of an accent.

"Mama," he says, intertwining our fingers. "This is Emerson."

Her dark brown eyes go from him to me, and she smiles, saying, "I told you she wouldn't miss your birthday."

My eyes fly to Mateo. How could he not tell me it's his birthday? He just shrugs, giving me a smile, and my mind flashes to the package in my suitcase. This has to be divine intervention—a gift for him. His mother reaches out to me, cupping my face, then pulling me down into a hug. She's a petite woman, so I really have to hunch over.

"I'm Isabel," his mom says, taking my hand and opening up the door. "You must come meet everyone." Stepping into his apartment, I don't have time to take it all in. The scene is a blur: there are kids running around, a baby crying, two men arguing over something in Spanish. Isabel claps her hands. "Everyone, this is Mateo's Emerson." They all seem to yell hello at the same time, and his mom starts pointing to them one by one, telling me their names.

I'm so overwhelmed that I only catch the father's name, Martin. His hand at the small of my back, Mateo leads me towards his dad. His fatherly eyes flash to his son, and I'm not sure if it's approval or not. Maybe he doesn't want his son with someone older, or divorced, or with kids. Then another thing hits me, something I hadn't even thought about before—about Mateo and me being an interracial couple. Hispanic and Caucasian? Is that even considered interracial? I don't know. He's just Mateo to me.

I need to focus. I'm about to meet his father. It's been forever since I've done this. Do I call him Martin or Mr. Reyes? He and Mateo have the same initials. If I married Mateo, my initials would be E.R. That can't be a good sign. Why am I thinking about marriage? Still, I've debated changing my last name back to my maiden name of Montgomery since Ryan and I divorced. I kept my married name, Baker, so the kids and I would have the same last name. But if I ever married again, my last name would be different from theirs.

Before I have time to decide the best way to address him, he's right in front of me. "Thank you for having me at the party," I tell his father. "It means a lot to me to celebrate this day with your son and meet his family." He says something to Mateo in Spanish, and Mateo nods and grins. "What did he say?" I ask.

"He told me I couldn't tell you."

I look at his dad, a mischievous grin on his face. "I can see where Mateo gets his charm from."

He leans forward, patting my hand and grinning. "Happy you could join us."

"Now where is Celia?" his mother asks.

"Right here, Mama," Celia says, stepping away from the front door she just snuck back through.

"Oh good, come meet Emerson."

Celia gives me a bright smile, like she's meeting me for the first time. "Happy Birthday," I say, playing along.

She thanks me then walks over to the baby girl crying in her father's arms. "All the kids are mine," she tells me before pointing to a couple boys. "Our oldest set of twins."

My eyes bulge. "You have more than one set?"

"We had twin boys, then two years later, another set of twin boys." She kisses the baby's belly. "Then finally I got my girl."

His mom grabs my arm again. "You must be starving. Mateo didn't think you were coming, so we ate already."

"I'm . . ." I start, but Mateo shakes his head at me, making an eating motion with his hand. "Starving."

She doesn't ask me what I want, but instead just fills up a plate of food for me. "I'm so happy we didn't cut the cake yet."

Mateo kisses her on top of the head. "Can you give us a minute, Mama?"

"Of course," she says, patting his cheek.

As soon as she disappears, he leads me to the farthest corner of the kitchen where no one can see us, and leans in for a kiss. But I playfully hold him off. "It's your birthday? Why didn't you tell me?"

"I didn't think you could come in today with your kids leaving. And I knew you'd feel bad if you couldn't make it." He shrugs. "Besides, I'm too old for birthday parties, but my mom insists. She makes it just like when we were kids." His arms cinch around my waist, forcing our bodies together. "I can't believe you're all mine for a whole week," he says.

I hope it's for much longer than that.

I CAN SAFELY say I love all of Mateo's family, but mostly Isabel. She's like my mom's twin. It was the cutest thing seeing Mateo and Celia blowing out their birthday candles. Yes, his mom actually had thirty-three candles on each cake. Mateo's was yellow cake with chocolate frosting, and Celia's was chocolate cake with strawberry frosting. She even had them in party hats. Mateo in a striped cone hat is a sight I will never forget.

Watching Mateo today, I got to see another side to him: the brother who still teases his sister, the uncle who is goofy and silly, the son who is respectful and loving. Getting to see him in the context of his own family was a nice little glimpse of how he'll hopefully fit into mine.

After Celia and her family went home, his mom and dad hung around longer. His mother insisted she clean up, even though Mateo reminded her he has a cleaning lady who does it. She didn't care. And when Mateo and I offered to help, she shooed us away with some nonsense that guests shouldn't clean and neither should birthday boys. So we simply have to wait her out. But I sense Mateo's patience is waning. If he shifts and adjusts his pants one more time, I'm not going to be able to keep myself from laughing out loud.

My cell phone rings from my purse, and I answer to Connor in tears. "You didn't answer your phone," he cries. "You said you'd answer if I needed you. I called you three times."

Huh? I look at my phone and see three missed calls. I guess I didn't hear with all the noise at the party. Now I feel terrible. Mother guilt to the Nth degree. It's like I can hear his lip pout through the phone. "Are you okay? Did something happen?"

"No," he cries. "I just miss you."

I talk to him for a few minutes until he calms down. Mateo's parents give me silent kisses on the cheek before they leave, and I mouth that I'm sorry. I don't want to be rude, but my kids come first. Given how they are with their own kids, I think they understand.

Mateo whispers, "Take your time."

"Let me talk to your brother and sister," I say.

"Daddy wants to talk to you first," Connor says. "Love you, bye."

"Love you."

"Emerson," Ryan says, his voice harsh and cold, "I know you're busy with Mateo, but for fuck's sake, take a breather and pick up for your kids."

"I hope you didn't just say that in front of them," I say, causing Mateo to come over to me. He sits down beside me, rubbing my leg a little.

"Of course, I didn't," Ryan says. "Unlike you, I care about how . . ."

"Don't you dare," I bark and stand up. "When Ava caught you with that woman, I completely supported you. I expect the same damn thing from you."

"That's not going to happen," Ryan says.

I look into Mateo's concerned eyes, knowing I have to put an end to this drama. "Go to hell, Ryan," I say, then end the call. This is the bad thing about cell phones. I miss being able to slam the phone down. As a teenage girl, that was always fun.

My body shaking a little, Mateo sits down beside me, taking my hand. "You okay?" he asks.

I've got a couple choices here. I can let my argument with Ryan bother me or give Mateo my full attention. I've got a chance at something real with a good man, to have some fun with my list. And when I think about it that way, it's an easy choice.

Trying to shake it off, I say, "Yeah. No more of that. This week is about us. Besides, I haven't given you your gift."

He pulls me to straddle his lap and kisses me. His hand grips the back of my neck, like he couldn't bear if I pulled away. There's no chance of that happening, but then he begins to slow down, lessen his grip. "It's been a long week," he says, kissing me between each word.

"I missed you," I whisper.

His wicked little smirk appears. "I want my present."

Giggling, I lean back slightly. "It's in my suitcase."

A quick kiss on my lips, and he's moving me off his lap to go fetch my suitcase, stashed away in his car. "Be right back."

Smiling, I start to roam around. I've only seen the kitchen, guest bathroom, and den area, which are very impressive. The place is modern, masculine, with clean lines. Everything looks professionally done—the design, the knickknacks, a collection of black and white family photos on one wall, all with coordinating frames. There's an office downstairs with a wall of books and a telescope. I look through the eyepiece, seeing a few stars. A metal stairwell leads upstairs. I know that's where his bedroom must be, and I only make it a few steps up before hesitating, wondering if he'd mind me snooping, if it's too nosy of me.

Hell, the man bypassed my house alarm and snuck into my bedroom. So I keep going. When I reach the top of the stairs, I'm greeted by double doors. There are no other doors. The entire upstairs must be his master suite. Pushing the doors open, I feel my eyes bug out. I've never seen a bigger bed in my life, the headboard upholstered in a soft, suede-looking fabric. The whole room is coordinated in steel blues and grays.

Running my fingers along his sheets, I imagine him sleeping here each night, wondering if he's ever thought about me while lying here alone in the dark, wondering if he ever thinks of me when he pleasures himself, the way I think of him.

Suddenly, my stomach flips flops. I'm going to be in that bed with him shortly. The stretch marks, the cellulite, the saggy breasts—the whole mom of three kids body.

After we first had kids, Ryan would always tell me how sexy I was, how beautiful my body was, what a wonderful gift it had given him. But even he lost interest along the way. What if Mateo doesn't like what he sees? What if I gross him out? What if he can't even get hard? After all, he's never seen me completely naked.

I scream at myself inside my head. Old habits are hard to break. But these negative voices won't bring me closer to Mateo. Just like I won't let Ryan ruin this, I won't let all the crap in my head do it, either.

I hear the heaviness of his footsteps as he comes up the stairs and turn, seeing him filling up the entire doorway. Judging by the sexy grin on his face, he doesn't seem to mind finding me in his bedroom. He places my suitcase down, then slips his hands around my waist.

I step back, tugging on the waistband of his jeans. "I need to give you your gift."

Walking to my suitcase, I pull out the package. I really should've wrapped it, but I wasn't planning on letting him see it. After all, it was something for me. I thought I'd be the only one seeing it.

I hold it out to him. Holding my eyes, he rips through the cardboard, exposing the black leather. A moment of fear grips me. Maybe this wasn't a good idea. I haven't even seen the finished product.

He looks down, opening up the leather cover. His eyes grow dark and wild. I've got no idea what he's seeing. All I know is, I'm either fully naked or in lingerie in those photos. I try to peek, but he won't let me. It's killing me not to look as he slowly flips each page. I wonder if he's seen the one of me hooking my pearl thong into my sexy stilettos.

The book drops to the floor, and the next thing I know, I'm flat on my back on his bed, clothes being ripped off left and right. There's no time to think, no time to feel insecure. There's barely time to breathe as he kisses me with greed, the hot length of him rubbing between my legs. Then he stops and sits back on his heels, staring down at me, with a look that says what's to come isn't just about him or some primal need he has, but about me, him, us.

And it's going to take more than five minutes. From the way he's looking at me, we might be late for work tomorrow.

He starts at my neck, his warm tongue ever so slightly touching my skin as his lips move along my jawline, each kiss lingering just long enough to make my heart skip a beat. When his teeth find my earlobe, I can't help but tremble. So he does it again. I hook my leg around his waist, wanting him inside me.

"Fuck, baby," he moans but doesn't give me what I want.

His head lowers slightly. I hate my breasts. Okay, there, I've said it. I've nursed three kids, and nature wasn't kind, leaving me with two deflated balloons on my chest. With each pregnancy, they just got worse. I even saw a doctor about a lift, but he said I'd need an implant too, and I could never justify putting myself through all that.

And when you're married to someone as long as Ryan and I were, you just sort of get used to each other. I mean, my breasts fed his children. There was some sort of appreciation. But now, I've got a new man whose tongue is dangerously close to my fallen nipple. He cups my breast in his hand, probably because he had to dig it out of my armpit.

One suck, one lick, and I don't care how low my boobs hang as long as he keeps doing that. I get the feeling he could stay there all night, but the ache between my legs is demanding, unrelenting. "Lower," I whisper.

I feel him smile. His eyes lock on mine as his tongue blazes a path down my cleavage, circling my belly button, sending shivers throughout my body. A few more inches to go, the man is driving me insane. He's getting close then veers off path, angling to my hip, kissing me. Holding my eyes, he lifts his head slightly then kisses my other hip.

I know he's going to get there, but he's enjoying the tease too much. My legs fall open, inviting him, and frankly, I don't give a damn if I look slutty or wanton. He moves down my leg, sucking and kissing my inner thigh, using his hand to massage. I can feel the muscles between my legs clenching over and over again.

Without warning, he slips his arms under my legs, lifting them to his shoulders, and gives me one hard suck. Hands down, receiving oral sex is my favorite. There isn't a vibrator or masturbation technique on the planet that rivals a man's tongue between my legs.

"Oh God!" I cry out, hoping slow and gentle time is over. And I get my wish. His hands on my ass, he devours me. There's no other way to describe it. With every swipe of his tongue, he makes his hunger for me known, like he's trying to temper some long starvation.

My thighs on his shoulders, he works me over, licking and sucking and driving me crazy, but then he stops, and my eyes dart open. Gently, he kisses a path up my body, slow and sweet until we are eye-to-eye. "What do you want?" he asks.

I'm not Poppy. I've never been one to take what I want in bed. I usually just took what Ryan offered and either it worked or it didn't. But this is the new, adventurous me. "I want . . ."

I can't say it, even though I'm thinking it.

He lowers his lips to my neck, whispering, "I'll give you whatever you want."

Closing my eyes, I say, "I want to sit on your face."

I can feel him smiling. "I was hoping for that," he says and rolls to his back, pulling me into a straddle over his face. He gives me one little lick. "Grab the headboard," he says, "and fuck my mouth, baby."

At first, I feel self-conscious about the way my body looks, but he takes hold of my ass, massaging my cheeks, making me clench around his tongue, and I don't give a flying fuck anymore, and before I know it, I'm not thinking about whether I'm smothering him. I thrust and clench, a warmth spreading over my body, my legs tightening. I feel myself ready to explode, and my vision goes white. I cry out in pleasure, not sure the words coming out of my mouth are even English.

Mateo gives me no time to recover, flipping me under him, sinking himself deep inside me. I'm not sure how I have anything left, but my body starts trembling, pulsing around him.

"You got more for me, baby?"

My neck arches, and my second orgasm comes right on top of the first. As I come down, he kisses my neck gently, his dick still rock hard inside me, and gives me a moment to catch my breath, my body still jerking from the aftershocks. When my eyes open, he slowly starts to move in and out, waiting for me to settle before thrusting any deeper.

A soft, sweet smile crosses his lips as he leans down to kiss me. Our eyes locked on each other, we start to move together, slowly at first. The man is taking his time, savoring me. I know Mateo's waited for this moment for a long time, so I figured it would be fast and furious, but I was wrong. Instead, it's like he waited so long that he wants to make it last and last.

"Fuck, you feel perfect," he groans.

I always thought Ryan had the perfect dick. I had nothing to compare it to until this moment. I shouldn't be thinking about my ex-husband. I'd hate to think Mateo's comparing me to anyone else.

But I've never had sex with someone who hadn't said they loved me, until now. I know what sex was like when Ryan and I were madly in love, and I know what it was like towards the end when I didn't feel loved by him anymore. There is a huge difference. Whether that difference is just in me, how I felt, or something more—it's still there.

Right now with Mateo, this feels much more like the madly in love sex than the empty sex just because you need to get off. This is slow, sweet, full of promise, passion and possibility.

Poppy's going to be disappointed we aren't hanging from a chandelier. To her, this would be boring old missionary sex, but it's anything but. We don't need crazy positions, toys, videos, or any of that stuff. Don't get me wrong, all that is fine and good and keeps things spicy, but sometimes this is all you need—to feel the warm weight of a man's body on top of yours—to have your bodies moving together in rhythm.

This time when my orgasm hits, it rolls down my body like an ocean wave. As soon as it crashes ashore, Mateo's teeth gnash together, the strength of my muscles clenching, pulling his orgasm from him. He rests his head down next to mine, keeping most of the weight of his body off mine, his dick still inside me.

Suddenly, I don't know what to do. The sex part came right back to me, but the after-sex part is causing some anxiety.

Ryan used to get up so quickly, it was almost like he was throwing me off, then he'd disappear to shower or brush his teeth. It wasn't always that way, but it's been years since a man held me after. I shift, causing Mateo to lift his head. I try to move again, and his dick twitches inside of me.

"You're not going anywhere," he says playfully, twitching again.

The man knows exactly how to make me smile, pinning me to the bed with his cock. I tighten my muscles, giving him a hard squeeze, and am rewarded with a delicious groan.

"Now you're definitely not going anywhere," he says, leaning down and giving my bottom lip a gentle bite.

He gently moves to my neck, kissing and nibbling, his fingers playing with my hair. "If you keep doing that, you better be prepared to fuck me again," I say.

I feel his smile as he buzzes me with his dick again. He's torturing me, so I tighten around him as hard as I can. "If you keep doing that, you better be prepared to get fucked again," he says through clenched teeth.

Oh yes, I am.

I DON'T KNOW that we'd ever make it out of bed except that all the panting made me thirsty. I get up, stretching, and step on my boudoir photo album. Bending down to pick it up, I flip it to the first page—a silhouette of my naked body lit from behind. I slowly flip through the pages, unable to believe it's actually me in the photos.

Looking at myself, it's like an out-of-body experience. Everything I see is one hundred percent me—the real me, not a lick of Photoshop anywhere. And because my face isn't in a lot of the photos, I can look at this woman without judgment, to see what others see.

Mateo's arms slip around my waist, and he buries his nose in my hair. My feet shift side to side, and he squeezes me a little tighter. "I love my gift," he says. "You surprise the hell out of me."

"Which picture is your favorite?" I ask, and he lifts one hand from my skin and turns the page, landing on the tamest picture in the album. "Really?"

"It's the only one where you're looking right at the camera."

That is the sweetest possible answer. Dropping the book on the bed, I turn around and kiss him softly. He takes my hand, leading me towards the bathroom.

His bathroom is the best room in the house. There's a fireplace, a huge glass shower with all kinds of jets, and what I can only describe as an infinity tub. I'm not sure that's a real thing, but the tub is set against a huge glass window, so it looks like you're bathing in the sky.

I do a little spin. "I may never leave this room. It's heaven."

He chuckles. "I've never even used the tub."

"You're kidding?"

He shakes his head. "Guys shower."

I guess that's true. Ryan never bathed. Jacob stopped bathing. Wonder why? Is the bathtub a girly thing? "Well, today you're bathing," I say, bending over to start the tub water and throw him my best flirty smile over my shoulder. "With me."

I don't have to ask twice. He steps right inside the tub, offering me his hand, and sits behind me, letting me lean back on his chest, his arms around my waist, and we relax down into the warm inviting water.

Neither one of us say a word. The man just saw me naked, did amazing things to my body, and I oddly can't think of one single thing to say. But that feels completely okay in a completely weird way. It feels good not to be running around, organizing, chauffeuring my kids, planning, working. It feels good to just be—still and quiet, focusing on nothing but the sound of his heart beating strong and steady.

When the water is high enough, he stretches up his foot to turn off the faucet. "I wish we could skip work tomorrow," I say, yawning.

"Me, too," he agrees so easily it makes me beam. "I think there's some things on your list that need to be done."

"Guess I can cross off sleeping with a younger man," I say. "I still can't believe you read it."

"Baby, I have it memorized. That was number 20."

"I need to get it back from you."

"You don't need it," he says. "Because anything you want to do on it, you'll do with me."

"Anything?"

"All but one thing."

"Never took you for a prude," I tease. "Which one bothered you?"

"It didn't bother me."

"Which one?"

"Threesome."

I bust out laughing. "Layla, Poppy, and I were so drunk when we made that list. Poppy insisted I hadn't lived until I've had two men servicing me at the same time."

"Not gonna happen," he says, and his possessive tone sends goose bumps across my skin.

"Of course, I think Poppy also has done a little girl on girl. I'm sure you wouldn't mind that."

"Nope," he says, tilting my face to his. "I'm not sharing you with a man or a woman."

"I wouldn't share you, either," I say.

He flips me over in the tub, water splashing over the side. "As for everything else, we're good."

I raise an eyebrow at him. "That's very generous of you."

"You'll find me a very generous man," he says and leans in to kiss me.

CHAPTER NINETEEN
SPANKING

Usually, the first time I wake up in a new place, I feel a little disoriented, off balance. But I did not feel that way waking up in Mateo's beautiful room and soft bed. It feels good here, like I belong.

But it's three in the morning, and I have to pee. The pressure from his arm lazily thrown over my belly isn't helping the situation. It feels like it weighs twenty pounds, all pushing down on my bladder. I'd much rather lay here and admire how cute he looks when he sleeps, his chiseled face relaxed, his breathing soft and rhythmic. Instead, I move his arm to his side and scoot off the bed, careful not to wake him.

As soon as my feet hit the hardwood floors, I'm reminded why I don't sleep naked. Without the warmth of his body and the warm comforter, it's freaking freezing all of a sudden, which takes the bathroom emergency up a few notches. Scurrying to the bathroom with my legs clenched, I quietly shut the door behind me.

I'm not sure if it's a mom thing or not, but I can empty my bladder in ten seconds flat. I think it comes from years of having no privacy and no time for yourself. My ten seconds turns into thirty when the great debate starts in my head. To flush or not to flush, that is the question. Ryan and I had a rule that we didn't flush in the middle of the night. Sleep was more important. But I'm not sure Mateo and I are at that point in our relationship.

Is it better for him to wake up to my pee in his toilet or to wake him up with my flushing now? Such are the deep questions of any new relationship. It's important to know the answers to such questions—like whether you are a cat or dog person, whether the ketchup goes in the refrigerator or cabinet, and whether it's okay to take home the shampoos and soaps from hotels.

But right now, it's the great pee debate. If the roles were reversed, I'd want him to leave it. I need my sleep. But I don't want to be gross and I know Mateo functions on little sleep, so I say a quick prayer and flush and wash my hands.

Cracking the door back to the bedroom, I hear his slow breathing. There will remain a little mystery in our relationship. I lift the covers and crawl back into bed, resting into his side, his arm coiling around me tightly, and I say another little prayer, this one that the morning doesn't come quickly.

Unfortunately, I don't get my wish. And to make matters worse, it's a Monday morning, and my phone is already ringing—with Ava's boy band ringtone. "Ugh," I groan, and Mateo reaches over to the nightstand and grabs my phone for me.

"Ava, it's a little early."

"There are a lot of cute boys at the beach," she shrieks. "I'm sitting outside watching them with their surfboards."

This is her way of letting me know it's over with her and Justin. Ava's figuring out her love life, and I look over at the hunk of possibility currently slipping on his boxer briefs. Damn, I just barely caught a glimpse of that ass of his. He turns around, mouthing he's going to make me some breakfast. I lean up in bed, lifting his shirt over my head, then listen to my happy teenage daughter. These are rare moments, when teenage emotions are in perfect alignment. I talk to Connor briefly, too, and learn that Jacob is still asleep. Even the fresh ocean breeze can't energize that boy.

Mateo returns and kisses me on top of the head like it's completely normal for me to be here, for us to wake up together. He mouths to me, "Where are your keys?"

I point to my purse, watching him dig them out, adding another key. Turning to me, he gives me a little wink. He doesn't need to tell me it's for his place, and he doesn't make a big deal out of it. I mouth, "Thank you," to him, and he points to the smoothie and plate of food waiting for me before disappearing to take a shower. I really wish we could play hooky, but Gage is in the office and holding a big meeting in a few hours. We both have to be there, and we both need to prep.

By the time I finish the call, I'm running late. Mateo must be, too, since I still hear the shower running. Maybe I can catch another peek at him. His shower is glass on two sides, so I have a perfect view, except the steam from the shower is blurring things like a censored porn clip.

I open up my toiletry bag and place it on his bathroom counter, catching my reflection in the mirror, *au naturel*. Sex with Mateo looks good on me. It didn't cure my wrinkles or tame my mane of hair. But I'm smiling. Smiling from a place I didn't think I'd ever smile from again.

His strong arms snake around my waist, nothing but a towel around his hips, and he leans down to rest his cheek next to mine, gazing at our side-by-side reflection. He's wearing the same smile I am. My heart has that weird growing pain again, making room for the enormity of what I'm feeling.

His warm lips lower to my neck, but his eyes stay locked on mine in the mirror, watching him kiss a path, his tongue gently teasing me. Lifting my hair, he makes his way along the back of my neck, a shiver running down my spine. As soon as he gets to the other side, his eyes are fixed on mine again.

His towel drops to the floor with a thump, and the outline of his muscles frame my body. He reaches to the bottom of his shirt I'm wearing, and he begins to lift it up, slowly at first, revealing my breasts. I don't make it a habit of staring at myself naked, but it's like I'm hypnotized by him. He could tell me to bark like a dog and I would.

I'm temporarily blinded as the shirt goes over my head. But as soon as my eyes are free, they find his again. No one has ever looked at me like this before—pure, raw. I watch his hands slide up the curves of my hips and waist, his fingers gently toying with my nipples, feeling him poised at my entrance. He guides my hands to the vanity, leaning me slightly forward. This is not a good position for a woman over forty. Gravity is not kind.

My eyes close. "Watch," he commands. "Watch how good we are together. Never forget."

He invades me, my mouth falling open. One of his arms is coiled around me, the other is between my legs, demanding my orgasm. Our eyes lock on each other, and I'm not sure what I'm enjoying more—losing myself in this man or watching him lose himself in me.

"HOW DO YOU want to handle this morning?" I ask. "I mean, do you want to stagger when we leave so we don't walk in together?"

"Fuck no."

Not even a regular no, but a *fuck no*. And he's got the fire in his eyes to match the fire in his tone. "I don't think we should flaunt our relationship in front of everyone."

"Walking in together isn't exactly throwing things in people's faces."

"I guess not. But what do you plan on saying if someone asks you?"

"Damn right, she's my woman," he says, cracking a smile and taking my hand. "I think if we are relaxed about it, then everyone else will be, too. We might be water cooler talk for a few days, but that's all. If we try to keep some big secret, it just gives everyone something to talk about."

"God, how do you always make so much sense?"

"The better question is, how do you come up with fifteen thousand different scenarios with plots and subplots and alternate endings for each?"

"I think it's a woman thing," I say. "It's how we can multitask so well."

"You don't seem to mind my singular focus."

Oh God, I absolutely do not.

✦ ✦ ✦

I CAN'T SAY I wasn't nervous pulling into the office parking garage with Mateo. As much as I tried not to look around to see who might be watching, I did. But Mateo and I are both professionals. We didn't walk in holding hands. We didn't make out in the elevator up to our offices. He didn't smack my ass as we went our separate ways, even though I know he wanted to. And if there were any rumblings around the water cooler, I didn't hear them. The true test is coming, though.

Certain executives and other personnel begin to gather for our big meeting. I take my place next to Gage's chair. Mateo usually sits opposite me at these things, but he's not here yet. There are about a dozen other people filing in. So far, no one seems to be looking at me any differently. It's not like I'm wearing a sign that says I'm screwing Mateo, but it sure does feel like it.

Suddenly, Mateo's warm breath lands on my neck, causing my toes to curl, as he leans over and whispers, "I keep thinking about how you taste." Then as casual as ever, he takes his seat. To everyone, I'm sure it looked like nothing, but the muscles between my legs clench hard. He takes a seat and flashes me a little smirk, his eyes darting down quickly.

Shit, my nipples are hard and erect and poking right through my blouse. Damn this stupid flimsy lace bra! I pull my cardigan tighter, crossing my arms. Smiling, he shifts slightly in his seat to let me know he's hard and just as uncomfortable and horny as I am.

Gage comes in, and everyone comes to order. I put on my glasses, and for the next ninety minutes, we are all business—Mateo, me, and everyone else. It surprises me a little how easily Mateo and I shifted gears. But as soon as the meeting ends, the gears shift right back, and getting into his bed and working on my list are the only things I can think about.

It's not too early for me to sneak away, and Mateo put that key on my key ring. That's perfect. A plan forms in my mind. I sneak out of the office, call a car service, and am back to his place before anyone notices.

I strip down and crawl into his bed, typing him a text once I'm settled.

I'm naked in your bed, waiting.

Placing my phone down on the nightstand, I wonder how long it will take.

"Now that's the kind of service I like," I say, trying to catch my breath. "I call, and you come."

He flips me over, smacking me on the ass. "I seem to recall a spanking being on your list."

I look over my shoulder at him. "Will you really do anything on my list?"

His eyes spark. "Will you?" he asks. I give him a little nod. There aren't many things I wouldn't try, especially in a committed relationship. "Pick one," he says.

Biting my lip, I roll over to my back. "Let's make a sex tape." Never in a thousand years did I expect that to come out of my mouth. I'm a mom, for goodness sake. If that ever got out, I'd be humiliated, and my kids would be mortified.

"You're quite the exhibitionist," he says. "First the photos and now this."

It's weird. I'm so self-conscious about my body, but those photos, even though I still have my hang-ups, have made me feel powerful. "We'll just watch it once, then we'll destroy it," I say.

This is the high-stakes, adult version of pinkie-swearing, becoming blood brothers, a complete trust necessary between two people. This is the exact kind of thing I'd warn the kids never to do, and probably murder them if they ever did, and here I am suggesting it.

"You sure you don't just want to have tantric sex?" he asks. "That was number 4 on the list."

I start laughing. "I was so drunk when I made that. I mean, honestly, the point of sex is the orgasm."

"I love that about you," he says.

I've lost count of how many times he's used the word *love*. It's never that he loves me, exactly. But my heart notices each time. "How about this? Let's make tantric porn."

"We're tantric sex failures," I say, lying naked across his bed, recovering from multiple orgasms.

I know it's all my fault. Five seconds in and I was begging him to make me come. And like a good man, he wouldn't deny me pleasure. So screw the lovemaking without crossing the finishing line. I know it's supposed to bring you closer together, take you to some high plane of connection or something, but Mateo and I are just fine in our un-evolved state of sexual bliss.

As for knowing I was being filmed, that was a little nerve-wracking, to be on camera in the most intimate way. But I got past it, and it certainly didn't hold me back. It was also a little nerve-wracking that the man had a video camera at his disposal, but he is the head of security, so I guess it makes sense. I didn't want it recorded on his phone or computer. God only knows what cloud it would end up on in cyberspace.

"Should we watch it?" I ask before a little yawn escapes.

He cuddles me to his chest. "Tomorrow. You can barely keep your eyes open."

He's right. Sex makes me tired, and we've got work tomorrow. "Think I'll go in late," I say. "Turn the alarm off."

"Already did," he whispers into my hair.

When my eyes close, my heart, my mind, my body are all at peace again. That should've been the first sign all hell's about to break loose.

CHAPTER TWENTY
SEX TAPE

My phone rings much too early. It's Ava again, the second morning in a row. Is she trying to ruin my sex afterglow?

Mateo stretches out his long arms and legs, flashing me the smallest grin before his phone starts ringing, too. "Gage," he mouths to me, getting up to walk to another room.

I answer to Ava talking a hundred miles an hour. This time she needs fashion advice. Apparently, the color of her toenail polish is clashing with her swimsuit, and she left some shade of blue at home. I spend a few minutes with her snapping photos of nail polish options. I love the names of nail polishes. Whoever has the job to name those must be the coolest person on the planet.

Listening to Ava, I watch as Mateo walks back in, no longer on the phone, but he doesn't look at me. No sexy smile, no wink, no pat on the ass, nothing. I hear him turn the shower both on and off in under two minutes, obviously in a big hurry.

Doing my best to hurry my daughter along, I hang up as he walks into the bedroom, buttoning up his shirt. His dark tan skin peeks through the opening, the edges of his muscles seemingly cutting through the material. "I thought we were going in late?" I ask.

"Gage needs me," he says, not looking at me, finishing up the buttons on his shirt and tucking it in.

"I'll come with you," I say. "Just give me a couple minutes."

"I need to go now," he says sharply, walking straight out the door.

All the air leaves the room, and I'm left with the voices in my head. And the first ones, of course, are negative. What did I do? What's wrong with me? I guess he fucked me a couple times, and now it's over. The call from Gage was probably just an excuse to leave as quickly as possible. Screwed the old bitch, time to move on.

"No!" I yell at myself, flying out of bed. It's clear he's upset with me, but it's not about sex or my body. I can't let myself go there, and I won't let myself be treated like crap. If he's pissed at me, he should tell me why, not give me the cold shoulder and run off. That's how a relationship dies. It's not the fighting that screws up two people. It's the silence. When Ryan and I stopped fighting, that was the real end; we didn't care enough to expend the energy. That's when you know it's over.

Throwing on some clothes, I grab my suitcase, searching for the stuff I've taken out, then pack up and roll it to the top of the stairs. Ugh, why did I pack so many pairs of shoes? My size nines weigh too much, I think, as I grip the handle to pick it up.

"Don't you dare lift that," Mateo's voice bellows from the bottom of the staircase.

I grip the handle tighter. "I can do it."

He starts up towards me. "Where are you going?" he asks, taking two steps at a time. He's in front of me before I know it, his hands on the handle.

"Let go," I demand.

"As long as I have it, you won't leave," he says. "You're too anal to leave it behind."

"I'm not anal," I snap.

He throws me a devilish little grin. "Is that why anal sex is missing from your list?"

He's struck a soft spot without even realizing it. When I started to sense things were bad with Ryan, I tried really hard to make things work. I gave him space, planned trips, bought sexy lingerie. After almost twenty years of marriage, things can get routine. I thought something was wrong with me. He didn't seem interested in me no matter how many sex toys I bought for us, so in a lame attempt to peak his interest in me again, I suggested we try anal sex. What can I say? Not even the third input could save my marriage!

"I'm leaving," I say.

Mateo's whole body blocks the stairs. His message is loud and clear. I'm not going anywhere without permission, but I've got a message of my own. A knee to the groin would work. Too bad Layla and Poppy aren't here, because I could sic them on him. But it's much easier to play on his soft spot. I know the man's weakness—me—and it just takes one little word.

"Please," I say.

His dark brown eyes quickly soften, and he takes a step back, making room for me to pass. It's a striking reminder how powerful I am, how much he cares for me.

He hooks his pinkie finger with mine. "Don't run away."

"You're the one who left all pissy."

"I came back."

"Good for you. I'm leaving."

"Emerson, you want me to run all over the fucking city looking for you? Because I will."

"No, you wouldn't," I say and start down the stairs.

"I'm not Ryan," he barks at me from behind. "Stop testing me. I don't deserve it."

I stop on the stairs, frozen, a cold burn raging inside me from his words. The truth really does hurt—it burns like a mother.

Ryan never came after me when we fought. He would say he thought I needed space, which always felt like a cop-out, like he just didn't care enough. But I wanted him to chase me. I know it's old school and went out of date with the cavemen, but it's ingrained in me somehow. I think it's ingrained in all women to some extent. We want the man to pursue, to hunt, to fight, to capture us and not let go.

Mateo has the old school thing down. And I *was* testing him. Maybe I have been the whole time. Did I do the same to Ryan? Did I test him so much he got tired and stopped chasing me?

"I'll always find you," he says, his voice growing gentle. "I'll always be here. I'm sorry I stormed out."

I turn around on the stairs. "Why were you upset with me?"

Releasing a deep breath, he says, "Gage wants me to do some background on a competing airline. When I asked why, he told me he's considering selling to them."

Dammit, I really wish Gage would've given me a heads-up that he was going to tell Mateo. "Oh."

"Guess this isn't news to you?"

The sarcastic tone of his voice causes my guard to go up even higher. "Gage told me he was *thinking* about it. We discussed it as a family."

"Why didn't you tell me?" he asks.

"I wasn't sure there was anything to tell," I say, walking back up the stairs to him. "I thought maybe Gage was just upset after the incident with Dash."

"You've known that long?"

Ugh! This is why it's not a good idea to date an employee. It's rough. "Yes, but I couldn't tell you. It was confidential. It still is." I reach for his hand. "I wish I could've been the one to tell you. I'm sorry you found out that way."

He gives me a little nod, but not enough to make me feel he accepted my apology. "I need to get to the office."

"I'm glad you came back," I say. "Thank you for talking to me."

Another little head nod, and he turns for the stairs. I'm not sure he's ever been upset with me before, and I don't like the feeling. But I love that he came back. I have to remind myself that fighting doesn't mean the end of anything. Fighting, though I hate it, is normal.

Rushing down the stairs, I call out to him as he reaches the front door. "I never answered your question." From the look in his eyes, I can tell he knows exactly which one—the missing item on my list. "I didn't mind fingers," I say, lifting my eyebrows at him.

He smiles wide, and with that, I know I'm forgiven. He walks towards me, unbuttoning his shirt, and I actually squeal a little as he catches me by my waist. "You can explain to your brother why I'm late."

✦ ✦ ✦

I CUT OUT of the office around six, and it's past ten now. Mateo's still not home. I blame myself because I made him very late this morning. I also blame Gage. He's holding Mateo hostage with work. I should have Layla call Gage and say she needs him. Gage would fly out of the office then. Instead, I get her and Poppy on a three-way call. With Poppy out of the office and Layla busy with the baby, we are long overdue for some girl talk.

"Perfect timing," Layla says. "It's Greer's last feeding of the night. I'm hoping she sleeps at least three hours straight."

"Damn," Poppy says. "That's horrible."

"I think it's her name," Layla says. "When we were going through baby names, Gage fell in love with the name Greer. Similar to his name, I suppose. But Greer means 'alert' and 'watchful.' I should've known she'd be a terrible sleeper."

"I bet Emerson's not getting much sleep, either," Poppy teases. "Spill! How's sex with Mateo?"

"Poppy, some things are sacred," I say.

"So he's a god?"

"Completely," I say as we all bust out laughing.

"Oh my God," Poppy cries out, interrupting our giggles. "I just searched the meaning of the name Mateo."

"And?"

"You aren't going to believe this."

"What?"

"Mateo means 'God's gift!'" she squeals.

"No, it doesn't," I say, immediately pulling up my search engine on my phone. Holy shit, she wasn't lying.

"You lucky bitch," Poppy laughs.

Thank God, Greer is a slow eater. We spend the next twenty minutes laughing and catching up. Poppy fills us in on Dash, who is recovered and just waiting to be cleared to go back up in the air. She sounds happier and more content than she has in a long time, and

Layla has settled into her mommy role. The three of us seem to have this kickass woman thing down pat. When we hang up, I'm counting my blessings for my beautiful friends as well the man walking through the door.

I turn to see Mateo dragging himself inside. He looks exhausted. His eyes meet mine, and he smiles. "My dad is a smart man."

Walking to him, I wrap my hands around his neck. "You going to finally tell me what he said?"

"He asked me if you were the woman that could make me smile while my dick was still in my pants."

"Well, am I?" I ask, laughing.

He nods. "He said that's how you know you're with the right woman."

His dad might be on to something. A litmus test for relationships based on smiling with and without clothes on. I say it works both ways. Mateo makes me smile while naked and while dressed.

"I know it's kind of late," he says. "But what do you want to do tonight? I'd like to take you out. Maybe a late dinner?"

"Watching TV sounds good."

He chuckles, grabbing my ass. "I think we do have a movie we need to watch."

CHAPTER TWENTY-ONE
SEX, INTERRUPTED

MORNING THREE, AND I'm awakened by Ava's ringtone again. Bleary eyed, I reach for my phone. I can't deal with another round of nail polish issues or whatever. I'm going to tell her not to call me before eight unless it's an emergency.

"Ava, honey, it's a little early."

"Ma'am, this is Officer . . . Are you the mother of Ava Baker?"

Hearing the words every parent fears on the other end of the line, I dart out of bed, wide-awake now and freaking the fuck out. This is the phone call no parent wants. This is the reason why I'm programmed in her phone as I.C.E, or In Case of Emergency. An officer would not be calling if she was alright.

"I'm afraid your daughter has been in an accident."

"Oh God, tell me she's alright!" I beg.

Mateo's arms fly around me. I'm trembling so hard the bed is shaking. I listen for a few minutes then hand him the phone. "Please get the address." I jump out of bed, looking for my clothes.

A few seconds later, I'm still naked in his room, pacing around, unable to function enough to even locate my clothes, much less dress myself. He sees I'm lost and grabs my arms. Somehow he's already dressed, keys in his hand. "I gave them Ryan's number," he tells me. "You should call him."

"Right, yes. Why wasn't he with her? Did she sneak out again?"

"I don't know," Mateo says, pulling a shirt over my head. "I'll call the airline to get us on a flight. Hilton Head is just an hour or so by air."

The trembling grows worse. "If I was in Savannah, I could drive there quickly. Oh God, I'm not there. I'm here. We were . . ."

"Emerson," he says, holding my face in his hands. "I'll get you there quick. I promise."

My phone rings, and I know it's Ryan. Mateo drags me and my suitcase out the door. As I listen to Ryan, Mateo gets me out of the building, into his car, and on our way to the airport. Mateo's on his phone with Gage, getting the corporate jet ready. It's a complete abuse of power and company assets to use the jet right now, but I don't give a fuck. And neither does Gage, apparently.

"I'm on my way, Ryan. I will just be about an hour."

"Where are you?" he asks.

"I'll be there soon. What happened?"

Ryan tells me the boys wanted donuts for breakfast, and Ava drove off to get them. He swears it was only a mile away. Other than the fact that she was hit head-on by another car, we know nothing. He's on his way to the hospital and will call when he knows more, though I'll probably be in the air when he does.

I won't know how my daughter is for an hour.

"EMERSON," MATEO SAYS as we start our descent, "how about some juice or a snack."

I can't even manage a simple "no."

"Just a little?" he asks.

I pull out my phone and put my glasses on. "Maybe it will work. I need to try."

"Baby, we're still too high up."

I try, but there's no signal.

"I'm sure Ryan left you a message."

"She's hurt," I sob. "And I'm not there. You want your mother when you're hurt."

He wraps his arm around me, and I rest my head on his shoulder. "We'll be there soon. You're a great mom."

I pull away. "A great mom who was fucking her boyfriend while her daughter is in the hospital."

Rationally, I know it didn't happen that way. Rationally, I know I didn't do anything neglectful, but the heart is not a rational organ. I try my phone again—still nothing. If something really bad has happened to my daughter, I'll never forgive myself for being so far away, for being selfish.

"Hey," he says, "nothing you did was wrong."

This is officially the longest hour of my life, longer than laboring to deliver my kids, longer than all those nights after Ryan left, longer than my father's funeral. Why does that happen? Why do the minutes when we are afraid seem longer than any others? Fear is such a little word, yet it seems to last longer than any other. And right now, it seems infinite. Time is standing still. It feels like the plane isn't moving. I know it's going several hundred miles per hour, but it doesn't feel like it.

I stare at my phone, willing it to come to life as we fly lower and lower. It finally dings. A voicemail from Ryan appears. It's thirty minutes old. I listen with my hand over my mouth, my eyes closed. I feel the plane touch down, the jolt as we slow down, but the only thing I hear over and over again in my head are three words Ryan said.

Unconscious, head injury.

THERE'S A CAR waiting for us when we land. The hospital is about ten minutes from the airport. I call Ryan on the way over, but he doesn't have any other information—except that Ava's in stable condition. How can my daughter be "stable" if her head is injured and she's unconscious?

Part of me is angry this happened. Part of me is scared shitless. Part of me can't believe this is my third trip to the hospital/urgent care in the past few months. It's absurd. If it's not my toe, my friend getting hurt on the job, it's my daughter. It's ridiculous. I don't live on the edge and consider myself a careful person. My kids constantly tell me I smother them and am over-protective.

But from what I hear from friends and family, this is part of normal family life. Some other moms I know are on a first name basis with the ER doctors, they're in and out so much. Being a mom means any disposable income gets spent on copays and deductibles. So while this may be a normal part of life, my baby girl being hurt and not being by her side is anything but normal.

By the time I rush through the emergency room entrance, I'm about to lose my mind. I spot Ryan in the waiting area. He's got his arms around me in a few seconds, stroking my hair as I cry into his chest. "I know," he whispers, his voice cracking.

"Our baby girl," I sob. "Where is she?"

"She's back in the ER. She's going to be . . ." Ryan stops mid-sentence, and I look up, his eyes zeroed in on my traveling companion and my suitcase. His eyes shift back to me, and he finishes the thought, "Alright. She'll be alright."

I can't be concerned about Mateo right now. Ava is all that matters, and Ryan's words didn't sound too convincing. Mateo rolls the suitcase to a chair near me then gently touches my arm. "I'm going to find the cafeteria and get you something to eat." I give him a thankful nod, then his eyes shift to Ryan. "Can I bring you anything? Coffee?" Ryan shakes his head, and Mateo disappears.

I feel the sting of Ryan's eyes. I don't need his judgment right now. I'm doing a good enough job of beating myself up. "I want to see Ava."

"A nurse will come out to talk to us in a minute," he says.

"I need to see her. Is she okay?"

"I'm waiting on an update," he says. "They think she will be okay."

"*Will be?*" I cry. "Is she okay *now*? Is she awake? How bad is it? Have you seen her?"

"She's having scans, so I haven't seen her. They haven't told me much else."

I pull at my hair and stifle the urge to scream a string of curse words to be heard from one end of the hospital to the other. "Where are the boys?"

"Jacob's watching Connor at the condo," he says. "Connor doesn't know about this. I didn't want to scare him."

"Good, that's good," I say. "I told Gage and my mom I'd call them as soon as we heard something. They both are ready to come if . . ."

I stop speaking when I see a nurse heading for us. I try to read her face. Is it good news or bad? This is the moment before my whole life can change. For all the wishing we do for things to change—to have more, do more, travel more, learn more, be more—I'll settle for business as usual today.

"She's awake," the nurse says. "She has a concussion, but the scans and tests show nothing else. She's fine."

Ryan and I both exhale, and then he grabs my hand as I start sobbing. The nurse goes on to say that they want to keep Ava overnight for observation, but aside from a nasty seatbelt bruise and bump on the head, things look good. The nurse says we can see her, and Ryan and I rush back into the ER.

When Ava looks over at us, she immediately starts to cry. "I'm sorry," she says. "I'm not getting a ticket, am I?"

"Oh, baby," I say, smothering her in my arms and laughing. Ryan comes over to embrace us both, and none of us lets go. My head tilts, Ryan's face just inches from mine. His fingers gently line my cheek, and I know if Ava wasn't right here, he'd try to kiss me. I'd shut that shit down, but still, I know he'd try.

A knock forces us apart. A young, hot doctor enters to check on Ava before she moves up to her room for the night. I see her blush a bright red. Like mother like daughter, checking the guy out in the emergency room. He makes small talk for a moment then gently lifts up her gown to peek at her bruise, the hot pink print of her panties showing, and I swear Ava almost dies.

I'm so thankful she's okay, that she's still the Ava I know and love. Ryan places his arm around my shoulder, kissing the side of my head. I turn a little and catch Mateo's eyes, finding him standing in the doorway. He's excellent at hiding his emotions. I don't know what he's feeling, but I can guess.

When the doctor walks out, Mateo knocks and peeks his head in then looks to Ava for permission to come in. Her eyes fly to her father, but Ryan offers nothing. Ava gives Mateo a little smile and waves him inside. He hands me a styrofoam box, which weighs like five pounds and I can only assume is filled to the top with food.

Mateo flashes an angry look to Ryan then plasters on a bright smile for Ava, holding out a plastic bag for her. "How are you feeling?" he asks her.

She just gives him a nod, too busy with the bag, pulling out a handful of girly magazines. "Thank you," she says.

"I figured you and your mom would need something to keep you busy while you're in here," he says. "One of them is full of quizzes. My sister used to love to take those."

"Me, too," Ava says.

"She used to make me take them, too," Mateo whispers through a grin, and she giggles. He gives her foot a little pat over the covers before flashing me a look to follow him into the hallway. I give Ava a little kiss and tell her I'll be right back.

Mateo and I step into the hall, closing the door, so we're away from Ryan's prying eyes. "I'll call Gage with an update," Mateo says. "What else can I do?"

"Nothing."

"Let me help. I can go check on Jacob and Connor."

"Ryan would never allow that."

"Fuck him."

Mateo's not the type of man to play second fiddle to another man. But he has to understand that Ryan and I have to work together, and the last thing I need is a fight with Mateo to top off this day. "He's the father of my children."

"And I'm what?"

He's the man I was screwing when my daughter was hurt. Why did something so great have to turn to shit? He's also the man I know I'm starting to really fall for. "Please," I beg. "Ava could've died. Please don't do this right now."

He releases a deep breath, hugging me. "Then you don't do this, either."

"Do what?"

"Feel guilty," he says. "I watched what guilt did to you before. One kiss and you punished yourself for years." He pulls back to look into my eyes. "I will not be something you feel guilty about."

"Emerson," Ryan says, slipping his head out the door.

"Is Ava okay?" I ask.

"She's fine," he says, eyeing Mateo's hand around my waist. "I need to get the boys."

"Okay, tell them I'm here and will take them home as soon as I can."

"It's my week," Ryan says. "I still have them for a few more days."

"I know, but with Ava in the hospital," I say, "I just figured you'd head back to Savannah when she gets out."

"I plan on finishing out the week here at the beach with the kids," Ryan says.

"But I need to be close to her right now."

"You're welcome to stay," he says then gives Mateo a smug smile.

"Just go deal with the boys," I huff.

An arrogant grin on his face, Ryan struts past Mateo and down the hallway. I'm glad he's gone. Two more seconds together, and no telling what would've happened. I really don't need this macho shit right now.

"I know you aren't leaving Ava," Mateo says.

"I can't."

"You've met my mother. I get it," he says, giving me a little smile before adding, "I can stay, too."

"That's sweet, but one of us should be at the office."

"You and the kids are more important."

"I need to focus on Ava. I won't have any time to see you."

His eyes narrow just a hair. "Because you plan on staying with Ryan and the kids at the condo?"

"Yes," I whisper, taking his hand. "Please understand."

"I'm supposed to be alright with you staying with Ryan?"

"I can't deal with you being jealous right now."

He takes a step towards me, pinning me to the wall with his eyes. He's not even touching me, but the heat between us is so hot, they're liable to call the burn unit. "I know the way you moan, taste, move. I meant it when I said I don't share. I meant it when I said if I had you, I wouldn't let you go. The moment you shared my bed is the moment I earned the right to be jealous."

How does he make jealousy sound so hot? "You don't need to be jealous of Ryan."

"It's not unheard of for exes to fuck each other after they've broken up."

"No, it's not unheard of," I say, my voice giving away my and Ryan's little sexcapade.

"You slept with him?" he snaps.

"It was before you and I . . ."

"When?" he barks.

"None of your damn business," I bite back.

Mateo leans back, crossing his arms over his chest. The man puts up with a lot of shit to be with me. I'm not doing a very good job of showing how much I appreciate it. I reach out to him, my fingers playing with his shirt. "Look, I'm exhausted and stressed and being a bitch."

"Hey," he says, uncrossing his arms and pulling me closer. "Think I might be the bitch here." I laugh out loud for the first time all day. The grin he gives me is unforgettable.

He rests his chin on top of my head, holding me close, playing with my hair. His muscles tight, his heart loud, I can feel a struggle in him to fully understand. I give him a little squeeze, feeling him take a deep breath.

"Okay, tell me what you need," he says. "I can stay, even if I never see you, even if you only sneak out for a goodnight kiss. If you feel like you need me close, I'll stay. Or if you want me to go, I'll do that, too."

As much as I want him to stay, I need to focus on my daughter for a few days. And I don't want to feel torn between her and Mateo. Plus, I don't want Ryan starting any bullshit with Mateo around. "Go back to Atlanta, but call me," I say then kiss him sweetly. "Call me a lot."

"Promise me you'll take care of yourself."

"Try not to worry," I say and give his hand a little squeeze. "Plan on coming to Savannah next weekend."

CHAPTER TWENTY-TWO
QUICKIE QUEEN

I'M THRILLED THE doctor releases Ava the next morning, but spending the rest of the week with Ryan is not so thrilling. I try to focus on Ava and the boys, but Connor makes that impossible almost every second of each day.

He's constantly saying: "Look, Mommy, isn't Daddy so funny?" or "Look, Daddy, doesn't Mommy look pretty?" And if he's not saying those things, he's trying to get us to sit by each other or touch each other. It's tiresome. Thank God, tomorrow we're all heading back home.

I knew staying with Ryan and the kids was going to be difficult, but I didn't think how difficult it would be for Connor, who seems to think this is his chance to have his nuclear family intact and create some memories of his dad and me together, even if it's forced.

The thing is, it's not completely forced. It's always been easy for Ryan and me to fall into our parenting roles. And Ryan's always been a good dad. There's something inherently sexy about a good dad.

At times during the week, like over a family dinner or when we were all laughing while watching a movie together on the pullout sofa, things felt like they used to—maybe too much like they used to. I'm sure that's what Mateo was worried about, the inherent danger in those moments. But I didn't find them dangerous at all, but rather so very revealing, eye opening. It's what my marriage was for years—me pretending one thing while feeling something else.

I step out onto the beach, needing some air. I can see the condo from here, see the kids all playing a board game together inside. I didn't think kids did that anymore. The beach is always good for simple fun. Ava learned to hopscotch and hula hoop at the beach. At home, it seems we're always too busy for simple fun, all consumed by school, activities, blaring electronics. It's a pleasure to see them all playing together instead of ripping each other to shreds for a change.

Clearly, this week of family time was good for the kids. I want them to have happy memories of Ryan and me, even if we aren't married. They should see us happy and getting along. And it was fun to ride bikes, spend the day doing the lazy river and water slides. It's never a happy time when I have to put on a swimsuit, and wearing one in front of your ex-husband is even more unnerving, especially when I'm pretty sure I caught him staring at me a time or two. There were women half my age and twice my cup size—why wasn't he staring at them?

My cell phone rings, as I knew it would. Mateo calls at this time every night, which is another reason for my walk on the beach. And I've decided the list is useless. All I really need is him naked. Of course, I won't object to handcuffs, blindfolds, nipple clamps or . . . Okay, so basically, I won't object.

I answer to him saying how much he misses me, to which I sappily agree. It's completely mushy and something I'd roll my eyes at if Ava were talking like this to her boyfriend. We fill each other in on our days. He always asks how Ava is feeling and about the boys. And I avoid the subject of Ryan as much as possible.

"You sound so far away," I say.

"Sorry," he says, "long day at work."

"What's going on?"

He starts telling me about the work he's been doing on the sale of the airline, that he's pretty sure Gage is going to go through with it, the details of some of the negotiations. But I completely zone out. The only thing I can think about is how this will affect me. More specifically, how it will affect my and Mateo's relationship. I don't want to be one of those people that makes everything about them, but I can't help it.

The thoughts in my head are going record pace and are so loud that I don't notice when he stops talking. "Emerson," he says softly, knowing I'm unsettled.

"I'm here," I say, looking out onto the black night sky, the dark ocean waves crashing. "I'm listening."

"What's wrong?"

"Nothing."

"You know I'll wait for you to be ready to tell me whatever's bothering you, even if I have to sit on the phone with you all night."

I giggle a little then draw a deep breath. "If we keep seeing each other," I say then start over, not liking the "if" word. "I know I'm getting ahead of myself. You know I have a tendency to think too much."

"Spit it out," he teases.

"I'm never going to be able to move to Atlanta. That won't ever be an option. The kids' schools are here. Ryan would never allow it. Not to mention, my house is the only home they've ever known."

"What are you worried about?"

"That the airline will sell. I won't be working there anymore, so I won't be coming into Atlanta. You may or may not be working there. It's hard enough to make time to see each other now, what will we do . . ." I stop myself, hoping he doesn't think I'm a crazy person. Maybe I shouldn't be thinking so long term?

"If the sale of the airline goes through," he says, "that will change things for me."

"What does that mean?"

"I talked to my old security firm."

"They're based in Atlanta, right?"

"Yes." He pauses, taking a deep breath. "I talked to them about me being based out of Savannah."

My mouth falls open then turns into a huge smile. "You'd move for me?"

"For you and for the kids," he says.

My heart feels like it's about to burst. "You just made me miss you that much more."

✧ ✧ ✧

IT FEELS SO good to be back from Hilton Head. The forty-five minute drive to Savannah felt like forever. Even all the space in the Suburban Ryan rented after Ava wrecked his car wasn't enough. The time never seemed to move.

The same thing is happening now. Like a schoolgirl, I look down at my watch for the thousandth time this morning. Still two hours until Mateo's supposed to be here. I haven't seen him in forever, and I've got everything lined up for the day. We'll spend a few hours here with the kids, then my mom is coming over to watch Connor so Mateo and I can go out. Ava and Jacob are capable of watching him for short periods of time, but I don't want to have to rush. Perfect plan!

Not wanting to hit the kids over the head with Mateo the second we got home, I decided to give them a day to unwind. It was torture for me, but they come first. Besides, I thought it might go better if they were well rested and not cranky from the trip.

I've got some stuff for work I can catch up on. I did a little work from the beach, but there's always more to do. Reaching for my glasses, my hand hits the nightstand. Where are they? I hope I didn't leave them at the beach. I really should get a second pair.

Two paragraphs into the latest advertising statistics, the doorbell rings. I leap to my feet. I'm happy to answer the door myself for once. I find Mateo standing before me, looking sexier than ever in a t-shirt and shorts.

He briefly glances over my shoulder then takes my hand, yanking me outside and closing the door behind me. He pins me to the door and kisses me. The last time someone kissed me like this on a front porch, I must've been a teenage girl.

The kiss starts hard and fast, but soon falls into slow, tender strokes of his tongue, his mouth moving over mine softly. It ends with a few gentle pecks to my lips, and then his hands cup the sides of my face. "All this time apart is killing me."

"Me, too," I say. "I'm glad you came early. You must've left at the crack of dawn." He shrugs like it's not a big deal, but it feels like a big deal to me. I appreciate it. I love how eager he is to see me. But the look in his eyes indicates he's eager for something else, too. I love that even more. "Little time with the kids, then just me and you," I say, giving him a flirty smile.

The door opens. "Mommy, I'm hungry," Connor says before his eyes land on Mateo. "Never mind."

"Connor!" I cry out and reach for him, but he's already back inside.

Mateo grabs my hand. "Don't force him. I can wait him out."

Nodding in agreement, we walk inside. "Hi, Mateo," Ava says, skipping down the stairs. She's unusually happy this morning. She plants a kiss on my cheek, grinning.

"Okay, who's the boy?" I ask.

"There's no boy," she says, giggling. "You always tell me my happiness shouldn't depend on boys."

"Okay," I say, kissing the side of her head, then see Mateo smiling like a damn fool, apparently finding my children amusing.

"There is, however, a music festival," she says.

"Ava."

"Please, Mom," she says. "A couple of my friends are going. You camp out. It sounds like so much fun."

"Bonnaroo?" Mateo asks.

"Yeah, how'd you know?" Ava asks.

My eyes dart to Mateo. "You've heard of this?"

He nods, pulling out his phone and starting to type. Turning back to my daughter, I say, "Ava, there's so many drugs and drinking at these things. You're a little too young. Maybe in college."

"Mom, please."

"Any parents going?" I ask.

"No, but my friend's older sister is going with some of her friends. She's in college."

"Boys going?"

"Not with us. Please! It will be so much fun to take a road trip. Just with my girlfriends."

"How many?" Mateo asks, still looking down at his phone.

"Six, I think," Ava says. "Why?"

But he doesn't answer. Ava spends the next few minutes pleading her case. She should consider being an attorney. As she's winding down her closing argument, something about the unfairness of her life and how this trip would make everything better, I see that Mateo continues to be consumed by his phone. I don't expect him to help parent my kids, but it's unlike him to be so detached. "Mateo?" I say, waving my hand a little.

"The guy who owns the company who does security for a lot of these festivals is a buddy of mine," Mateo says. "I was checking with him to see if they've had any threats."

"Oh my God," Ava screeches. "I don't need another dad! I have one!"

"Ava! You apologize to Mateo, right now."

"I will not!"

"Young lady . . ."

Mateo rubs my shoulders and says to Ava, "I was only trying to help. He said security is in place. He even offered to keep an eye on you girls if your mom lets you go, and upgrade your tickets so you'd have air-conditioned bathrooms, a place to shower. It's not my place to say if you can go or not. That's up to your mom. I was just trying to make her more comfortable if she decided to let you."

Ava is speechless other than to say, "Oh." She quickly looks down, and her eyes well up.

"I guess you're sorry now," I snap, which causes the tears to well over.

"Why's she crying now?" Jacob says, coming down the stairs. "She cries all the time."

"Shut up, Jacob!" Ava barks. "I do not."

No wonder Poppy doesn't want children. They are exhausting. But Mateo doesn't seem to mind, giving me a little wink. "Come on, Jacob," Mateo says. "Let's go watch TV. Give the girls some time."

"I want to watch TV," I say in our code, and he flashes me a smile. "I promise to watch something with you later."

✧ ✧ ✧

LET ME TELL you, dating with kids is not for the weak. No decision was made about the festival, but Ava had a long cry. We didn't really talk, unless you count her tears as a language, in which case she's fluent. She didn't want to hang around, and I wasn't going to force her. Before she left, she gave me a big hug then walked into the living room and apologized to Mateo. I stood back watching, giving them some space. There was no hug, not that I thought there would be, but maybe one day.

Jacob and Mateo seem settled. I couldn't join them if I wanted to, both of them in a full man spread on the sofa. You know, the way men sit with their legs spread apart to give room for their balls. That leaves no room for me, so I go to find my little man. Connor is glued to the computer again. He doesn't even speak to me. He was such a happy little guy last week trying to corral Ryan and me back together. It's like night and day.

"Hey, Mom," Jacob calls out, "Mateo and I are going for a run." I nearly fall over that my lazy teenage son is volunteering for physical exercise. "He said he'll help get me in shape."

Jacob bounds up the stairs to change, and I look at Mateo, who apparently is a magician. It should be Magic Mateo instead of *Magic Mike*. Hmm, he definitely has the moves for that movie. "What did you do to my son?"

"I don't know," he chuckles. "We were just talking about guns and . . ."

"Guns?"

"Well, my work. He was asking what I do exactly, and what I used to do. Then he just sort of asked if I'd train him. He says he wants to get into shape." Mateo winks at me. "I think there's a girl involved."

"A real life girl? Not a porn star?"

He cracks up laughing as Jacob comes running down the stairs. Mateo pats his back, and they head out the door. Smiling, I wonder how Jacob went from playing with super heroes to admiring super models. Pretty soon, Connor will be the same. It goes by too fast.

Jacob hasn't worked out in forever, and the Savannah sun is high in the sky today. I can't imagine they will be running very long or very far, so I retreat to the kitchen to make some sweet tea and sandwiches. I try again to coax Connor, to no avail. Reminding myself this is all still new, I refuse to let his behavior get me down.

When Mateo and Jacob return, they are both soaked in sweat. On Jacob, it looks and smells disgusting. Pinching my nose, I order Jacob upstairs to shower. On Mateo, on the other hand, it looks sexy and rugged.

"Want to use my shower?" I ask Mateo.

"I don't have anything clean to put on," he says, raising an eyebrow at me.

Taking his hand, I pull him towards my room. "I'll wash your stuff."

"What will I wear in the meantime?" he asks, locking my bedroom door.

Giggling, I reach into my closet and throw my fluffy baby blue bathrobe at him. He catches it then lifts his shirt over his head, the edges of his muscles dripping with sweat and making me moan a little. "Shorts, too," I say, motioning with my hands, and in one swoop, he steps out of his shorts and boxer briefs. He's hard as a rock. The thing is like a beacon pointing right at me. "Uh, I'll just . . ."

I can't finish the sentence because my mouth is suddenly dry. I need to get out of here before I fuck him with my kids at home. Quickly, I walk past him, retrieving his clothes, and head to put them in the laundry. Thank goodness that I have a speed wash and dry cycle. I don't think I could stand knowing the man is hard without underwear on in my house for any real length of time. If it wasn't for the kids, I know I'd be mounted on top of him right now.

Then it hits me. I've had sex plenty of times with the kids at home. Granted, it was with their father, and I was married—though I wasn't the last time. Truth be told, I've never been good at quickies. It seems to me quickies were designed for the guy. Sure, my vibrator can get me off in under two minutes, but I've never been successful with a man under pressure.

Tiptoeing to the bottom of the staircase, I listen. The shower is still running upstairs. Maybe it's time to try again. After all, with Ava gone, only two kids are home now—and Jacob's showering, and Connor's frozen in front of the computer. I'm going to go for it.

Sneaking back into my bedroom, I lock the door behind me then hear the shower turn off. This is even better! I don't want to get wet. That would be too obvious. Shower sex will have to wait. He steps out of my bathroom, his back to me as he's drying off. God, the man's ass is a work of art, his muscles flexing as he moves.

"Two minutes," I say. He turns around as I yank down my shorts. "We've got two minutes."

If the man were a swimmer, he'd have an incredible start time. In like a hundredth of a second, he's got me pinned to the bedroom wall. Hiking my leg up to his hip, he pushes into me. God, it's been way too long. He yanks my hair, granting him access to my neck. How he manages to kiss me so gently while fucking me so hard, I'll never know. I suspect he's probably one of those people that can rub their belly and pat their head at the same time.

He withdraws until he's almost out of me, then thrusts hard. Withdraw and thrust, withdraw and thrust. Over and over again. I'm never sure how far he'll go, how hard, how deep. It's driving me crazy, and he knows exactly what he's doing to me. How close I am. And he's loving it.

"Oh God!" I cry, and his mouth slams into mine, muffling my string of curse words while I come quick and hard.

Add Quickie Queen to my resume.

He follows right along behind me, his head on my shoulder as he pants, "I'm sorry, baby."

Huh, is he kidding? Could he not tell I finished? Ryan used to always ask me whether I did. I hated that. It made me have to verbally lie. It was easier to just fake it than lie to his face. "Why?"

"You only finished once."

I stifle a laugh. "Well, I did *only* give you two minutes."

He raises his head. "I think we have thirty seconds left. You have more to give me, baby?"

WE WENT A little over our two-minute mark, but it was totally worth it—at least for me. Sticking my head out of my bedroom door, I make sure the coast is clear before motioning for Mateo to wait a minute before coming out. Smiling and feeling refreshed, I walk out of my bedroom. I don't make it two steps before a little voice startles me.

"Are you going to marry Mateo?" Connor asks.

My heart leaps into my throat. Did he hear us? Would he even know what he was hearing? No way. "What are you talking about, honey?"

"Because if you marry Mateo, then you may have a baby with him someday."

I exhale—he obviously didn't hear us.

Connor continues, "And I like being the youngest. I don't want a baby brother or sister."

As a mom, I'm never quite prepared for what my kids will say. They never give me warning, and they don't always bring up heavy subjects at convenient times. This is a perfect example. I don't know what to say.

Connor's eyes shift to Mateo, coming out of my bedroom, wearing my bathrobe. He freezes, seeing Connor and me. Shit! Did he hear what Connor said? Mateo's face isn't telling me anything.

"Connor." I start, but he quickly turns and runs towards the stairs. I look over at Mateo. "He was just . . ."

"Asking about a baby sister or brother," Mateo says, eyeing my belly. "Is there something I should know?"

"No, nothing like that," I say, thankful he apparently didn't hear the marriage part.

I wrap my arms around him and rest my head on his chest, remembering that Mateo once told Poppy he didn't need to have his own children. Is that true? This is not the time to get into that issue with him.

I wonder if I would ever be open to more kids. I knew I didn't want more kids with Ryan. We never even considered a fourth. At my age, the window to have kids is closing. Would I reconsider for the right man?

He kisses the top of my head. "Are you sure there's nothing you need to tell me?"

I shake my head, laughing. "I'm sure, but I have no clue what to do about Connor."

"Maybe he'll take a bribe," he teases.

"How much you got?" Jacob asks, coming down the hallway and walking into the den. "Cause I could take a pic of you in that robe and post it all over the place. Probably would go viral."

"You know, I think I liked you better when you just grunted," I tease, and Jacob laughs before assuming his position in front of the television. "Mateo, I'll go check on your clothes."

Throwing the clothes from the washer to the dryer, I walk into the den to join Mateo and Jacob. Jacob is sitting on the leather chair, and Mateo's on the sofa. They're playing some terribly inappropriate, violent video game where the object seems to be killing the other person in the most violent way possible—like ripping off their head, shoving it down their neck, then pulling it out through their chest. I think I may have bought this one for Jacob for Christmas last year.

Don't get me wrong, I hate all the violence in the video games, but all of Jacob's friends have them, too. And he talks to his friends while playing them. I don't want him not to be able to talk to his friends. I want him to have a social life, and this is what most teenage boys seem to do. Still, I'm conflicted about it. I guess I've just learned to pick my battles with my kids over the years.

Jacob holds out his remote to me. "Mom, play Mateo."

"How do I play?" Before I know it, the game has started. Mateo obviously knows which button combinations to push to do some cool moves and counter moves. Without my glasses on, I can't even see the letters on the buttons, so I just randomly start pushing things. Suddenly, my psychotic character begins to levitate and electrocutes the other guy.

"Go, Mom!" Jacob says, laughing. "You are a complete badass! She lit you up, Mateo!"

I'll let the cursing slide since it was compliment, I suppose, and we're having such a good time. Mateo is beaming with pride, looking at me like I just won the Nobel Peace Prize, and leans over and kisses me on the lips.

It's closed-mouthed and brief, and I know it was spontaneous, but the room goes silent just the same. Mateo and I both realize what happened at the same time. Jacob's been the one that's handled this the best. I hope we didn't just ruin it. I can't believe this happened—and on the heels of the awkwardness with Connor.

We turn to Jacob together and see he looks completely stunned, having never seen anyone other than Ryan kiss me, if he even remembers that from several years ago. I look up at Mateo, his eyes searching, neither one of us knowing what to say or do, compatible even in our insanity.

Jacob fills the dead air, asking, "Do you love my mom?"

Before I have time to freak out, Mateo answers, "Very much."

Jacob's eyes shift to me, the shock evident in my face. He gives me the same mischievous smile he did when he was a little boy. "Would now be a good time to ask for fifty bucks?" he asks.

I laugh through a few tears, and Jacob gets up and hugs me—really hugs me, like he hasn't in a long time. "I love you," I whisper in his ear.

"Love you, too," he whispers back, pulling away then adding in typical teenage boy style, "What's for lunch? I'm starving."

CHAPTER TWENTY-THREE
COMPLICATIONS

MATEO'S GETTING DRESSED, so I've got a few minutes alone. And I need it. Stepping out onto my back porch, I wonder if my yard is big enough to hold the many thoughts in my head right now.

Ryan was the first boy who ever said he loved me. And he's the only man who's ever said those words to me—until today. Mateo's in love with me? I wonder when he first felt it. What does this mean for me, the kids?

When you're young and use the "L" word, it's a lot simpler. I think love in general is simpler when we're young. Perhaps as we age, we complicate love—and everything else—so unnecessarily.

I feel Mateo come up behind me, his hands on my hips. "I'll be working from home this week," I say, not looking at him, the love comment hanging over us.

"You're thinking way too much," he says.

"You told my son that you love me."

He turns me around, forcing my eyes to his. "And how do you feel about that?"

"Well, I think that . . ."

"No," he says, planting a small kiss on my lips. "Not think. Feel."

I gave him a smirk. Why do I always try to process, itemize, categorize? I'm the queen of organizing, of lists. For goodness' sake, I even made a sex bucket list—and I did it when I was drunk! I get plastered and still can't shake my Type A tendencies. Don't get me wrong, I adore that list, though, and it's served me well—wherever the hell Mateo has stashed it.

As for love, Mateo's right. Love's not something you decide or think through. If I'm going to love again, it's not going to be because I processed something or because of a list. You can make a list of a thousand traits you want in someone, and if you ever happen to find that person, you may actually feel nothing. It may make sense on paper, but your heart could care less.

I know I need more feeling in my life, but I can't help but trust my head over my heart. My heart has made me stupid before. My planning, my lists, and my rational brain never let me down. Mateo's asking me to use an organ that's broken. It's like I'm being asked to dance without any legs. How can I trust my heart?

"Mom, the doorbell's ringing," Jacob yells, opening up the backdoor.

"Well, answer it." I say sarcastically. "You can walk to tell me someone is at the door, but you can't walk to the front door and answer it?"

Jacob shrugs, so I head for the door, motioning to Mateo to give me a minute. He nods and heads back inside to the den with Jacob. The doorbell rings again, and I move a bit faster. "Coming," I say.

It's probably my mom coming over to babysit. She's got good timing, as Mateo and I obviously need to finish our conversation. The doorbell rings again. Hurrying to answer, I fling the door open. It's not my mom.

"Ryan?"

"You left your glasses in the car on the drive back, and I thought you might need them," he says, holding them out.

"I've been looking for them," I say, walking out to the front porch with him and closing the door behind me. "You didn't need to bring them by."

"You okay?" he asks.

I give him a quick nod. "Good, yeah."

"No, you're not."

Leave it to Ryan to finally grow some insight. Shrugging, I say, "I'm fine."

"Talk to me," he says, touching my hand for a second. "You used to always say we never *really* talked."

"We're divorced. Now's not the time for a heart-to-heart."

"Guess not," he says, and I turn to head back inside. "Fuck it, Emerson!" He grabs me by the waist, turning me to him.

I try to wiggle free, but he pulls me closer, our hips pressed against each other. "Ryan, let me go."

"Never again," he says, his eyes softening, and I suddenly stop struggling, even stop breathing. "I made a huge mistake when I left. I still love you, and I think you still love me."

"You divorced me," I say.

"I tried to stop loving you. I swear I did, but I still believe in us."

"Ryan, you don't mean that," I say. "It was an emotional week with Ava and playing house at the beach with the kids."

He flashes me that dimple smile, the one that caught me all those years ago. "You aren't hearing me. I want you back. I'll do anything."

Holy shit! Where is this coming from? I know he's needed time to *think*, and sleeping together may have confused things, but this is entirely different. He's not hem hawing around. He's dead serious. Why now? After all this time? This has to be a reaction to our week with the kids. Or maybe it's just because he's jealous of Mateo. Either way, I closed this door.

"Aren't you seeing someone?" I ask.

"That's long over—never really went anywhere," Ryan says. "There's only one woman I want."

"I'm not yours anymore."

"Because you slept with him?" he asks softly, and the tears in my eyes are enough of an answer. "I don't care."

Who is this man? "But one kiss and you . . ."

"I know. I was so stupid, prideful. I'm sorry, baby. I'm so sorry. Please come back to me." Ryan takes my hand. "I promise I'll make you happy this time. We can do counseling if you want, whatever you think is best. We aren't over. I think we owe it to ourselves to try again. Hell, we owe it to our kids."

"I have to go inside," I say, turning for the door.

Ryan catches my waist. He's serious about not letting me go this time. "The kids were so happy this week. You can't deny that. We can give them that again. Think about it."

"Emerson," Mateo's voice startles me.

I wiggle free from Ryan, but he captures my hand. "What the hell is he doing here? With my kids?"

"Think you need to go, man," Mateo says calmly, though I can feel his anger vibrating like an aftershock from an earthquake.

I don't recall ever seeing Ryan look like this before. His eyes say he's sad, but the rigidness of his posture points to only one emotion—pissed off. I can feel him digging in his heels. For once, Ryan's not going to bail.

"We would be back together if it wasn't for him," Ryan says, "and whatever the hell you two are doing with that sex bucket list."

I roll my eyes. "It has nothing to do with the list."

"Then it has everything to do with him," Ryan says.

"Ryan, a lot of time has passed," I say.

"Tell me that's not true," he says, his voice cracking a bit.

Mateo's deep brown eyes shoot to me, clearly wondering if there's any truth in what Ryan's saying. I can't think it's entirely untrue. Before Mateo came along, I still had a soft spot for Ryan. We even slept together again. I still loved him in some weird way. I probably always will.

"Tell me our kids wouldn't have us back together if he wasn't in the picture," Ryan continues, his eyes welling up a bit.

I close my eyes, remembering our kids this past week at the beach, each of them happy and content. I haven't seen them all look that way for that length of time in years. A week with their mom and dad together did that.

"Daddy," Ava says, coming up the path to the house, her eyes darting between the three of us.

"Go inside with your brothers," I tell her.

"What's going on?"

"Now, Ava!" I snap.

She looks at the pain on her father's face. "Daddy, are you okay?"

"I'm fine, honey. Everything's fine," Ryan says, reaching out and squeezing her hand. His eyes go to me. "I'm going to take her in the house for a minute."

Ryan and Ava disappear, and I turn to face Mateo. "He just showed up."

"He seems to think you're trying to work things out."

"No, well, I don't know. I mean, he just asked me to think about it."

"Don't fuck with my heart, Emerson," he says. "Did something happen with you two at the beach?"

"No, of course not. I wouldn't do that to you."

He doesn't respond. It looks like he's hurting. I'm standing only a few inches from the man, but it seems much farther. The wedge Ryan just drove is big. Perhaps that's what he wanted, though he seemed completely sincere. This isn't a game. I feel my body start to tremble before I realize I'm crying.

"You need to believe me," I say.

"I believe you," he says, reaching out to me. "Talk to me."

"What do you want me to say?" I ask.

"Tell me how you feel."

"There's something to be said for seeing your kids happy," I say through tears. "There's nothing better than that. Especially to see Connor the way he was, it was special. How am I supposed to deny them that?"

"I want you, Emerson. I'll fight for you. You know that."

"I know," I say. "I have to think."

"Ryan knows how to get to you. He knows he's too late, so he's trying to guilt you, use the kids, into giving him another chance."

"I'm not sure he's doing that," I say and look off into the distance, thinking about Ryan, how I've known him for decades, and that for all his faults, this isn't some stunt. His feelings are real. "I need to think," I say again.

"Was he thinking about the kids when he left you?"

Before I can answer, Ryan opens the front door, and I find myself standing in the middle of these two men, a pair of blue eyes staring at me, and a pair of brown doing the same, my heart screaming, my head yelling, but my mouth mute. One man is my past, asking for a second chance, and the other is my present, hoping for a future. And they couldn't be more different: from the way they look—one, strong and tan; the other, softer and lighter with those dimples—to the way they love me—one, like I'm his whole world and the other, as history loves, through a lens that may not always be accurate.

I suddenly realize I'm going to hurt someone. The pain of knowing that is unbearable. How did it come to this so quickly?

"I need you both to go," I cry out softly.

They open their mouths to protest, but I hold up my hand. Ryan quickly closes his mouth, but Mateo can't be silenced so easily. "There's no way I'm leaving with things like this," he says.

I gently reach out for his hand, and he locks his fingers with mine, the warmth of his hand leading me down the steps of the porch for privacy. "I'm sorry," I whisper.

"I love you," he says, his voice soft but firm. "I don't just throw those words around, Emerson."

"I know," I say. "And if this were just about me, it would be different."

"So Ryan was right? If it wasn't for me, you'd give him another chance?"

I don't see the point in answering that question. We both know the answer already. "Please don't do this."

"Emerson, I need you to tell me what to do. My instinct is to fight for you, beat his ass, and claim you as mine. I'm not the type to bow out."

"Part of me wants you to do just that. But then there's my kids, so . . . " I say, my voice trailing off. "I don't know."

"I don't want to fight so hard that I hurt you. I'm incapable of doing anything that would hurt you or them," he says. "I feel like my hands are tied."

"If you could just give me a little time to think," I say, hating I'm breaking his heart. Plus, I feel like a hypocrite, remembering how hurt I was when Ryan asked for "time" a few months ago. It seemed like chicken shit then. I'm sure it rings hollow to Mateo now.

He looks me straight in the eye. "*Time* wasn't on your list," he whispers. "I hope it's not the last thing I give you."

Without another word, he walks to his car and drives away. I can't bear to watch another man leave me, even though I asked him to. I turn back towards my house, where Ryan is waiting, finally ready to offer the life I once wanted more than anything.

CHAPTER TWENTY-FOUR
MAN SANDWICH

I SENT RYAN home after Mateo left. I hope Mateo realizes that. Maybe I should text him and tell him. But I don't. I can't. I have to figure this out before I talk to either one of them again. Throwing myself into bed, I stare over at my phone on the nightstand. Every time it buzzes, my heart leaps into my throat.

But it's just my mother each time, wondering why I cancelled her evening with the kids, asking if everything's okay. I give her brief, nondescript answers, which only lead to more questions. The buzzes keep coming, and I stop answering her eventually. I don't have the time or energy for that.

A tightness strikes my chest. I feel like I'm trying to get into a pair of jeans after they've been washed and dried. Honestly, I almost never wash my jeans. I know that sounds gross, but it's because they're too tight after. Ever notice how your favorite pair of comfy jeans all of sudden feels like they don't fit anymore once they've been cleaned?

Guess that's how I feel about Ryan. He was always so comfortable, so dependable. Perhaps with a little time, he'd start to feel good again. Or maybe it would always be work to try to make us fit together. Either way, he was right: if Mateo wasn't in the picture, I'm sure I'd give him another chance. The kids would be so happy if we got back together. But could Ryan and I fit together again?

People are like puzzles. Everyone has certain edges, some sharper than others, and some pieces fit together, and some just don't. Some are certainly easier to figure out than others. And just like a puzzle, you can break them in a second, but it takes a lot longer to put them together.

When I was a tween, I remember doing a puzzle of my favorite boy band then putting some rubber cement over the top to try to preserve it. It held together for a little while, but eventually started to crack. No matter what I did, I couldn't hold all the pieces in place. I closed my bedroom door real hard one day, and the whole thing shattered.

Just like Ryan and me, I couldn't hold us together. One wrong move, and the whole thing fell apart. Is love supposed to be so fragile?

Ryan asked me to *think* about giving him another chance. When I think about it, it does make sense. We are a good team. We owe it to the kids. But when I *feel* about it, there's only hurt and pain. You can't make someone feel your love. That person either feels it, or they don't. Ryan would say he loved me, but for the last few years of my marriage, I didn't feel it in my heart. I'm not sure if the problem was with him or with me. Either way, it didn't work. And there's no reason to think that would change.

Mateo's words echo in my head. *Don't think. Feel.* When he told me he loved me, I felt it deep in my heart. And it's not just the words, it's the way he looks at me, touches me, cares for me. It's like the man was made to love me. He knows just how to do it. My stomach tightens, knowing I never said the words back to him. Do I love Mateo? I've only said that to one man. But I know the answer. Every part of my body knows the answer.

But is love enough?

Isn't that the age old question?

All moms feel torn—torn between their work in and out of the home, between their duties as a wife and as a mother, between being in the boardroom and in the classroom as room mom. There simply aren't enough hours in the day to be a mom, wife, daughter, friend, sister, boss, worker, and volunteer. What usually happens is we put ourselves last on the list. We forego sleep, exercise, nutrition, new clothes, haircuts, friendships—anything in the name of being a "good" mom and wife. The pressure and guilt are overwhelming.

And now out of nowhere, I have a chance to give my kids exactly what they want—their dad and me back together. Shouldn't I do that for them? What kind of mother would it make me not to do that? The question haunts me the entire night, and by midafternoon the next day, I've stuffed myself with carbs, eating every piece of bread in the house, called in sick to work, and faked one too many smiles for the kids. And I've got nothing left.

Walking to my backyard, I sit down on the back porch steps. The Savannah sun's rays feel like little embers on my skin, providing warmth but little comfort for all the burning I'm doing inside. I continue to agonize: Make my kids happy? Make myself happy? I hear the door open behind me, knowing it's one of my kids, but I can't even bring myself to turn around, wanting a moment to just be a woman, to be Emerson, not a mom.

I hear Jacob's voice. "Grandma's on the phone," Jacob mutters behind me.

"Tell her I'll call her later."

"I called her," he says, causing me to turn my head to him. He holds the phone out to me. "For you."

"I don't feel like talking," I say and turn away. "Apologize for bothering her, and tell her I'll call her later."

I hear him say a few words to my mom before the click of the phone. Then he tells me, "I just thought you could use your own mom."

Everything melts—my heart, my anger, my sadness. I turn to him and hold out my hand, and he plops down beside me, wrapping his arm around my shoulder.

"How'd you get so smart?" I ask.

He shrugs a little. "Even moms need moms."

"I'm okay, Jacob. You don't need to worry about me."

"I like Mateo," he says with a firmness to his voice that I wonder whether I've missed before.

"Me, too. He's a good man. What did you like about him?"

"You smiled a lot when he was here," he says. "I liked seeing you smile."

My hands fly over my mouth in a weird mix of happy and sad. Sad that maybe my kids haven't seen me smile and laugh enough the past few years, and happy that means so much to my son. "I love you, Jacob," I say and throw my arms around his neck, hugging him tight, hard, as long as I can, never wanting to let go, until the inevitable happens.

He starts to wiggle free, trying to escape the prison of my maternal embrace, groaning, "Mom, okay, that's enough."

THE DAYS COME and go with no word from Mateo or Ryan. I asked for time, and boy am I getting it. *Be careful what you wish for* has been given a whole new meaning.

I keep telling the office I'm sick, trying to explain why I'm not doing a damn bit of work. They probably think I'm dying at this point. But I'm too paralyzed by analysis to do anything and can't chance having to face Mateo.

I'm not someone who shares a lot while in the middle of something. I've always found it easier to share an old story than one I'm living through. Ever notice that? I tend to put on a brave face and power through. It's why I haven't reached out to Layla and Poppy or my mom, why I haven't reached out to anyone.

But Poppy and Layla are the same way. We all know that about each other, so we know when it's been a while since we've seen or talked to each other that something could be wrong. All things considered, my drama basically just started, so I'm surprised when I look through the peephole and see Layla banging on my door, holding Greer on her hip.

I open the door and find the culprit standing right behind her. My mom's eyes send me into a sort of adult time-out. My head sags, my shoulders slump, and silence takes hold of me. It's like I'm ten years old again. I'm sure she's upset I never called her back after Jacob's phone stunt a few days ago.

Before I can get any words out, my mom's hand flies up. "We'll talk later," she says.

"Poppy needs us," Layla says.

"What's going on?"

From behind some bushes, Poppy jumps out in front of me. "Bachelorette party!"

"What?" I scream and pull her into a hug. "You're getting married?"

"Tomorrow!" she says, her breath heavy with excitement.

My eyes pop out of my head. "Tomorrow?"

"Damn straight!" she shrieks. "So tonight we party!"

"Okay!" I say, full of happiness for my friend but also so many questions—like how did this happen so quickly, where is the wedding, how in the hell did she pull a ceremony together in a few days?

"I'm watching my grandkids tonight," my mom says, tickling Greer's chubby belly. "Even you."

Layla smiles and pushes me towards my room. "Go pack a bag. We've booked a hotel. And don't forget to pack a black dress."

"Black?"

"I'll explain later," Poppy says.

A thousand excuses not to go explode in my head, ranging from silliness like laundry, to the fact that I'm supposed to be sick from work and shouldn't be out partying, to the hardcore truth, that I don't want to discuss Mateo or Ryan. But they are so happy, so high. And I wouldn't miss out on that for the world.

I stand in my room, unable to start packing. I'm completely frozen and know I'll stay this way until I work through this stuff with Ryan and Mateo. "Mom," Ava says from behind me. I turn around and see her holding out a Vera Bradley duffle bag. "Thought you might want to borrow this."

"Thanks, baby," I say, giving her a little hug.

Her feet shuffle a little. "You know how you let me decide about Justin?" I nod, opening up a drawer. "I knew you didn't want me to be with him, but you were going to let me make my own decision, remember?

"I do."

"Were you just saying that? Would you have let me see him again?"

I gnash my teeth a little before turning my head turn to her. If she's dropping the Justin bomb on me right now, I'm going to lose my shit. "I was being honest," I say. "You know, I wouldn't have liked it, and I would've policed you to death, but I was prepared to let you make that decision."

She sits down on my bed, playing with the comforter a little. "I know Daddy wants you back. We all heard him say it the day Mateo was here."

"What does this have to do with Justin?"

"You know I'd rather you be with Daddy, just like I knew you'd rather I not be with Justin. But you were going to let me decide. I know this is your decision, not mine." Tears roll down her face. God, she's trying to be mature, but it breaks her heart. I wrap my arms around her. "It's not that I don't like Mateo," she cries. "It's just *Daddy*."

"I know how much you love your dad."

"I do, but I'll be going to college in a few years."

She can't even finish her thought. And that's not exactly a glowing recommendation for me to be with Mateo. Best-case scenario, it's half a blessing. She dries her face quickly, takes a deep breath, and sucks it all back in. I hate seeing her do that, knowing she gets it from me. I wish she'd just let it all out. I wish I could. I can't seem to give myself permission, either.

I kiss her on the forehead, then she helps me throw some things together. Jacob yells goodbye from upstairs. I hear Connor giggling in the living room with his grandmother, but as soon as he sees me, he crosses his arms over his chest and turns his head away. My friends' eyes fly to me, wondering what that was about, having no idea what a scattered mess my family life is.

I walk over to Connor. The boy hasn't spoken to me since Ryan left, apparently believing his silent treatment can force me and his father back together. I bend down in front of him. "Connor, look at me." He doesn't.

"Connor," my mom says firmly, "look at your mother."

His eyes turn to me, holding in tears. "I love you," I say.

"No, you don't," he cries.

"Connor, I love you very much."

"You stopped loving me just like you stopped loving Daddy!"

That's rough. It's a tough thing to hear. But Connor is hurting, so I need to stay calm. And I need to watch what I say. I can't tell him I never stopped loving Ryan. That would just confuse him. And it wouldn't do much good to say that his dad left me. "Moms can't stop loving their kids."

"Well, kids can stop loving their moms," he says. While I know he doesn't mean it, my heart starts to hurt and not in the growing pain way. It hurts like I'm about to lose someone I love.

"If you loved me, then you'd let Daddy come home. I love him!" he screams. "I won't ever love Mateo. Ever!" He bolts up off the sofa, his feet pounding up the stairs.

Covering my eyes with my hands, I rub my face. "I can't go," I choke out. "I can't leave him like this. I'm sorry, Poppy."

"It's okay," she says.

"You're going," my mom says. "He'll be fine in five minutes."

"Look at him," I say. "I can't. I can't do this to him."

Layla rubs my back and throws my own words back at me, the ones from Greer's baptism. "A good mom knows when to take a break," she says.

ONLY POPPY WOULD have a surprise wedding. Other than celebrities trying to avoid the press, I don't think anyone does that. But once Poppy decided to marry Dash, it was a race to the finish line. So tomorrow they are having the most unique wedding in the history of the universe. As for tonight in our hotel room, Poppy settled for the standard fare.

"Last time we had a bachelorette party, I ended up with that damn list," I say, picking up my wine glass. "This is so much better."

Poppy hired a half-dozen male strippers. She jokingly said it was her gift to me—a good girls threesome. I certainly hope Dash and Gage don't get wind of this. They would flip their shit if they could see their women right now getting lap dances and rubdowns from two extremely hot guys while sexy stripper music is blaring.

Lucky me, I've got twins working on me.

Poppy laughs, "The guys were going to drink beer and watch sports!"

I have no doubt that's exactly what they're doing, having long ago traded in strip clubs for suburbia.

I lean back in my chair, as lap dance twin is grinding and thrusting up on me. I take a look down, and while my eyesight is not the best at the moment—we've been drinking over an hour—I see that the man is really hung. Unless he's stuffing his drawers, but I don't think so. The song changes, and he pulls me to my wobbly feet.

As I gain my balance, I find myself in the middle of a hunk sandwich. I feel like a ping-pong ball. One twin thrusts, forcing me into the other twin, who thrusts me right back. Perhaps any other week of my life, this would be fun and sexy as hell, but being caught between two men leaves something to be desired at the moment.

I take a glance over at Poppy, clearly in her element. She's like a kid in a candy store. I still can't believe she'll be getting married in a few hours, and not just because she has her hands all over her two mostly naked guys, and their hands are all over her. I look over at Layla. She has her eyes covered and looks like she might be praying her breasts don't leak.

An hour later, our company is gone, and we're all giggles and smiles in our pajamas. It doesn't matter how old women get, we still like sleepovers. But now instead of doing each other's hair, Layla pulls out her breast pump, asking, "How much do I need to throw away since I drank that glass of wine?"

"Google it," I say, "but I think you're supposed to toss the milk produced the first two hours after you drink. But double-check me. I can't remember exactly."

"Wait! You can't drink when you breastfeed?" Poppy asks. "This pregnancy and baby thing keeps getting worse and worse."

"You and Dash come to some agreement about that?" I ask as the sound of sexy stripper music is replaced by the vacuum sound of the breast pump.

Poppy smiles. "After Dash got hurt, all I could think was how much I wanted to spend my life with him. I actually asked him to marry me."

"You asked him, Poppy?" I cry.

"Sure, why the hell not? I felt like it, so I did it," she says. "I don't care about any PC crap. Dash doesn't, either."

"What about kids?" Layla asks.

"He told me he realized something when he was hurt, too. He said that having kids wasn't worth losing me. He said he'd rather spend his life with me and no kids, than have a life without me."

"And I guess you believe him?" Layla asks. "You don't think he'll change his mind down the road?"

She shrugs. "Maybe I'll change mine."

"Really?" I ask.

"All I know is that we love each other and that's enough," she says.

With that, I lose it, crying into my hands. Poppy and Layla both start saying my name over and over again, no doubt thinking I'm a crazy person. I try to pull myself together, hating I'm now shitting all over Poppy's night. "I'm sorry," I say. "God, I'm sorry."

Layla wraps her arm around me. "What's going on?"

"Does this have anything to do with Connor?" Poppy asks.

I wipe my face and take a deep breath, and then, after apologizing some more, I fill in the missing pieces about Ryan, how I haven't heard from Mateo, how I'm torn between my kids and my heart. "Whoever thought a sex bucket list would lead to this?" I half joke.

"You know the list was never about sex, right?" Poppy says, and I look at her, confused. "It doesn't matter how many things are checked off. It's about putting you first in your life. Making yourself feel good."

"You heard Connor. He's never going to accept Mateo," I say. "How can I feel good if *my kids* don't?"

Poppy quickly responds, "How can your kids feel good if *you* don't?"

"All I know is that I'd sacrifice anything for my them," I say.

"Maybe that's the problem," Layla says.

"Huh?"

"Emerson, you know I love you," Layla says, "but Poppy's right—for once."

"Thank you," Poppy says.

"Being a mother does not mean being a martyr," Layla says.

Poppy touches my hand. "Maybe being with Mateo is the best way to love your kids."

"How's that?"

"You want your kids to love passionately, or just settle for convenience?" Layla asks me. "You need to show them the kind of love you want them to have. Show Connor and Jacob what a real man loving you looks like. Because God knows, they haven't seen it from their father. And what about Ava? Do you want her to settle for what you had with Ryan, or fight for what you could have with Mateo?"

I absorb all these words, so grateful for these women in my life. They're my tribe, my heart, my wisdom. And as usual, they give me a lot to think about.

THE NEXT DAY, giving new meaning to "until death do us part," Poppy and Dash get married in Bonaventure Cemetery. Sure, it is a beautiful and historic place in Savannah, resting peacefully along the Wilmington River, but I hate thinking about death and don't much like being surrounded by it. Poppy looks beautiful in her white gown, while the rest of us wear black. The guest list is small, just close friends and family. And since the setting is more than a little odd, there are no kids in attendance. Even amongst the revelry of the ceremony and reception, I can't help but notice that another person isn't in attendance, either. I've felt his absence all week. Something about the stony grave sculptures and majestic oak trees of this wondrous place is telling me that if I don't pull my act together fast, I'll be feeling his absence for the rest of my life.

CHAPTER TWENTY-FIVE
THE LIST RETURNS

Pulling onto my street, I look towards my house. It's been a long day and night, but for a moment, I think I'm seeing things. My house looks different. I blink a few times, and then my eyes fly out the windshield to my garden. Some of the old bushes have been removed, and standing in their place are some I recognize immediately, the same ones my dad planted for my mom so many years ago.

"Rose bushes," I whisper to myself, as I pull into the drive, admiring the beautiful red hues draped in front of my porch. I instantly know who did this. He knows just how much it would mean to me.

My mom meets me on the front porch. "The gardeners just showed up this morning. Mateo was here, too. He told me to tell you this was for all the times he never sent you flowers. And asked me to give you this." She hands me an envelope before she leaves. With trembling hands, I put on my glasses and sit on my front steps. I slowly pull out a folded notecard and have to smile. It's got the Southern Wings logo on it. Of course it does. Men don't keep stationary. Lifting it open, a folded piece of paper falls out.

My list.

He's giving me back my sex bucket list. Why? I look down at his handwriting, hoping for some answers. He gives me seven words.

Even if my love is not enough.

He wants me to be surrounded by his love even if I don't choose him. This is his way of always being there for me, of us always being together. What the fuck have I been doing the past week? I don't need to think about it because I feel it. I feel his love.

There's an art to loving someone. And just like real art, it's subjective. One person's way of showing love doesn't work for everyone. It's delicate. And just like real art, sometimes you mess up and have to start over. Sometimes the piece can be saved, and sometimes it can't. And right now, Mateo feels like an artist trained in the art of loving me.

I don't need to think anymore. I feel his love. I've always felt it.

Some won't agree with my decision. Some will say I could've tried again with Ryan, and I'm making a selfish choice. But somewhere deep inside, I know it wouldn't have worked out with Ryan, and that my kids would only end up hurt more.

It's Ryan's week with the kids, so when he shows up, I meet him on my front porch, the pretty rose bushes all around us, and he looks me in the eye. Whether it's the fresh bright colors in our midst, or something he sees in my face, he knows I've made my choice, and that it's no longer him. He closes his eyes and whispers, "It's always going to be you. For me, it will always be you." He opens his eyes, his lips in a tight line, and his fingers gently graze mine.

Before I know it, he's hugging me tightly, his head buried in my neck, his arms all the way around me. We both seem to know that this is it, the last time we'll hold each other. This is the real goodbye. Sometimes you have to hold on tight before you can totally let go.

I know I'm making the right decision, but this hurts. My arms cling to his shoulders, and I hear him sniffle. Slowly, he pulls back slightly, his arms still wrapped around my waist, his head leaning on mine. He knows he was too late. He decided to fight for me too late, and it's hurting him. I hate seeing it. I don't want my kids' father to hurt. His hands slide from my waist to my face.

"Are you sure?" he chokes out.

I've never gotten how people go from loving to hating each other so quickly. I'm not built like that. My heart prefers to focus on the good times we shared. If I could hate him, this would be a lot easier. But I won't ever hate him. The truth is, I'll probably always love him. But there's a big difference between loving someone and belonging with someone. Tears roll down my face. He walked away the first time. I need to do it this time—that's the only way he'll know it's really over.

"I'm sure," I whisper then disappear inside, sending the kids out to their father before pulling out my cell phone.

I need to look into Mateo's eyes. I need him to hold me and kiss me, to wipe away the feel of Ryan, of my past, of my stupid indecision, and this whole horrible week. Maybe more than anything, I need to apologize. I suspect he's been waiting for this call—for me to need him, bring him in, accept his love.

I dial and only one word comes out: "Mateo."

"On my way," he says, then the line goes dead.

It's a four hour drive from Atlanta, an hour plane ride plus commuting to and from the airport, so I figure I have at least ninety minutes or so to stop crying and compose myself, freshen up, take a closer look at the roses, straighten up the house. But I'm not able to do any of those things.

Mateo barrels through my front door within fifteen minutes, finding me with my eyes all red, snot running out of my nose, my hair in knots. And the sight of him shooting inside like a man on a mission, calling out for me, only makes me cry harder.

I head into the foyer to meet him, and he instantly, magically, knows what I need. He moves towards me and, without saying a word, wraps his arms around me, holding me tight, protecting me while I cry.

It's a gift to know what a person needs without them having to tell you. Mateo is blessed with such a gift. I'm the opposite, second-guessing the flowers I send for funerals, any words of congratulations or condolences I utter.

After I tie myself up, Mateo has a way of untying me. I'm not sure if he's this way with everyone, but he knows me, knows my heart so well that he knows what it needs before its next beat. He must want to talk, but as usual, he puts my needs before his own, letting me cry. We stand that way so long the light changes outside. Finally, I look up at him and whisper, "Hi."

Smiling, he strokes my hair. "I was wondering if this was a hello or goodbye."

A cry comes from the back of my throat. "I'm sorry you found me like this. I didn't expect you to get here so fast."

"I never left Savannah," he says. "I've been at a hotel. Called in sick the past few days."

"Me, too," I say, crying again. "I'm so sorry, Mateo. I'm so sorry about everything. You have to know, I always wanted to be with you. It was never about that."

"I know that."

"There's just a lot of guilt with divorce."

"I want your kids to be happy, too."

My heart melts, and he embraces me again, pulling me to his lips this time, kissing me sweetly. When he releases me, he asks, "Did you decide how you feel?"

I reach for his face, holding his eyes. "I feel very loved."

Smiling, he says, "You are."

EPILOGUE
SIX MONTHS LATER

MATEO

U̲n̲t̲y̲i̲n̲g̲ ̲h̲e̲r̲ ̲w̲r̲i̲s̲t̲s̲ and ankles, I can't help but grin. One look at her—just the sight of her, and my body comes alive. I lean down, undoing the last knot on her wrist, and she whispers, "I love you."

It took her a long time to say those words to me. It didn't happen in the foyer that day, or in bed that night, or over breakfast the next morning. She didn't yell it out while we were making love. She didn't say it casually as we said goodnight.

Instead, she waited a few weeks, until Ava was packing for the music festival. Ever the mom, Emerson made sure Ava prepared like the zombie apocalypse was coming. She had lists everywhere—things to do, places to park, emergency numbers. She had lists for her lists, for goodness sake. But my sole task was to communicate with my buddy to make sure his best security guys kept close watch on Ava.

As she was finishing packing up, I remember Emerson walking past me and handing me a folded piece of paper. I expected it to be a list of instructions for my buddy, but it wasn't. It was her sex bucket list. I scanned down the list, check marks here and there, still a few open items, wondering why she was giving it to me at that moment. I kept looking over it and found a new entry at the very end, with a huge red checkmark beside it.

Fall in love.

When I looked up, she smiled and said it out loud.

That was several months ago, but it never gets old.

Now kissing her wrists and cradling her naked body to my chest, I whisper I love her. "Since you aren't allowing threesomes," she teases, "I guess we're officially done with my list."

We spend the weeks when the kids are with Ryan scratching things off her list. I know she dreads the weeks the kids are gone, but this has given her something to look forward to. And I'm not complaining.

"It just so happens," I say, letting my fingertips roam the curves of her naked body. "I've made my own list."

Her eyes brighten. "Your own sex bucket list?"

"Not exactly."

"Then what kind of list is it?"

"It's more of a traditional bucket list," I say, reaching for my jeans, pulling out a piece of paper from the pocket, and handing it to her.

Mateo's Bucket List

1. Emerson—Notice you are first on my list. Just like you are first in my life. You are what I desire most in the world.
2. Jacob—I'm putting him second only because as the middle child he never gets to be first.
3. Ava
4. Connor
5.
6. I'm leaving No. 5 blank just in case Connor's fear of a baby brother or sister comes true.
7. A house for us to make our own memories.
8. I really want a dog. A big dog.
9. For you to make another list!
10. For you to be my wife.

I watch her eyes scanning the page, a soft smile playing on her full pink lips. I think she thinks it's cute that I made a list, that I'm trying to speak her language. I know the exact second she gets to number 5. She's hinted at having a baby with me once or twice, seemingly unable to believe I'm satisfied with just her and the kids. But I am. Still, I left it open, just in case.

Number 7 may be a sticking point. She loves her house. She likes being able to tell me where each kid took their first step, who bled where, exactly where she likes the Christmas tree. That's all well and good, but Ryan's somehow involved in each of those memories. It's not that I'm threatened by that. I just think it would be best for everyone to start fresh. I have no desire to take his place, and if I ever moved in, it may seem like I'm trying to.

She keeps on reading, and her breath catches, just like it does before she comes. Number 10! From the look on her face, she's completely taken by surprise. She reaches over, grabbing her glasses. I'm not sure what's cuter—her in those naughty black secretary-looking glasses, or that she thinks she might've read the list wrong.

She lowers my list to her lap, her eyes lifting to mine. I know that look. I've seen it from her before. She's going to fight me, but I'm going to win. She just needs to think things through. So I'll talk it out with her. And if all else fails, I can fuck her into seeing it my way. Maybe I should start with that?

I've spent so much time before and during our relationship letting her set the pace. It didn't come naturally to me. I normally pursue what I want until I get it, but not with Emerson. It's taken every ounce of training I've had to have patience, to wait for my shot, until she's ready.

There've been several starts and stops along the way. But it was the only way to go. Because there were three other people involved, people who mean everything to her.

The airline sale will be completed in a few months, and I'm moving to Savannah. I've already listened to Emerson's dissertation twice about why we can't live together, and I get it. But this is what I've wanted from day one, so it's time to make it happen.

I get down on one knee, completely naked still. "Emerson, will you ma. . ."

She hops up and starts to talk really fast, interrupting me, bringing up things we've discussed before: if she should get an annulment, having a different last name than her kids, wondering how my parents will feel if we're not married in the church. All valid concerns she's going on about, but I'm confident it will all work out.

She throws a shirt over her head, making it hard for me to understand what's she's saying. Eventually, she has to slow down and take a breath.

"Was this planned? Do my kids know? Do you have a ring?"

"You see the list. So yes, it was planned. The kids don't know. I hope we'll tell them together. And yes, I have a ring."

Her eyes dart around. "Where is it?"

"Say yes first," I say, getting to my feet.

Her smile reaches all the way to her eyes. "You won't show me the ring until I say yes?"

"That's right." I plant a little kiss on her shoulder and wait. It's what I do with her.

Her eyes close as she shakes her head at herself. "I should be jumping up and down. God, I'm sure this isn't the way you thought this would go."

"This is exactly how I knew it would go."

"Connor," she whispers.

"He'll have to talk to me if we all live under the same roof," I joke, though it's not funny.

That kid is a tough nut to crack. Ava is coming around more and more, and Jacob and I have gotten really close. I don't think of myself as their father, which I think helps all of us. My role is to love and support their mother. Once Ava and Jacob realized that, things have been pretty smooth.

Connor is another story. He's barely said a dozen words to me in the past few months. It's ripping Emerson apart. We started doing dinner with the kids once a week, hoping things would improve, but Connor simply eats, nothing more. He's no longer being rude. He'll answer if I talk to him, but that's it. He never laughs or smiles with me, or anyone else, really. If I try to do something with him, he refuses.

I also started going to some of the kids' activities, but that backfired. Ryan refused to sit anywhere near us. Of course, Connor saw that and took it to mean his dad's being forced out. I tried to talk to Ryan about it once, but that didn't get anywhere. He's not causing trouble for Emerson anymore, but he's not going to help, either. Not that I would expect him to.

I pull Emerson to my lap on the bed. "Number 8 could win Connor over."

"You want to bribe my kid to like you with a dog?" She rolls her eyes at me. "Nice try. No dogs."

I take her hand. "I don't want to wait." Her perfect pink lips part, and I know I'm about to hear a litany of excuses. "Baby, I've been waiting on you for years. From the moment you hired me to guard Layla." Her mouth closes. "Did you know I almost didn't take that job?"

"No, you never told me that."

"I knew I'd be distracted if you were around. I knew I wouldn't be able to do my job." She looks down, smiling, her skin pink. "Same thing when Gage asked me to come work for the airline full-time. For months, you'd breeze in and out with this wall around you. You took off your wedding ring, but the vibe you gave off said you were very much off limits. I think I first noticed a difference that day in the elevator when you bumped into me. Remember that?"

"Yes."

"But my dick was so damn hard I couldn't be sure."

She playfully elbows my side. "It was not!"

"The next time I saw you was outside Poppy's office."

"You came on pretty strong that day," Emerson says.

"And you bolted out of the office. I figured I blew it."

"You weren't the reason I bolted."

I could press her about what happened that day. God knows, I cursed myself enough over it, but if she wanted to tell me, she would.

At this point, I don't really care, and I'm trying to move forward with her, not get stuck in this little walk down memory lane. "Then you hurt your foot."

"And you found my list! Why were you snooping around in my office anyway?"

"After our time in the stairwell, I had to ask you out. I came by your office to do that. Imagine my surprise when I saw that list just laying there."

"I think you felt something other than surprise."

"I was relieved nothing was checked off," I say, "and also frustrated because I knew you still weren't ready for what I wanted."

"I don't recall you complaining," she flirts.

"I did complain. You just were never around to hear it." I say. "Remember that night when you, Layla, and Poppy were going out, and I came by your house as you guys were leaving? I complained to my scotch the entire flight home."

"So you came over that night to see me, not hang with Gage and the kids?" she asks.

"Of course, it was to see you."

"Then why didn't you tell me to stay?"

"Because you needed to go out with your friends. Just like you needed time to decide you wanted more with me. Just like you needed time to choose . . ." I stop talking and shake my head, not wanting to bring up bad memories, realizing we are getting way far afield from my end game.

"You know how sorry I am."

I raise my hand, her apology entirely unnecessary. "You still don't get it."

"Get what?"

"That I'll always give you what you need," I say. "No matter the cost to me."

And I paid a high price that week in the hotel. I struggled every minute with whether or not I should be doing more, fighting harder, while also reminding myself Emerson is a grown woman, not a child who needs a man to make decisions for her. The best thing for her was to make the decision on her own, so it didn't matter that I didn't sleep or eat. It was what she needed. And I will always give her what she needs, no matter how much it fucking hurts me.

"And you think I need to marry you?" she asks, a huge grin on her face.

"I know I need to marry you," I say, getting down on my knee again, reaching into the nightstand for the little square box, but not opening it.

Her lips land on mine. We've been together long enough that I know her kisses—which one means "this is just a kiss" and which one means "we'll be naked in two minutes." This is her "yes, I'll marry you" kiss. And it's the best yet.

Emerson's Sex Bucket List

1. Give panties to a stranger
2. Bondage play
3. Threesome with two men
4. Tantric sex
5. Make a sex tape
6. Learn to twerk
7. Give myself multiple orgasms
8. Selfish sex
9. Pole dancing
10. Unselfish sex
11. Reverse cowgirl
12. Ask a man out
13. Give a strip tease
14. Spanking
15. Take naughty pictures of myself
16. Go without panties all day
17. Use a blindfold
18. Use nipple clamps
19. Orgasm in a public place
20. Sex with a younger man
21. Feather play
22. Work through all the Kama Sutra positions

Coming Summer 2017!

Meet the woman who invented Emerson's new vibrator.
It's sure to be a buzz.

ALSO BY PRESCOTT LANE

The Reason for Me
Stripped Raw
Layers of Her (a novella)
Wrapped in Lace
Quiet Angel
Perfectly Broken
First Position

ACKNOWLEDGEMENTS

I'VE GOT TO thank my husband first, because he's the one that I woke up at one in the morning in tears threatening to scrap the whole project. He's wonderful, but it's the tribe of women at my side to whom I owe this book.

Nikki Rushbrook, my editor, my advisor, my friend—without your help and constant support, my commas would be semicolons and my mind would be Jell-O.

Robin Bateman, beta reader extraordinaire—thank you for listening to my incessant bitching about blurbs. The back jacket would be blank without you.

Sommer Stein, my cover designer—it got done! You are a saint among saints for enduring my constant back and forth as I jumped from concept to concept.

Becca from Bibliophile Productions, thank you for bringing my story to life with your amazing trailer.

Nina Grinstead and the team at Social Butterfly PR—thank you for helping to bring my vision to life, believing in Emerson's story, and guiding me through the crazy process of publishing.

To my daughter—thank you for telling everyone who will listen that your mommy writes books. And believing whole-heartedly in me.

To my son—thank you for not being like the character Jacob, and still talking to me. You have no idea how much that means to a mom.

To my amazing sister, who listens to me drone on and on about my characters while loving and supporting every word I write.

Bloggers—I wish I could list all the blogs that have ever done a shout out, post, or review for me. But the list would be too long. Thank you for loving books. But more than that, thank you for loving romance books, and the authors who write them.

Readers—thank you for sharing my characters' tears, their laughs, their hopes, and their love. Thank you for taking them into your hearts and loving them as I do. Thank you for taking them into your lives where they will live forever. And thank you for allowing me—a simple Southern girl—to live her dream.

Hugs and Happily Ever Afters,
Prescott Lane

ABOUT THE AUTHOR

PRESCOTT LANE is originally from Little Rock, Arkansas, and graduated from Centenary College in 1997 with a degree in sociology. She went on to Tulane University to receive her MSW in 1998, after which she worked with developmentally delayed and disabled children. She currently lives in New Orleans with her husband, two children, and two dogs.

Contact her at any of the following:
www.authorprescottlane.com
facebook.com/PrescottLane1
twitter.com/prescottlane1
instagram.com/prescottlane1
pinterest.com/PrescottLane1

Made in the USA
Columbia, SC
23 March 2018